Stradella

Stradella

by James Sherwood

Revised Edition

Grove Press, Inc.
New York

1

Once, meeting a girl whom it was fun talking to—whom, actually, I'd talked *at*—three weeks were spared from misery by her company. No longer did I ache from loneliness. I used to sit in my little black hole and carve soap. I used to get the neighbor's cat and feel its pelt for fleas to snap. I used to drip some wax on flies and burn their wings off. But no more. That all was dispelled by this girl.

The three weeks with her came to an end when I went to her apartment one evening to talk. In her haste, in her enthusiasm, she had forgotten to lock her door, though she'd shut it. Yes, I tried the knob in my one-minded intention, her intention never having occurred to me.

As her apartment was a one-room with bed that pulled down from the wall, I could not help walking into her private affairs. There, on the bed, she was flattened by some brute heap of naked stranger astride her. The memory of my three weeks ended with a quiet and polite little bow. Softly I shut the door, went home, and then to another film. Sometimes I went thirty miles to find a different theater.

When I made no commitments, the commitments made me, so I got a job, bogged down on the primal mudflat of employment, earning food and rent which I paid to mother. It was a tiny ripple of discontent in confinement—confinement without giving birth—which produced my little blurt forward to friendship with Russell and Gussie.

I worked as a shipping clerk, a menial job in a firm for mass-produced dishware. Daily I labeled the dishes to customers duped by the door-to-door salesmen.

The office was small and my shipping room occupied most of it. The office manager, I guess, had the sole function of helping me, and answering his wife on the telephone. He had a dish face. His secretary, a cunning woman of very stately size, with a narrow mouth, did his work. The regional sales manager, a chirping and chipper dapper man, had an ulcer and talked fast. He had saucer ears. His secretary had an ulcer too. She would cry in the office when the boss spoke abruptly to her, which he did after he talked with his wife. Later, the ulcer got so bad she became pregnant and the ulcer cleared up.

For three years I went to work there early, went out at noon for lunch, and at the end of the day walked with my boss to the corner where he bought a paper and I crossed the street.

For these same three years I never had a girlfriend, but I thought a great deal about it. I watched it in movies and read about it in papers. Spying rather than vying was the only reward I savored.

On payday of January 14 I was dismissed with one week of severance. My boss bought his paper, shook my hand, thanked me, and said I would not have to come in again.

My clothes had not a clean stitch among them, nor a matching pair of anything, nor a contrast anywhere, but all spots and bruises, creases and loose buttons. I failed to shave that night as I scurried from my room, neglecting to turn off the tap.

My regular coffeehouse was inhabited by actors. Noisy, colorful, it was a constant whirlpool of people, flashing hairdos, studied gestures, stylized voices, and flamenco flooding the air. I purchased a cup of tea. Tea was cheapest on the menu.

I sat at the largest table in the coffeehouse. All the little tables around me were cluttered with cups and packed with people. There was enough room at my big table to spread out several sheets of paper.

I needed the big table to write my friend who was at a resort with his wife. He had been gone twelve days, 260 miles away. My friend was a psychiatrist in a toy factory.

"Dear Russell," I wrote. "It has been a warm day here. Wish Happy Birthday to Gussie. Show her this letter. I'm wishing you well, Gussie. She might even want to write me, a little post card or something. Don't bother. It would mean a trip to the souvenir shop and then the problem of deciding which card was right— which card would appeal to my personality, you know. Actually any card would appeal. Don't bother. I saw a paralyzed bird today in the street. Traffic rushed by. The bird flapped its wings, but it leaned at an angle with its eyes into the sun, even when the nearest cars ruffled its feathers. I watched for a long time. Some woman came along. I showed her the bird. She stopped the traffic. Why didn't I do that? She threw it on a lawn and there it stood. So did I. Well, your one friend's hoping you're having a nice time. Oh yes, I got fired today. I worked there three years two months and three weeks. They gave me one week severance. Bring me back a pine needle or a piece of dirt from the great wide outdoors. One week severance wasn't enough--"

At this point the waitress removed my teacup though I'd only drunk a sip of it. I called her back.

"You'll have to sit somewhere else. This table's taken. There'll be no single seats for a while. You can wait by the door."

"I'll just—all right," I said. I was collecting my thoughts.

A woman at the next table spoke to me. She wore a red dress, was platinum blonde, and her palm was open toward me. A puppet man was with her.

"What are you looking for?" she asked, grinning, gushing.

My answer, I thought at the time, was rather debonair. "I don't know," I said. "Maybe I'm looking for you." I bowed slightly.

When the waitress came back to seat the group, the woman asked me to sit at their table. I was introduced to the puppet but because of the noise could hear nothing. I was conscious of the fact that her forehead was a little too small for her jaw. Then she told me her name was Stradella, which meant very little. After a few moments I gazed straight in her eye. It was a trick I had seen in the movies. It was supposed to evoke profound feelings. "Your eyes are—lonely," I said, looking deeply into them.

She drank her water and asked for my number.

I said, "I've had enough of these I'll-Call-You promises. If you want, give me your number. I'm very busy, always out and seldom in."

"What do you do?" she asked.

"Well," I felt my bristly cheek. "I'm a poet."

"Thank heavens you're not another actor. I wouldn't have talked to you. I'm a poet too."

"A poet?"

"Yes, a poetess. Call in the late morning, my answering service. Here, write down the number."

When they left, I left. She acted as though we'd never spoken, even though I held the door. She wore a fur jacket with a high collar and a diamond wrist watch. Her fur brushed me as she went out. Her puppet dusted it off. She was waving over the heads, "Wallace Brenner darling!"

I waited in the shadows till they drove away. My car was in the parking lot too. Ignoring them that long walk to the lot would be absolutely ungentlemanly, and being ignored would be even worse. I did not wish to finish in humiliation a meeting begun in daring.

The puppet sped from the parking lot, Stradella on the middle of the seat beside him.

I went to my own car, a jalopy. The battery was dead. I had to go back in the coffeehouse to telephone a tow service. I was embarrased because I was conscious of the glances different people gave me now.

The telephone was near a table where three made-up actresses were flirting with each other, and I knew they were listening to every word I said to the dirty tow company. The actresses didn't even glance up as I went out. They went on flirting and teasing each other.

When I realized I'd left some small change by the phone, I went back to get it, but the change was gone. I started to look around for the thief, and interrupted the actresses. They looked up and paused. Then I felt it in my other pocket. I went out and waited in my jalopy. I listened to the coffeehouse laughter.

I waited almost two hours for the tow service to come. Women in mink walked by with big men as the tow service filled out the form and got my money on the hood in coins. Then they pulled me off with a jerk.

2

I had already planned to attend a first-run theater Saturday evening and after that a midnight horror

show, so I told Stradella we could go out sometime
that afternoon, when I called her in the morning. The
Van Gogh exhibit was at the museum.

Dressing meticulously in my best baggy pants and
my whitest frayed shirt, I even had my jalopy washed,
which last gesture made me arrive late. I was told
her girlfriend was going too. We drove to her girlfriend's.

"He's one of these poor boys, Rita. Do you mind
his old heap or do we go in your car?"

"I'm ready for his old heap. I'm willing to leave
my Thunderbird home. Do you think I'm a gold
digger? Who'd I impress today, Van Gogh?"

All the way to the museum Stradella was attacked,
accused and bawled out by Rita. "That's right, my
only apparent pleasure, so far as you can see, is
making you feel smaller, less around the bust, more
around the waist, and less around the hips, with knock-
knees, Stradella," said Rita.

At the exhibit, Stradella and I walked alone. Rita
vanished, looking for Van Gogh. At one rare canvas
Stradella said, "Mmmmmmyyyyy—." With her red nail
she chipped at the paint like polish. "I wonder what's
underneath that bed?"

A nearby art lover whispered in the ear of a Van
Gogh-ophile who delicately nudged me to ask the
pretty young lady, Please Couldn't she?—and so I
did.

"They're afraid of me, with all that caution. I'm
a stoplight of flesh appeal." She smiled. "Like a
lady Van Gogh." All the same she withdrew her nail.
Then we left the exhibit. Rita was gone.

At Stradella's apartment, prepared to thank her, to
smile, to bow quickly, and leave, I was implored to
stay and eat.

She noticed the missing button on my shirt. "I have
a replacement. Would you please take off your shirt?"
I squirmed. She took my shirt into her bedroom.

After eating my pudding, I shuffled in after her and my shirt. The only place to sit was her bed.

She sewed very slowly, and said very little, and once or twice looked at me with an equal amount of slowness. I wanted to get to that show. I moved closer. This only slowed her sewing down more.

I glanced at the clock. It was 7:45. In 15 minutes the movie would start. I couldn't get in without my shirt. What should I do? In a fit of desperation I put my arm around her, my lips to hers and she fell back on the bed, suddenly moaning and setting the needle flying.

But I sat up. "I'm supposed to be at this meeting by eight." I pulled my sleeves down. "I didn't mean to take advantage of you," etc., etc. Somehow we both got to our feet.

"What do you mean? I wasn't letting anyone take advantage of me," she said. I got into my shirt. The new button dangled. I just tucked it inside. At the front door I turned to thank her. She was standing so close I swallowed her lips by accident. Offering to shake hands, I stroked her buttocks with my free hand. She quivered and asked me, and her voice filtered through my collar, "If I let you come back tonight will you kiss me all over?"

"All over?" I asked. "Oh! All over!"

She clasped me tightly. "I'll leave the door unlocked."

I left.

I followed the first show with concerted intensity, enjoying every minute, and my popcorn. It was first run. Finally I saw the horror show. Monsters were eating each other.

At three o'clock I drove by her door. It was dark. I tiptoed in and found a small night light on. There was a man's electric razor underneath with a note:

"Here's the way to razor yourself. Shave."

At this time of night, and the neighbors sleeping, I was definitely not going to shave.

Slipping into her bed, nude and quiet, my big toe touched one of her feet. She yielded her sleep and rolled toward me with the warmth and softness of lava, fully waking. I was not sure she had even been asleep.

I was enveloped in her. Every limb was burning. Every breath was searing. I was pinned to the bed by her onrush. My soldier rose like the sphinx, serenely taking its time. She was stuffed with sweetmeats.

She folded her arms around me. She lay on her back and buried my head in her cakes. Tentatively I kissed her candles, a weightless fly flitting over her. They hardened and expanded, a ripe fruit unpeeled in her bed and laid bare. She plucked me like a dandelion. I sank my toe in her apple. She spread me over the sides of the bed, and sat herself down on me, a sea wave, corking breath. I impaled her with a finger. On her knees she moaned into the cushions. I held her above me, speared on my thumb, and spun her. She clutched blindly at my stem like a lariat and whirled me. Every place that I touched on her skin broke out like a wound, ripe and rosy. The tongue in my head, not a word on it, tilled her furrows and curves. She became a ripe pasture. The wounds broke out in blossoms. The curves turned to creeks of sweat. Her whole body ran like ore, a mother lode of golden bronze tan.

Exhausted we fell into sleep in a heap, draped over each other amid discarded towels, awakening on the ceiling each to the other's summons, a faint breath like a cool wind blowing between my thighs, blood drained from her head and siphoned out like a silk kerchief through a straw. She waved her arms like wands of high magic. Lips groaning, the last bit of oblivion we greeted, parched and parting the cheeks of perdition as we went away into nothingness, faces fried to a fearful tingling.

I became invisible on the bed where our brightest light saw me nailed to the mattress, beard out.

We talked and shared her life story. She told me about her three marriages, to a gambler, to an actor, and a nobody. She showed me her scrapbook. She summed up her career.

For the first time I realized that this was not just a girl, this was *the* great Stradella who was known to the world as the star, Amourella, Goddess of Love, queen of midnight television, seductress of the latent libidos of the late-night audience. My God! I was in bed with a personality.

And on the morning of the seventh day I awoke to hear her talking across the country to Brooklyn.

"Yes, Daddy, I know, but if you could just send me a little money. Yes Daddy, I know, but it would only be a loan and I could pay it back in two years and besides, property here is going up. Property here is valuable. People are coming to live here from Brooklyn. Yes Daddy, I know, but couldn't you give me something? I want so much to have a housey, just a little housey-wousey, all my own. Don't you know that Daddy? Yes Daddy, I know. Well, all right. Why don't you send Mom and Dinky then, and come out yourself? I could take care of them and we could all three get a house together. . . ."

Et cetera.

3

Stradella got a phone call from an agent and scowled.

"What's running around in your busy little brain these days? Still peddling middle-aged virgins?"

Apparently he said nothing. Stradella looked doleful and damp on the line. She accepted my advice. She perked up.

"Talk to him with love, Stradella. Maybe he's lonely too, and he's only human. He won't hurt you."

She bit off a nail.

"I've been thinking of changing my hair color, dear. . . . Back to natural. . . . Soupy brown. . . . Turn the stoplight off."

The battle guns vanished. The warriors talked, and the lines that separated them drew them together. Her tone went down. Her eyes came up. She listened. She even slid down in her seat with her chin on her chest and the receiver coddled her neck.

"The title role in a movie? Who for?" she said. "What's the salary? $100 a day? At the mention of that price I'll cut my hair off first."

But she looked at me and her lids lowered. She scratched her bottom.

"You know that's scale wages, darling. How long have I been in this business now? Isn't it just a little depressing to have to take scale with a reputation to watch? You know how it must make me feel."

She paused. "You promise you'll try for the job at more money. You're sure I can sew up the part with one interview." The mention of sewing didn't make me suspicious. "All right, I'll go to the offices of Mr. Playbaum on Monday."

When Stradella hung up she had become a woman of mystery, a globe of contentment, an aura of radiance. "Here you are, and the bedroom's there. I've got plans for you," she said. Her eyes flashed.

The air became flurried with clothes, a blizzard of bras and underwear. She led. The magic, king-sized, inner spring mattress whisked away on a box-spring tour of paradise. She drove, and we returned, that seventh day, from our Sunday ride, breathless. I slept thirty hours.

To me Stradella's forehead was no longer too small for her jaw. The Brooklyn accent with which she tinged all talk was no longer the basement of eloquence but the highest Himalaya of elocution.

We babbled. We gootchied. We laughed. Our unfinished sentences were encyclopedias of prefatory sympathy that were consummated in glances that were no longer tricks or subterfuges. They were epics of communication capable of moving mountains. There really was a heaven and we knew, in those glances, where paradise was and how to find it on the map. We'd found it in the dark, and for us there was no doubt.

I threw her against a wall. She stuffed me in a drawer. I played in her pudendum, a kitten over pudding. She sighed and swung from a lamp. I crawled up the Venetian blinds. She whimpered and fell off the bed and split in sixty-nine slivers. I pieced them together nine times by seven and had six left over which I ate. She wiped her lips with a spoonful of ice cream. I polished her toenails with ear wax. She made rings with her locks and a collar of braid. Our heads bumped in a pillowcase, condemned Siamese twins, and we waltzed over the upholstery, jigsaw puppets. She became the wall clock and I the hands. I wound up her back and she chimed the beats by seconds. She had the pendulum and I had the weights.

I didn't even know her right name. But she told me soon enough. Not Stradella, but Isabella; not Fonteyn, but Funtberg. Those feet of clay I caressed, though those feet of clay had corns.

Stradella, I denied It. I refused then to say It even once. I detested you later, but expressed only It. But that was the time when I felt.

She reluctantly released me.

"I'm going to drive my sisters to the Girl Scout ski camp." I dressed.

She looked at me appealingly.

"I'd invite you along, but I won't because it would crowd the car. I'm taking my mother's. We couldn't all fit in with skis, schoolgirls and stuff."

"But . . . will you come back?"

"Yes . . . sure . . . I'll come back."

"How long will you be gone?"

"I don't know."

"When will you come back?"

"Don't ask me. I'll come back. As soon as I can. Is that good enough?" I agitated. "I've enjoyed myself very much, Stradella. Why don't you take the electric blanket to be fixed? You said it was broken."

She looked at me wide-eyed with a finger in her mouth. "I didn't need it repaired. I had something better than a blanket."

I returned to the bed, tossed off my clothes.

I stood on the mountains and knew the rumble of an earthquake, sir. Volcano Eruption and Sacrificial Flames Shook—giving headlines and spot coverage. *They jiggled like fruits ripe for falling and their peaks became like sword points, sir. And the ground broke apart and I was swallowed up in the crack in the earth, more ecstatically than Oedipus himself, sir.* I put out a thousand dailies and extras to cover this colossal hurricane in a double bed.

"You are a gusher!" she exclaimed.

"A monsoon!" I said.

"A typhoon not too soon!" she said.

Then I got dressed and went home.

When I returned to that room of scents on my second pilgrimage, the odors had become more clarified —talcum and lanolin and Red and White mouthwash, which was purchased on sale in the economy bottle, and Pepsodent toothpaste, and Stripe toothpaste, and Colgate toothpaste, and varieties of perfume and cold creams and face creams and the thick rich luster of Factor and others. I had never seen the real her.

Thank God for the manufacturers of unguents the

world over that make possible my Stradella. What they gave, I've preserved, in the glory of memory at the height of absolution, their genius, my pleasure.

As I drove to mother's place Stradella was still on my tongue. Was she pancakes or waffles? Every man knows that taste of that woman in that time in that place when there's breakfast and lunch and oatmeal and hot cream and marmalade and orangeade and pastry and gooey and runny cooked all together in the same long pot.

Open the cupboards to the infinite, how woman's kaleidoscopic stew tempts the cookbook man! But no man knows the recipe, nor ever will. Every woman is different. No woman tells. She has as many elixirs as men. They change with her mind and the moon. Her mind—she most denies it when most mindful—is brightest when opposed to her mood. The sun and the moon are brightest when directly opposing each other.

Stradella belonged to me the afternoon she thought she was losing me. When she knew I was going, she wanted me coming. My dreams were transformed, aspiration to perspiration.

But there was that one black hair on the toilet seat. That made me dislike her, eased the problem of leaving her. The rather vivid way she had of scrubbing between her thighs with a washcloth like she was scratching herself—that too put me off, especially when her next gesture was to pick her nose.

It was my fortunate position to see her not only as Amourella, Goddess of Love, in a hurricane wrap-around nightie of misty-mysterious white stuff, chimera-like and cloudy, which was her blossoming costume on television, but also soggy and soapy in the bathtub with the water dirty and the sad suds soaking around her sagging breasts, slick with slop.

Sometimes, when passion's flow was finished, the tired side of that rich baby's hot and self-taught vivacity took over. She opened up, you see, and like a flower, let off smells of all kinds as she burst like a rocket to the moon from the launching pad of the bed, so that once we were in orbit she was also breaking wind, and the wind-breaking set her laughing, and the laughing set her gasping, till at last she gave almost more than she ever thought she'd had, just short of mush, a bit softer than sponge cake, and cooked in her rear oven to golden brown.

The art of loving is concealing.
Those who love not are revealing.

My Stradella could dress up to be a captivating queen when she stepped in a room, the humming, purring, perfectly restrained and all-alluring woman. But when we stepped out, with me escorting her, I'd catch the devil for not keeping my necktie up, for ignoring her attempts to talk with intellectual overtones, and for somehow standing in her way, blocking those fierce sallies of hers toward being "A Great Lady."

But I'm getting ahead of my story. This narrative haste is due to mental contempt. I remember all the bad things about Stradella so I can imagine myself as I was when I walked out of the apartment after seven days into the harsh bright world of little girls going skiing at the Girl Scout camp, and the world of mother, and my deserted bedroom in her house.

I am remembering too that the beard was still on my face, and seven days longer, and I was feeling sated, reckless, powerful, completely sure I could not be unseated—and all because I had the gift of hating the thing I gave to, and of leaving the thing I'd return to.

Notice I call my Stradella a thing. That is part of the technique of keeping my aloofness, unity, strength. I recognized her, not as a human being, but a thing— "A Place To Stick It"—as Stradella informed me. I admitted it.

Stradella passed through me and I through her. We greased the ducts and eased the walls of each other, and made it easier to flow.

"Face it," she said. "It's no big deal. You bring on my period."

4

"Baby! What have you been doing? You haven't been home all week!" cried mother when I wandered into her bedroom. She was reclining.

"I've been—" I yelled and, grasping the air, swept on in proud triumph: "Sleeping with—Queen of Rutland!"

Mother set her vibrator aside. She'd shouted at me and I'd shouted in return because of the vibrator's noise. She fixed upon me her double-edged expression of long-suffering motherhood. It was supposed to be eternal and enduring and infinitely sublime. But she was finding it difficult to keep from breaking out laughing. The result was a smirk, and a fart.

"Baby—(pronounced: Baaaabbbyyy—)." She drew out the syllables, increasing their scorn, evolving a sermon of Thou Shalt Not's. At the same time she was pulling the bed jacket around her so as not to reveal her all too apparent muffins, thus embellishing the impression with some dignity. "You—haven't been seeing a—tramp—."

"No mother. Of course not. But I'm going to dress up now." I turned and went to my bedroom.

"Baby! Wait!" Mother struggled out of the sheets and blankets, pulled off a piece of scotch tape that normally slept on her forehead all night to ward away imagined wrinkles. "Baby! Come here and speak to your mother properly!"

I was already down the hall at the other end of the

house. Mother, with her bed jacket open and her transparent nightie spotted with spaghetti and oatmeal, marched into my bedroom barefooted, put her hands on her hips and stood in the doorway.

"Humpf. Baaabbbyyy—." She drew out the syllables. Her wild false hair stood on end, a lion's mane bristling with majestic superiority, the color of rhubarb. Her face creams were running down her neck. "What—is the meaning—of this?"

But I changed my socks and put on my black suit —the one which I'd had all my life with the sleeves —the one which I'd had all my life with the sleeves

Mother's hands remained on her hips. She shifted her footing slightly, invoking my name, my past, the long line of my ancestors, who all stood in the doorway of the bedroom behind her, barefooted, their hands on their hips too.

"Archimedes Flum—now tell your mother the truth."

I nearly laughed. I looked at her exaltedly. "I'm coming up in the world, mother. I'm going to be a gigolo. And someday—when I've finally made it and my services are wanted—world over I hope—you'll forget this moment, and be proud of me."

"Proud—of you? My son? (pronounced: suhuhuhun?) I could never look myself in the face, knowing you were—were—." On this particular morning it was highly probable she had not yet looked in her mirror. "You ought to be—ashamed. My suhuhuhuhun!"

"Well—I am—sort of," I chirped, and tied my shoes, which were the first pair of dress-up ones I'd ever had; we had bought them the time we went to New York on my twelfth birthday.

"To think—my son—turning out to be—A Typical Hollywood Bum." Her face was grinding out a gallery of grimaces. Her words crawled. "Not even manly enough—to go out—get a decent job—wanders around unshaved—like A Typical—Hollywood—Bum."

"Well," I speculated, and dropped the shoehorn my great-grandmother had given my grandfather on his twenty-first birthday, when he entered the world and stood up. "I guess you're right. And it feels pretty good, too."

Mother could not resist my smile. The urge to laugh, at the bottom of everything, was asserting itself. The best she could do to hide it was smirk, at the same time making a mighty effort to be dignified.

"Like playing the Hurt Mother Scene, ma?" I grinned. She grimaced.

My bedroom was littered with tapestries. I'm told they were worth a fortune, but what good were they to me in a bedroom? "But we have no place to store them," she'd told me. "Out in the garage they'll get dryrot and thousands of dollars will decay." Likewise with all the gewgaws from Hong Kong, Tahiti, and Bagdad. Mother'd traveled the world and returned with post cards, sore throats and walking shoes. But shipped back on her trail were all the triumphs of tour guides and mementos of souvenir shops from every city and continent. My bedroom was a storehouse of international keepsakes. The walls were lined with volumes of universal significance. "Despair, and Yoga." "How I Found Salvation Through Starvation." "The Spiritual Life of Your Dog." "Self-Realization Nuts, Staple Diet of the Prophets." "Slavery to Sainthood: My War with Onanism." "How High Society Found Orgasm Organically."

"Your room is the only place I can put them, Archie," mother'd explained about the books. "We can't let your little brother and sisters read them."

My closets were filled with totem poles. There was a large locked chest against one wall. When I insisted upon seeing what it held, since I had to sleep with the thing, I'd been given the key to the world's largest collection of astrological maps and palm-reading charts.

"I don't understand them but certainly they're very beautiful and the man told me they're very rare. Don't you think so, Archie?" mother'd said.

"You don't mind if we keep my mother's bedroom furniture in here, and my father's old writing desk do you, Archie? I can't have the children around them. They'll break them."

That was my bedroom. Yeah.

"Archie Flum," mother fumed. "I have a list of things I want done right away. If you'd come home earlier this week like a moral son should, I wouldn't have had such a list. First I want you to have the dogs clipped." Mother raised poodles as well as us children. Now she raised an eyebrow. "Then the garage needs cleaning out and I want you to lift the heavy things for me. You know how my back hurts. I can't lift anything heavy. I want the swimming pool cleaned. If you had a job like other boys maybe I could hire someone, but you're strong enough and have plenty of time. I want you to take some things over to the insurance man for me. You're growing up now and should start learning about business. I have no ability with those things and we need a man around the house. So you're elected, big boy. Get on with it now and don't disappoint your old mother. I've missed you all week. O yes—the fireplace grate needs emptying." She paused and fixed an angry eye on me. "Are you going to do it?"

"How's your love life, ma?" I tossed it off.

"Archimedes Flum—look at me." Mother was controlling her lip, trying not to smirk. She bit it. "Look me in the eye."

"I'm forever looking you in the eye, ma."

The front door banged and my little brother entered. He grasped the situation immediately. One look at mother, then at me, and the genius understood perfectly.

In deep, ominous, stentorian tones, he began the

monologue sermon that was destined to puncture anything.

"Oh—grr—anger now mother—grrurr—outraged—furious—possessed with an urge to murder—massacre
—monsters everywhere—fiends with heinous plans—
destroy us—look at her now how she bristles—rumpusy—Oh boy—filled with an impotent wrath—evil
everywhere—playing God on a mountaintop—Sheriff
G. Whippersnapper Doolittle can't save us—Rrrrreeeoowww (imitation of police siren)—Mother Flum to the
Rescue! Hooray! Hooray! Purity and virtue win out!
How did you do it Mother Flum? Oh yes, I know—
you just had your handy little Nevertire Incandescent
Flashlight battery ready—."

Mother went through all the emotions he described,
based on all the big words he'd heard, finally lighting
on laughter and did laugh. Then she turned on him
with a Whoop! and with an enormous slap across his
cheek dispatched his genius and all the big words.

The place was bedlam. Rodney was master of the
situation, governing it with immoderation. He kept
crying, "Eeeeeeooooooowwwwwww!" until our three
sisters, dripping wet from the swimming pool, their
bathing caps turned up, arrived clucking.

They greeted me with: "Oh, hello Archie," and
settled down, hovering hens, over mother and brother,
muffling the sounds and subduing the situation in their
oozing maternalness, trying out all the various tacts
and tenors for experience in the gathering buds of
developing motherhood.

"Archie? Are you going to drive your sisters to
Girl Scout camp like you promised?" Mother fired on
me from the fortress of her daughters and littlest son
in whom she was barricaded like an H-Mom-Bomb.
Her eyes were dancing fire.

The house was silent as it awaited my answer.
I faced them, upright and uncomfortable, in my
starched shirt and necktie.

"Well?"

They waited, watching. The refrigerator started up in the kitchen with a whirr. Rodney smuggled me a wink.

"What did you expect?" I tossed the ball back with casual indifference and shrugged.

"Very well then, you shall." Mother turned on her bare heel and walked out of the place, to return peacefully to the humming vibrations of the quaking vibrator.

"Is it true—" Rodney approached me. "You got mad last week at dinner and threw a baked potato at mother and she ducked and it killed a fly on the wall?"

I smiled with ineffable pride at my little brother.

A poodle in the pantry scuddled to the hallway, barking, as the doorbell clanged.

"Elmira! Quiet! Elmira!" My littlest sister slipped on the polished floor in the puddle formed from her bathing suit. She scurried to the hallway and a dozen poodles tripped her.

After a look out the window, she turned toward mother's room.

"It's Stoney, mother!"

In the windows of the front door stood a man of many teeth with a large bouquet of flowers and an eager expression.

"Tell him I'm asleep!"

My littlest sister, pushing the poodles back with one hand and opening the door with the other, relayed the message.

"Well, tell your mother I just brought her these, to commemorate our anniversary." Stoney squeezed the bouquet in through the crack. "Archie! What's the good word?" Seeing me, his face visibly brightened. "Gee, fella, it's good to see yuh. What's up? Got a girl? How's the love life?" He reached for my hand. I joined him on the porch and the two of us walked to my car. There was a deafening crash from the Home.

"How'd you get to the house, Stoney?"

"Took a cab, fella."

"I'll take you back down the mountain."

"I've moved again, Archie. I'm living in a little room over on Burton Way now. It isn't much, of course, but it's quiet and got a good clientele and they let me run my radio."

"What are you doing with yourself, Stone?"

"Well, I've got a little work project going."

"Yeah?"

"I'm preparing a series of safety messages. Called them Man and His Sincerity; Woman and Her Fertility."

"O yeah?"

"Sent them off to the California Director of Safety and Highways. I'm expecting a reply from him directly."

"Well—I'll be."

"I showed them to Mr. George R. Suching, who's the National Safety and Health Director, when he was out here on a goodwill campaign for Safety on the Sidewalks, Arch. He read my messages and thought very highly of them. Asked me to send them on to the State level."

Stoney spoke with a mouthful of peanuts at all times.

"Very good, Stoney. Yeah. So what else's new? Still drinking?"

He shook his head sadly. "No Archie—darn—I joined the AA. Your mother was driving me to drink, but she refused to see me again if I drank, so I had to get sober. Gosh, fella, but she's a hard woman to tame."

"Yeah. Haha! I know, Stoney."

Then we were at his place and he was getting out. He was asking me up to his room for a coke. If I couldn't today then some other time real soon because I was always welcome in his home. And Oh yes—his card.

The car behind me honked. Stoney said good-by.
The door was shut and I was driving. "Stonewall
Jackson Smith, Personal Consultation and Public Relations." The number to call was on the pay phone
down at the end of his hallway.

5

I couldn't remember her name when I returned to
her house and called her Estella, which is a bit like
Stradella, but unfortunately was the name of the girl
I have mentioned whom for three weeks I'd known
before. Stradella—Stradella, several times I repeated,
memorizing it carefully, and saying to myself over
again—face like a little girl, body of an Amazon,
Stradella—Stradella.

We went to a party. This party was blurring. She
was liked by the men. They were glad to see her,
telling black jokes, kidding with her, even whacking
her on the back.

Then the girls of the party began cloying me. One
squeezed my pants. Another invited me to join her in
bed; I decided she must be drunk.

In the car—my jalopy with the torn-up front seat
and the worn-out convertible roof—when we left the
party, Stradella seethed.

"Those girls were not interested in you for yourself
but in you as my boyfriend, since I was so popular
with theirs. But you didn't—good boy."

When we arrived at the apartment she clutched me.
I felt like a bird in the paws of a bear. Again I called
her Estella.

"Not here in the car Stella—Stradella. People will
see us."

Her cue to lead us inside.

Stradella had gone on a house-shopping tour that

afternoon I went to mother's. She'd seen half a dozen places to live.

"Since I've met you I've become so housebroken. This is just the cutest little house for me Archie. I already paid the first and last month. She wanted a one-year lease. Oh, it's wonderful. A bedroom, a bathroom, living room, kitchen and den, front and back door, garage, front and back yard, on a corner. It's just the cutest place in the world, with a tree on the sidewalk in front. Just think, a tree. It's a dream house, but we're going to have to fix it up. You've got your time set out for you now. I want to get the fireplace painted, and decorate the inside with wall-to-wall carpets and curtains and a shower instead of just a bathtub. O Archie! I can't wait till you see it. It's wonderful! And I've only got two weeks to get it ready. She gave me the two weeks rent free when I told her I'd remodel it. I gave notice to my cranky old landlord. He always looks in my windows here. I'm glad we're moving out."

"But how come you didn't show it to me before you paid the rent?"

"Oh—what?" She went in the kitchen and mixed up wheat germ and raw eggs with a beater and added some orange juice. "Here drink it. This'll make you healthy! I want to paint all the rooms too, and I've asked a friend of mine to help. His name is Rudolph Redpaw and he knows all about fixing up. That's his specialty. He promised to help me with my shower and everything."

"How come you didn't show me first?"

She slept, her expression as pure as an angel's. Our bedroom with colored lights was lit up all night. "Don't turn them out! Suppose I have to get up and go toitey?" The little blue and pink lamps glowed from snow bunnies and other toys around the room. Sometimes she reached up and turned on the red lamp.

Not this time. Her commands issued forth without
the bulb. My jaws ached.

"Not there . . . up a little . . . that's the spot . . .
now easy . . . no, lower! Lower! Oh! Oh!" She made
some joy sounds, then cursed. "I don't know what's
wrong! You hit the spot every night and morning last
week! Now you can't seem to find it at all!"

"But maybe it's just not there anymore."

"No, it is! It is! You don't know where to try."

"But I am trying. I did try. The spot's moved. Here
let me try again. My jowls are throbbing Stell—Stradella. I can't find it. I can't!"

"No it hasn't moved! It hasn't! It's still there! You
don't know where to look. Keep trying. Keep looking."

"Maybe if we turn the light on—"

Eventually the cannon fired and the fodder plopped
out of the barrel. As for me, I was a machine gun.
Stroke one, stroke two, ratatatat.

The next day we went to the house with a broom.
She drove in her lavender Thunderbird. "All the
young starlets have Thunderbirds now! But mine's my
own color. No one has one that's lavender." She left
me to sweep out while she went to sew up Mr. Playbaum for the title role.

Rita rolled up as Stradella was leaving, and parked
her cream-colored Thunderbird behind my lovebird's
lavender one.

"So this is the new little house, is it?" Rita glided
up the walk to Stradella.

"Oh, hello." Stradella, timid child before mama, held
her head bowed, completely shamed.

Rita rolled through the empty rooms, a steam roller
on spike heels. She made one complete circuit in
thirty seconds. "Well you've made another bad bargain, Stradella. The house's old and needs work. These
dark walls are thoroughly depressing. Every wall has
a door in it. Every room's in the wrong place. Your
closet's too small. The kitchen's backwards. You'll

be so cramped in there an egg wouldn't boil. Your garden's all weeds and the windows don't have screens. The bathroom's not big enough for a mouse. Oh, hello Archie. And besides it's a noisy neighborhood. Very bad for prestige. No class in this neighborhood. Children screaming all over. You'll be out in a week, or buggy."

"I like the house very much, Rita," I spoke up. "We're going to work on it now and completely fix it up, and I was born in this neighborhood, just three blocks away. If you stand in the middle of the street out in front you can see the house I was born in."

"And it hasn't changed a bit since then. Don't be so square, honey." She turned to Stradella and adjusted her white sunglasses that looked like cat's whiskers. "Well I'm off. Got a part on Alfred Hitchcock Presents. It's my English background. They want me for the lead. Got big things cooking, my series coming up this spring. We're working on the pilot."

That was her exit. With neither a farewell nor a thank-you-kindly, she walked down the walk to her Thunderbird, got in and blasted off.

Stradella draped herself limply and warmly over my shoulders, and asked me in tones submissive and endearing: "Do you like my little housey-wousey? You like it, anyway, don't you?"

"I do, Stradella," I said in my deepest and most kindly paternal tones. "Now don't you worry about a thing. We're going to fix it up to be your little dream house just like you want, and Rita who still has that apartment won't know what to say. You have a wonderful place here and need worry about nothing."

"You don't think the builders next door will make too much noise on the apartment building?"

"They've almost finished building that, Stradella, and you need never fear. The sign is out they're renting and pretty soon that place will be filled."

"Do you think I made a mistake, taking a year lease

with the option to buy? I thought they might want
to tear down the house and put up another apartment
like the one next door."

"That was smart, yes it was Stradella. That option
was good business. You're very right and intelligent.
And we're going to fix it up and be happy here ever
after."

"Do you think so?"

"Yes, I do," I, Daddy, assured her till she purred,
a kitten. "But you'd better go, or you'll be late to the
studio and Mr. Playbaum won't hire you."

"Oh . . . all right," she sighed, and went away,
dreamily wooed, warmed and secure.

I swept out the house, swooped up the dust, threw
out the mess the previous tenants had left, and a
young apollo-esque actor knocked at the door dreamy-
eyed.

"Stradella?"

"No, Archie."

"Oh. Stradella here?"

"No, just Archie."

I discovered the lock on the back door was broken,
found forty cans of sardines in the garage, and waited
around on the floor of the bare echoing living room
till way past dark, when my bird finally drove up in
her bird, only four hours late, with some "paint
brushes and spray cans and satin swatches of lavender
to be used for making curtains to cover all seventeen
windows. Is it seventeen? They're out in the car. I'm
bushed. Bring them in will you?"

This was not her last visit to Playbaumia.

6

"We're going to the schlock shop."

I asked her what that was.

"The junk shop, Archie, the junk shop. I'm going to fix my house up elegantly." She made arrangements to buy an old straw wicker chair which, "I'll make a cushion for and paint with gold leaf. We can put it in the center of the living room."

"Is that the most elegant place?"

She had found a pedestal which, though it supported no statue: "it's independently distinctive," and also a vase to go atop it and some colored cattails to go in the vase. "Pink and lilac, I like tails. They'll sit beside the wicker chair. Very dignified."

We then examined mirrors and went home and made some measurements. "I'm going to have a mirror on the big wall of the living room, so you can see yourself when you come in the door."

"I don't want to see me. Do you?"

"Got to have a mirror in the kitchen over the sink."

"So you can see yourself while you're washing dishes?"

"Dah-ling, I just do de cookin' roun' dis place. I want some full-length mirrors on the bedroom doors and three-way mirrors for the dressing table and some mirrors all around the bed."

"What for?"

"So I can see de action dah-ling. I don' miss a thing." She imitated Aunt Jemimah.

The want ads offered gold mines of mirrors and once more our jalopy went on the road.

We met a movie producer—"Stradella! Darling! You're looking so lovely, honey!"—who was selling his closet mirrors. "I'm producing a picture in Paris next month. You can have the mirrors for—I'll sell them to you for—" each pause was to examine her thighs and pick a notch in the dimple in his chin. "You can get away for a nice five fins each."

Complete change of pace next, leaping up. "How's that now, darling? You'll excuse me if I have an appointment—."

Though she had been on the best of terms with him only a few minutes ago, and was, apparently, a life-long companion, Stradella now turned into a servant and helped me remove the mirrors. The producer went into an another room where he apparently had a girl-friend. He forgot Stradella's name when he shut the door behind us. "Good-by—uh—er—yes."

We met a junk-shop dealer. "I always have a garage. I rent hundreds of garages for junk." Stradella ex-humed items from her copious list of necessities, written on little lavender pads with pink lead pencils. "O yes? I've got one just like that? You want to see it? I'll give you the key? We'll take a run over there? It's in a garage on Gardner?" or Sweetzer? or Poin-settia? or Marathon? "You can get it cheap? How much're you willing to pay?"

Stradella turned on his tactics so fast he blew over. "What do you mean, how much will I pay? I'm the customer. How much do you want, Jerry?"

To which Jerry the junkman hemmed seriously, and hawed, and started at a cheap thirty dollars and ended at five out of friendship, chipping the paint off his overalls. "Because it's you, Stradella, though I hope you won't tell anyone?"

"This is big on your part since we've never met before and I've not even seen the five-dollar item yet, Jerry."

"Yes, Stradella." He bowed his head.

We followed ads to the houses of old ladies whose husbands had died, leaving mattresses, iceboxes, wheel chairs and bureaus. From among the selections we got trinkets, like collections of little glass figures to sit on shelves somewhere, and conglomerations of window shades and fans. "Archie, isn't this cute? Oh, I must have this. It's so elegant." Sequins were pasted all over. It was a box. We met palsied old ladies with the eyes of mice who sat before television from morn-ing to midnight and hacked away in their hankies and made a sermon of spittle each hour, praising heaven they still had the strength to cough, the energy to die.

We shook the hands of relentless cigar-stabbed pawnbrokers, barterers with bent-over noses doing honorable trade, and curbside men of goodwill who had served their sentences and were now our friends, with darting eyes that could see around corners, selling tablecloths from car trunks and guaranteeing their value.

"Stolen, no doubt, from the factory, but I'll buy it, or turn you in if you don't cut the price."

The rugs that we finally obtained were an adventure complete in itself.

We'd gone to a carpeteer who offered to give us the best deal on earth and would send out a man in the morning to do the measuring. He was short and ugly with carpets as thick as his eyebrows.

Stradella signed contracts and the check for down payment, observing formalities up to the point of fingerprinting, "which you'll waive, because I'm Stradella, I hope." It was waived.

The rug mart was offering a complete "wholesale rug vamp," which would cost only one dollar a month for the rest of your life and it would be like money in the bank, because the rug mart guaranteed to undertake your funeral expenses as an incentive to buy their rugs.

As we left the mart Stradella requested a free rug. She was given one for her bathroom.

The next day she found an ad in the paper and immediately canceled her deal with the rug mart, which was done regretfully but vigorously, and the free bathroom rug forgotten—consciously forgotten— but definitely given, as the carpeteer assured her repeatedly on the phone. He called several times requesting she drop by to be fingerprinted so her record would be complete and they could close the deal.

We went to a house from which three Greeks were

departing and measured the rugs—they were green—
and pulled them up off the floors ourselves while the
wives of the Greeks watched TV behind us. "I'll have
them bleached." Stradella pulled. "My color scheme
will be white on white and lavender. I'll have the rugs
bleached white. Very pure and innocent."

We also purchased a grandfather's mantel clock
which had no key but happened to work, as one of the
Greeks tried to show us, but couldn't, until Stradella
said that whether it worked or not made no difference
at all. "It looks nice. I'll paint it gold like the chair,
and put it on the mantelpiece. It'll give real dignity."

We canvassed the town for a place to have rugs
bleached and finally found a bargain—two Mexicans
beating rugs in a garage for a man.

The man came around several times to dinner and
even brought tickets to a film, which Stradella
accepted and took me to, leaving him in his dis-
appointment to go back to his wife in the suburbs.
She waved as we drove off. "I'm going to need more
rugs. Keep looking."

During that time we hardly had time for the movies,
since our mornings were given to sleep, our afternoons
to shopping, and our nights to working. But the night
we did go, we held hands and cried over the drama.
Love made us free to weep. We went home to work.

"I'm going to make my housey so elegant. Look at
all my receipts. But we still need some more rugs,
with foam rubber matting around the bed so you can
spring in and bounce out—very comfortable. With all
the money I'm spending, it must be real class."

At one shop we met a registrar and sat down to sign
up to vote. There Stradella admitted, under oath, she'd
never registered before.

"Then you must be just over twenty-one, not more
than twenty-three! Oh Stradella! Stradella! I'm so
glad. Happy Birthday! If you're really that young,
then we can get married."

She acquiesced, quietly. "Um-yeah."

"My God but you've done a lot then! Twenty-three and married three times, been written up nationally in all the big magazines, appeared in twenty-odd movies and had your own TV series! My God, you must be a genius, Stradella! You're really going to go far!" Again I felt the crazy wild abandoned desire to propose.

Three days later I had thought it over. Someone who'd seen Stradella on TV laughed in my face at the idea. "She's thirty at least! Grow up, boy. You're dating a mama." Inside me something snapped. A mama?

"So you're thirty."

"Um-yeah."

"Well why didn't you tell me?"

"I didn't think that mattered, you seemed to enjoy it so much."

"As far as I'm concerned then, all is over, Stradella, and I should never see you again. How could I—older woman and all—not a genius—not even a future—going no place—probably already been—"

She sat down by me and circled my shoulder with a bronze arm and cuddled up next to my chest. "I need you and you're so warm, Archie."

When some colored men stopped her one day in the yard and said they would paint the house cheap, she didn't know how to say no. "Tell them you're my husband and we don't want them to paint, will you?"

"All right." So I did.

The colored men went away.

"Thirty-odd, my God! I'm broken inside. You're aging just like mother and older than I. It's killing!"

But she said it was of no concern and so I concerned myself not. There was too much to do hanging curtains and spreading on paint.

The color scheme was unique. We bought the cheapest paint we could find, lavender, and from the apartment painter next door got advice. He got inter-

ested in Stradella and came over often to help out
and bawl out and try to kiss her in the corners when
he could, where their brushes met. He told her she
was a terrible painter and would never have a stroke
like his.

He was only four feet tall and his voice was very
loud and when he tried to kiss her he came up just
to her bust. "But then all America's been told I'm
kissable, and so far all America only comes up to my
bust," she told me.

The kitchen and bathroom were lavender. The rest
of the rooms were white. I failed in teaching Stradella
the art of the long stroke, but she dabbled and drib-
bled and painted a bit, and started a sill which she
never quite finished, and half painted a door.

"You won't get this done without me," I informed
her. "In fact I doubt if we'll finish at all. There's so
much to do, and so little to do with."

"We'll finish," she said. "We'll finish and you'll just
see. I'll give a party to show it. We'll finish, I promise,
even if I have to finish alone, and I'll invite everyone
who helps me. You'll see. I'm not a quitter. I'll finish."

"You take that thought from We to I with a single
stroke of the brush. I'll help."

"Keep stroking."

Which again brought us around to the rest of the
rugs, bought sight unseen from an ad in the paper,
which were the last items delivered, by two boys in
a limousine who said they worked for a rug man—the
largest rug mart around. And the rugs turned out to
be the ones we had ordered from the great carpeteer,
except that we paid the boys poorly, and gave them
some drinks, and requested no receipt, and made sure
the coast was clear before they crept out into the dark
night.

"So the housey now has hot merchandise," grinned
Stradella.

"Your conscience worried for an alibi?"

"I'd love you to find one, with your poetic nature," she said.

I did: a Man had moved out and given them to her.

"I alibi well, don't I? I have a way of saying things innocently," she admitted. "Don't I, hm?"
We had to cut them ourselves to fit, which task was directed by the ardent rug cutter who still came around for dinner and "anything else he can get," she said. We had enough for two complete coverings of rug. The house was wall-to-wall rug. Even the bathroom was carpeted. The toilet was upholstered with leftover cuttings, as was the back porch, and the garage, and the car floor, and the front porch, and the walk all the way from the porch to the sidewalk. We even thought of carpeting the curb. We thought of carpeting the outside of the Thunderbird, and dyeing the carpeting lavender, but there was already a starlet around town who had carpeted the surface of her Thunderbird, so the remains of our carpets were rolled up and put on a shelf in the garage. "I won't be caught imitating that slut. It's a cheap idea, anyway."

We went to a dozen supermarts and got every house item on sale. Sometimes we used only a part of a paint can, a sample of gold spray, just enough for the chair and the clock—then Stradella returned it and got her money refunded.

"But you can't do that, we used it!"

"I know, but I told them I hated it, and so they gave me my money back. You don't have to keep things if you don't like what you buy. And besides, we only sampled it."

"I know, I know, but we're keeping the sample and using it."

To which she turned a deaf ear. "Oh, Archie, don't be so square. Get hep to what's going on. That's business. That's how they operate. No one minds. No one cares. I'm not hurting their feelings. I'm expected to do that. And look at the money it saves."

So I looked, and once in a while she spent a little on me for a fancy meal in a restaurant between strokes on the paint brush, and each other, and somehow I began getting hep, just a bit.

7

I dreamed how much I was coming to depend on Stradella, how helpless and small I was, and my efforts to save myself were futile. I dreamed of a monster deep within me who was a snail in a garden of gardenias. Because of Stradella's kisses, he ventured out in the light—into her arms—and drooled on her. He was a toothless thing who drooled when Stradella entered the room, and dripped, I dreamed, when she passed on the street. I dreamed his saliva became a torrent, until it was a cesspool of watery eyes.

In order to finish the house quickly, Stradella invited helpers. They wanted, like me, to become suitors, though none knew I already was.

She brought in twenty-one helpers to dabble in paint and dig in the garden. They all were male but there were only a few I could think of as manly. All were young actors and handsome.

"My studs," she called them, and laughed and they laughed and grew hungry with their jaws dropping open and their tongues slurping out—I swear I saw their tongues slurping out. Everyone laughed, except me, because I did the dirty work and finished the jobs they started.

One stud came in, saw his jobs, and leaned on the fireplace mantelpiece. He occupied Stradella in talk thirty minutes while I painted door trims. Finally I had to paint the mantelpiece. I asked them to excuse me. I was interrupted by the stud who said, "Let's buy you a cup of coffee and a tired bone, baby." I've forgotten the stud. But the tired bone I have never forgotten. I chewed that tired bone, trotted to the garden with that tired bone and made the supreme effort of burying that tired bone, and it still survives that stud.

"We'll let him finish this," said the stud, "him" referring to me. At first I thought he said "it" not "him." He didn't. Luckily for Stradella, she refused, but that night did no more work. We retired to the bedroom for reasons which I was never quite fully able to understand. She spoke of the stud in bed.

A few hours later she accused me: "Archie, you waste too much time. When I send you out on an errand you get stopped on the corner by the first stray person who comes along and tell him your life story and never get any further. You're just available to anyone who wants to use you and take up your time, aren't you?"

The twenty-one studs came and went, looking for something much easier than work, as studs are prone to do, pulling their tight pants on tighter and combing their hair and getting to the beach for a tan while I in my baggy pants and old shirt worked away at fixing the toilet which broke down, and emptying the garbage and washing the dishes, so that Stradella could rest in peace after the laborious day of group enterprise.

"My little houseboy is tired. My little black houseboy's too tired to make love to mama tonight." She had me sleep somewhere else, though I insisted I wasn't tired, but she said I was, and resisted.

Rudolph Redpaw was the first and last of the helpful helpers. I was his first and last helper. We worked in the rain on the roof with the antenna for the television set and sweated together installing a shower in the bathroom.

The fireplace had a chimney and grate, but one evening when Stradella eagerly lit the first, showing off her house to the old hag next door and to the old hag's old hag friend, billowing smoke poured out of the hearth and blackened the living room and all the white curtains and all the white rugs and the white walls and white leatherette seats and even the pink and lilac cattails. The chimney, we discovered, was sealed.

Together Rudolph Redpaw and I unplugged it and worked with concrete and chisels to repair it, while Stradella cooked dinner for us in the kitchen, burning a steak black like charcoal.

Stradella burned food. She'd leave it in the oven, deliberately remembering to forget it. She burned unbreakable glassware too. It broke. I think I forgave her, crunching my teeth on once-tender meat and picking glass chips from charred meatloaf.

She was making this a home, but every month the bills came around.

"How can a girl have a home and no man? I've got to pay for these bills myself, because I won't let anyone take care of me."

Rudolph Redpaw saw differently, and began trying ardently to seduce her. He had a perpetual bulge in his pants, apple cheeks and hair that stood up like feathers. Everytime he saw her he hugged her, then slapped his thigh and guffawed. He was one-half American Indian. The other half worked as a janitor regularly and a policeman partly. He drove a great big old Cadillac, his initials engraved on the dashboard. He wore turtle-necked sweaters and black-and-white sport shoes, and his calling card called him the Crimson Indian.

Everytime Stradella resisted him, and she resisted Rudolph because he burped quite often and apparently his breath was bad, she told him some new ill had befallen her poor little housey.

"I'll fix it!" he burped. "That's my specialty. I know all about that. Do you know I used to be a repair-

man? Specialities are my specialty!" Burrapp! He
danced to it. "I'm the pixie fixer!" Urrup! "I've studied
everything! I'm probably the only man in the world
who has completely and successfully psychoanalyzed
himself. That's an almost impossible feat you know.
(Burp.) But I've done it. Self-analysis, that's really
my specialty. That's what's made me so free. I've been
married eleven times. That's also a record. That's
right."

"Eleven times he's been married, Stradella."

He would nod. "Stick with me, Archie. I'll teach you
all you'll need to know."

"Eleven times. Imagine—eleven, Stradella."

With that Rudolph Redpaw, little suspecting that I
was the lover of that great big she whom he wished to
catch, slapped his thigh once more and guffawed,
crying, "Yippee!" and he pinched Stradella's seat as
she removed a plate of burnt meat. He bolted out the
door to fix something.

Stradella put a finger on my nose. "Just play along
with him, Archie, and never tell him about us, because
then he'll stop helping out, and he really does know
everything about repairs. That's his specialty."

When evenings grew rather late, Rudolph Redpaw
regaled us with stories. "A beautiful body. Oh yes,
but my God. She was so small. Do you know we
wrestled for an hour and she wanted it so bad she was
crying, but I just couldn't get inside her, I was so big?
We finally had to give up." Burrapp!

Stradella and I had each other to wash, but Rudolph
paddled by hand.

"Used to masturbate as many as twelve times a day
when I was your age, Archie. Never did a man have
the sex drive I've got. It's been my curse and my
glory. I can't escape it. Ruined me everywhere. At the
same time it's given me the only pleasure I've ever
gotten. Wow! Yahoo!" He would grab at Stradella,
and his hair would stand straight and his pants would

bulge out and his apple cheeks would ripen, then drop.

Cooingly Stradella would laugh.

One night I heard this going on in the kitchen. "That tickles, Rudy!" He guffawed loudly. "Woman is a glove, and there's always another woman!" He burst from the kitchen, a blushing splash through the door. "They come and go like taxis. You get in one and ride as long as you keep the flag down, but eventually you've got to pay and get out, because they're after all only taxis. They want to ride someone else somewhere. You never own them like a car. No, Archie."

"You mean women are a means of conveyance then, for you."

"That's right Archie, convenience, and—wow! Yahoo! Women! They're my specialty!"

"Rudy is a Yahoo, Stradella."

"I'll bet I've had more women than you've lived days on this earth, Archie. And I've never had a disease. Got a constitution like iron. Never been sick a day in my life. They've never gotten the better of me! Wawhaww! Women!"

Stradella said to me when we were alone, "Don't kiss me now. You're not shaved. Don't you know you'll scratch my thighs? O Archie, your breath is terrible. Get some mouthwash. I know where you can get some on sale. Your breath's awful. Like Rudolph's."

Rudolph Redpaw taught me how to stand up straight and keep my face washed and fingernails cleaned. Stradella was wild about little pink cuticles and freshly scrubbed pores. She raved about Rudolph's manner of back-straight prim propriety. "He has such dignity." His feigned, constant control that vanished the minute he saw the curve of her rear end was a continual source of amazement. Then he broke down and slapped his thigh like any other hillbilly guy. She held him up as an example, so I emulated him with energy.

But she'd decided my breath was permanently gone bad, so she took me to her dentist and he charged me the equivalent of one and a half month's salary to completely repair my mouth. Stradella did not bother coming to my dental sessions. She just sniffed my mouth after. The dentist raved about her. "What hips! What breasts! What a mouth!"

Then she went for a filling. I did attend her sittings, and watched as he pried her open. Her teeth were like those in a Neanderthal jaw. I didn't like Neanderthal jaws at all. Thoughts of Stradella's Neanderthal jaw prevented me from eating for days.

Many times of an evening, when we were sitting alone, Stradella would look at me quietly in that way she could look, directly and deeply into my own eyes —knowing the soul, having glimpsed the eternal, sharing the secret of everything—and tears would well up in me and pour out, for which I was not ashamed. We had exchanged perspiration, smells blended.

"Going to cry again? The big crocodile tears going to fall? The awning about to drop?" she coo-wooed.

"Have I given you anything at all, Stradella? Have I loved you at all?" I would ask her, plagued by that Neanderthal jaw.

One night she came from her closet in the pink dress she'd made with her own hand which had the low cut in the back, right into a closeup and quietly before me stood on the brink of eternity.

"You've plumbed my soul," she uttered serenely, in a voice smooth and mellow, the Neanderthal jaw barely moving. "No one has done what you've done for me, Archie. Bless you, you're an angel."

I was a dog, with a tired Neanderthal bone.

Stradella repeated it again. "My little child of fantasy, an angel." I cringed. Child of fantasy! What did she take me for, Alice in Wonderland? Don Quixote? I was Archibald Flum to some, as my father before me, and Archimedes Flum to mother.

"Do you remember how we met, Stradella?"

She nodded, and then said to me:

But I apologize for the crude thing she said.

"Don't worry about how we met, Archie. With your licker license, you'll lick lots of pussies after mine. Now let's see. I'm going to throw a party for all my studs who helped out, just as soon as I've worked in the picture."

"What about Mr. Playbaum?" I asked with sorrow in the name of compassion, seeking out suffering with the voice of understanding.

"You're like a laxative Archie! Don't bug me!"

"And everything comes down on my head!" I cried.

"Now lay off. Lay off!" she said.

"All right! All right!" I replied.

She smiled. "That's my line, my little bearded house-boy."

8

"He's a funny little man." Stradella refilled perfume bottles. "Mr. Playbaum is the biggest little man I ever saw. He smokes cigars as big as his arm and he keeps them in a cigar box the size of a baby's crib."

"I know. But what's he like as a man? Did he make a pass at you?"

"Oh, now Archie. Did he make a pass at me! Is my little baby boy afraidsie-waidsie? Mr. Playbaum is a gentleman."

"I know, all right, but did he make a pass at you?"

"No Archie, he didn't make a pass at me. He's not my type anyway. You know I don't like little men. He only comes up to my bust."

"I know, Stradella. That's too bad. What did you talk about then?"

"Well he did all the talking."

"From three in the afternoon till 11:00 P.M.?"

"He has to unwind Archie. He's a very busy man and he's got a lot on his mind, so he has to unwind and he likes to talk so he talked, and that's how he unwound."

"He talked himself down eh?"

"He told me his life story and then asked me mine and said he'd bet he could guess it and then he guessed it."

"Was he right?"

"Archie, what is this, the inquisition?"

"No Stradella, I'm just interested. I don't have to know. I just thought maybe you'd like telling me. I want you to share everything with me. I understand, and I can take it."

"Well he didn't make a pass at me Archie."

"Oh."

"Is the little boysie-woysie happy now?"

"So—yeah—I guess."

"He made me sit on the couch beside him and then he got out one of those smelling cigars. O Archie, do you know how bad they smell?"

"—"

"So he paced back and forth and waved the cigar like a wand and answered the phone. That's all he did most the time. And people came in and out and he told them yes and no. Can you imagine how busy producers are? He started out as a copy boy on a newspaper and now he writes TV shows and magazine articles and produces movies and everything."

"Were you impressed?"

"Ummmm*mmmmm*—yes. Then he played me the theme music of the new movie and said he was going to have a popular song written to go with it."

"Can he make the song popular by having it written?"

"He can maybe. It's all big business. You know that Archie. He probably can make it a hit."

"This little man really did impress you, didn't he, Stradella?"

"This little man is a pretty big man Archie, so—yeah—I guess he did. He's a hard-working little guy. He's a real driver. He gets up and goes and knows where he's going."

"So did he give you the part, Stradella? That's what we're really interested in."

"Sure—yeah."

"What do you shrug it off for? We ought to celebrate."

"What's there to celebrate?"

"Well you got the part in the picture. Is he paying you more than scale?"

"Um—yeah."

"Don't be so passive about it Stradella. What's he going to pay?"

"Um—150 dollars."

"A *day?*"

"Sure Archie, sure. And that's cheap."

"—"

"For what I've got to go through."

"What you've got to go through?"

"A girl's got to keep herself in shape for a part like that. Upkeep—maintenance. Got to keep the old farm repaired. Got to keep the grass cut. You know. He didn't want me to change my hair back."

"You asked him about your hair?"

"Sure. I asked him about a lot of things. We talked quite a bit. He told me all about his wife, and his kids, and how when he was my age all he ever wanted was to get ahead and protect himself against a poor old age, and then he offered me 150 dollars a day. That's fifty dollars over scale. I think it's pretty good."

"Yes—it is—but what did you have to do for it

Stradella? Did you ever go to bed with a producer for a part?"

"How dare you ask me a question like that! You have no right. You're not my husband."

"Then marry me!"

"This has gone too far! I have a right to my privacy."

"Yes, Stradella—yes—sure you do."

"That's a woman's privilege, to keep her secrets. A woman's not supposed to tell all she knows."

"I know that, Stradella. I know."

"Well, don't ask me then."

"I couldn't help it, Stradella. I'm sorry. I just couldn't help it."

"Well what did you do it for if you knew you shouldn't? Don't you know it's rude? How dare you intrude on my privacy!"

"I'm sorry I made you angry, Stradella. I *am* sorry about that."

"You haven't made me mad. You've been rude. That's all you've been is rude. I have a right to be mad when someone is rude. A lady isn't supposed to be treated like that."

"You know, Stradella—you know—if I were you—"

"Well you're not. And you never will be."

"It isn't any of my business, these questions I've asked you. They're none of my business at all. In fact, nothing about you is any of my business, and I guess you know that as well as anyone. Only there's one thing Stradella. There's one thing I don't want to forget. You came to me one night in a coffeehouse, and you were lonely, and you invited me to join you—"

"I made a mistake."

"And we got together then, and we made love Stradella."

"You don't need to advertise."

"So we had some love, and we had some laughs, and it's a funny thing, Stradella, but I started to care for you a lot in there somewhere between the mouth-wash and the bedspread. That's when I got the funny idea that maybe we were sharing some things."

"I'm not like you, Archie. I don't have to go around telling everyone my life story."

"And I'm not asking you to Stradella. You're a lovely woman. Your feelings are deep and they're real. You're a genuine friend. That's what we really are, you know. We're friends, and I hope we always will be Stradella, after the lover parts of us have faded, and after we've gotten some gray hair. I hope that we still can be friends, and forgiving, and understanding."

"Yeah."

"I know how you feel Stradella."

"Yeah."

"And I understand too."

"Yeah."

"And I forgive you, no matter what you did, because it's the you that's down deep inside I love, the real you, the you of the heart, the you of good intentions, the you of meaning, and I can forgive the rest, can forgive all you might ever have done."

"Yeah."

"So I take that to mean you did go to bed with a producer once."

"Yeah."

"Just one?"

"Yeah."

"What was his name?"

"What's his name matter?"

I smiled, or leered. "I was just interested. What was it like? Why'd you do it? All's I was wondering was—"

"All's Archie? What's this all's word? Is that a word Archie? All's?"

"All's. All's. Let's see. Means all is. All is I want to know is—no—I guess it isn't a word then. I made a mistake. Grammar. Bad grammar, I guess. I ought to improve my grammar."

"Yes. Yes you should, Archie. And you with good manners and all that."

"That's true, Stradella. Grammar's important. But I was wondering—all's I wanted to know was—I mean —all I wanted to know is—"

"I did it for a part Archie. Is that what you wanted to know? I went to the producer's office and he asked me to pull up my skirt and I was hungry and needed the part and he had a big desk so I lay down on the desk and let him pull it up."

"Was it fun?"

"Was it fun, Archie? What is this, huh? Are you getting some sort of pleasure from all this?"

"No Stradella. No. I just wanted to know. You've probably never told anyone these things before. Probably never have, have you?"

"No."

"And I thought it might make you feel kind of good to talk about it a little, to get it off your mind where it's been even if you haven't been thinking about it."

"Even if I haven't been thinking about it?"

"That's right, because it's good to tell someone some of these things. And the person can forgive you, and then you feel better."

"It was only that one time I did it Archie."

"Only that one time. I see."

"So now are you happy?"

"Did you get the part Stradella? And did he pay you more than scale?"

"I didn't even get the part Archie. That's how far it goes on the producer's desk. I found out you've got to be different. He didn't even call me back."

"I see, Stradella."

"You do?"

"I see."

"Do you want to eat now?"

"Eat dinner?"

"I was going to make steaks, Archie. I was going

to broil them, but they kind of got burnt. We can grab a hamburger. I've got to go to The Akron."

"What for?"

"I want some wheels for the TV so I can take it into my bedroom."

"How many guys have you gone to bed with Stradella?"

"What?"

"How many guys have you gone to bed with?"

"How many guys? Ha! That's a laugh! Do you keep track? Is that the idea? Do you keep a little chart and mark them all down Archie? Is it some sort of record with you?"

"Some sort of record? Why it's—it's like a marriage with me."

"Like a marriage."

"That's right, Stradella. So naturally I never forget one."

"Oh, I see Archie. Well I'm a pretty big girl now and I don't keep track anymore. But I guess you can imagine. I've kept pretty well supplied."

"Well supplied?"

"Uhmmm."

"Are they just like supplies to you, Stradella? Just like meat?"

"That's right Archie. Studs. Studs, like meat. They're beefsteak. All they want is somewhere to put it. You know they say a stiff one knows no conscience. And I like to get my depth charge every two weeks or so at least. Otherwise the battery'd run down."

"So, if you've been making it for—Oh—fifteen years —is that too many Stradella? Or not enough? For fifteen years let's say—twenty guys a year let's guess— is that about right?"

"—"

"About twenty guys annually?"

"Yeah."

"Then—let's see—twenty guys a year for fifteen years

—gosh! That's 300 guys! My gosh, Stradella! Have you been to bed with that many different guys?"

"Um. Yeah. We've got to get to The Akron now, Archie. Come on. You can talk on the way."

"Talk on the way?"

"I'll tell you how Mr. Playbaum said I could write the hit song for his picture too if I wanted, only if he liked it I'd lose money by selling it to him because I'd have to join more unions and pay more dues than he could give me for the song, so it wouldn't pay me to write it."

"But are you going to write it?"

"Of course I'm going to write it, Archie. You're a dear sweet angel, Archie. Don't let anyone ever tell you differently. You're an angel. Bless you."

"Have you ever gone to bed with any celebrities Stradella?"

"Celebrities?"

"Yes—famous people."

"You get your thrill this way, knowing you're sleeping with a big star? Yeah, well sure. I've slept with celebrities."

"Who've you slept with Stradella?"

"Can't you guess?"

"—"

"With studs Archie. Studs. All the big studs. I've made it with all of them. A girl gets around when she becomes a celebrity."

"Who've you slept with then, Stradella?"

"You want to feel like you're sleeping with them too when you sleep with me, huh? That it Archie?"

"No Stradella. No. I was just wondering. I thought you might want to get it off your mind. You know. I do love you. I do want to share your whole life with you. I can forgive you for it."

"*Forgive* me! Well who wants to be forgiven? I didn't ask you to forgive me. I liked getting laid by the biggest stars in the industry. Wow! Could Jim

Barnstorm ever lick! He was wild! And Richard Crockett! He could never stop! I've tried practically every star with a series."

"So that's why you want wheels to take your set in the bedroom!"

"Only they're all more interested in their rating than their erection. Jimmy Barnstorm was always off to the golf course. Ralph Hubby—we had a thing going for a while. He used to get drunk and put me down. Then he'd get drunker and call me up at three in the morning."

"Really?"

"Yeah."

"When did he stop?"

"He still calls me, Archie. He called me last week, if you must know. He called me last Wednesday."

"And what did you say?"

"I said we were through. I said I was busy now, with someone else. And I didn't have time to get jilted by him."

"Is that true?"

"Here I am with you, Archie."

"Yeah, that's true."

"Friends, Archie, friends, remember? That's what we are. We're not a quick lay for each other. We're not a drop in the wastebasket and thanks. You're like my little brother. We're not just for sex—or for love. We're friends Archie. Friends. Remember?"

"Couldn't we get married Stradella? Couldn't we?"

"You think you could take care of a girl like me? Pay all these bills Archie? Earn 150 dollars a day from Mr. Playbaum so I can stay home in a nice big fine house with my own Victorian furniture and my own yard without a lot of little neighborhood kids running around screaming at seven in the morning? You think you could do all that, Archie? No Archie—no. I need a man, Archie. A real man. I want someone who can give a girl security, who can make a girl feel good and take her out to nice restaurants. You can't even afford a haircut, traveling around with your outcat friends."

"I know Stradella—I know but—"

"There's a lot more to this world than just being in love, Archie."

"And—yes I know all that, Stradella! There are things like trust—and encouragement—and faith—and help! I don't see you encouraging me. Who knows? Maybe I could stop writing poetry. Maybe I could write a book all about you. Maybe I could write you a play and then we'd be rich and then I could—but you've got to stand by me, Stradella. You've got to encourage me. You're not doing a woman's part. A woman is supposed to stand by her guy, and support him morally, and then he's her man and he becomes these things you're describing. Money's easy to get. I can get it, lots of it, only I need some reason to get it, Stradella. Just love me a little, and accept me, and stand behind me, and support me with all your beliefs and—and—don't you see how then I can become these things, Stradella?"

"But I'm not a prop, Archie. I did it all alone, all these things. I poured twelve thousand dollars down the drain on my first husband. Three times I bailed him out of jail. Who supported me all this time, Archie? Was it you? Was it him? I got up and went to work modeling—modeling naked by the way—at eight in the morning and quit at noon to work as a waitress by one in the afternoon until midnight. And where do you think I picked up my husband? At the tennis courts, where he played with his friends all day. That's the kind of support you need, Archie. But that's not the kind I'm willing to give anymore. Now let's get to The Akron before it closes. I want to get some wheels for my TV."

"Let's take my car, Stradella."

"Your car? Oh, no. Not this time. Wait till you

get it repaired. That smoke coming in from the motor is enough to knock you out. We'll take my car."

"—"

"Funny man," said Stradella. "Funny man. That Mr. Playbaum is a funny man. Do you know he's just about my father's age?"

"Your father's?"

"And I only met him once and he gives me all this money. But at least he's shaved."

"And your father?"

"My father? Why you want to ask me 'bout him? No. He never shaved. He was a bum, my father. He hated to shave. I still get a rash with a beard."

"So that's why you wanted me to shave, is it?"

"Ha! You, like my father? Oh, now come, Archie. You're practically young enough to be my son. Why do you think I chose you? So you could daddy me?"

"But that's what you want from this man who's going to take care of you someday isn't it? Just a daddy? Just a Mr. Playbaum who isn't married?"

"No Archie. No. I'd never marry a Mr. Playbaum. I told you about my studs. Can't you remember? Well they let the pressure off. They service me. What would I need a husband for?"

"When you got older. When you got gray. And to have babies, Stradella."

"Well maybe you're going to be my daddy, Archie. Maybe you're going to save me. You know I'm the only cooze in Hollywood who's never been pregnant a day in her life? I've never been pregnant once?"

"Is that good? Is that bad?"

"Well, it's funny. I'm the only one in Hollywood. That must be some kind of record or something for a big girl like me. I think—maybe—it's funny. But you know—people always laugh—but I once told my girlfriend I never did anything to disgrace my mother and father?"

9

I remember so clearly the torn end of a moment. We were tired and she didn't want to cook. Rudolph Redpaw stopped by. Poor old Rudolph. He was using her garage now, to assemble a headboard for his bed. He wanted a headboard like her headboard—one with cubbyholes for everything and sliding doors and secret panels, a place to live without getting up, where he could even install a hot plate and make breakfast in bed like her, if he wanted.

We were very tired and Stradella said, "We should all rush over to Mrs. Palmer's Kitchen!" Mrs. Palmer's Kitchen was a nice little restaurant we'd heard about for years and never tried. It was near. "It's the kind of intimate restaurant where only ten customers can be served at a time. Very dignified."

We went in our work clothes. My baggy pants had paint stains and Rudolph was wearing his carpenter's overalls. Stradella had on her tights, torn in one seam, shiny on the bottom and frayed from many washings. She wore these tights when watering the garden. "I think we look all right don't we, Rudolph? Archie, don't you have a comb?"

The three of us traipsed into Mrs. Palmer's Kitchen. The waiter looked us over. The customers—all ten of them—looked us over. They were in neckties and propriety, with their napkins in their laps and their hands in their napkins.

"I'm embarrassed, Stradella."

Rudolph kept his chin and eyes down.

"I thought you were hungry!"

hungry. I'm Stradella Fonteyn. Amourella, Goddess

"Waiter, we'd like to have dinner for three? We're

of Love."

"Pardon me, Miss. You must make reservations at least a day in advance. Our meals are prepared to order. They're custom cooked—."

"They'd never think of catering to fly-by-nights, Stradella."

We turned on our heels without, I think, so much as even stopping in the restaurant, and exited on the same wind we flew in on, brisking past the ten blank-faced customers, all patrons of a more stable world with a bit of cracker crumbled on their lapels.

"Mother duck and her two chicks, eh, Rudolph?"

"Keep your chin down, Archie. That's my specialty."

"I'm sure I saw my father inside, only every man there was my father, and they were all sitting judgment on me, Rudolph."

Burrapp. "Oh, really?"

One night I dared to take Stradella to meet Harry and Eleanor Hardy. They owned a drugstore. "Are these your friends, Archie?"

Harry and Eleanor were glad to see me, pleased to meet her. They gave us each a coke and asked what she did, asked me so that she seemed displayed, like an inanimate parcel in a pharmacy window. When I told how Stradella was a star who'd had her own series on TV and been in Life magazine several times, they said they never looked at TV or Life magazine—"Well, that's pretty good isn't it? What's their circulation now?"—as if Stradella was the circulation manager!

Then Harry turned to me. He put his hand on my shoulder to hold me off, and at the same time to keep me near. He studied me, leaning back at the end of his arm. "Well boy, you're sure coming up in the world."

Eleanor invaded. She wanted me to take some toothpaste. Perhaps I was eying the toothpaste counter. She pressed it into my hand and then gave Stradella a lipstick. She pressed it into Stradella's hand clandestinely like a secret, but Stradella held it up and marveled. "O my, thank you." Then she looked over to the shelf. "It's very nice of you to give me this, Eleanor, yes, but I don't ever have the opportunity to use this shade and I—" Eleanor cackled apologies like a scurried chicken gushing helpfulness, "—was wondering if I might try a sample of that new mouth-wash you have on the shelf there?" Bottles flew. "Oh certainly! Certainly!" Eleanor pressed the mouthwash into her hand.

Stradella turned around and made a tour of the pharmacy. "I've decided to buy lots of things." With her arms loaded she returned to the counter. "Will you take a check?" I was mortified. She was a harried and hurried and impatient customer making Harry and Eleanor, my friends, who had been on that corner twenty years, her clerks, wrapping and ringing things up and making the change. There was nothing I could do when we left but say good-by.

Harry stood at the door with one hand on his hip. "It was sure nice of your young lady friend to come around with you, Archie. 'Bye now. Come again any time!" Harry waved as we walked away up the curb.

"Here, carry these, Archie. Don't you know it's the gentleman's place to carry a lady's packages?"

I remember the look in Stradella's eye. There was something invincible about her walk. She'd gotten my number, "Always out and seldom in, eh?"

Only once did she refer to my, "Corny little corner friends. They give away presents like Santa Claus. Does my little black houseboy like friends who play Santa Claus with him? Is that his idea of friendship? Nice little friends who give away presents like Santa Claus?"

Stradella after that was quite quick to censure me for wanting to spend any time at all anywhere with anyone other than herself for anything. "Your friends are all right, Archie. They're just like you. They're okay. Only they're square. They're not hep. They don't know how to dress or anything. They're just not my kind of friends, that's all."

There were Monday night visits, as regular as clockwork at midnight, to Canter's on Fairfax. We drew the same waitress who smiled like a pink and saggy cupid. I went there once alone on a Thursday night and the waitress stopped me and said, "Where's your sweetheart?" If she'd chosen any word but sweetheart, I might not remember the waitress.

We sat in Canter's—noisy, clanging, banging, rattling, yelling, shouting, seasick, neonlit, clamoring Canter's Restaurant—and just ate each other up. Stradella's eyes were alive with the look. She was inhaling me, warming me over with her insides. She was understanding everything I said before I spoke. When I spoke she was answering even my pauses with nods of Yesses and Um-yesses and more Yesses. She was all woman, her big breasts, her tight dress, her little girl's face. She really liked best to sit on fire hydrants in the Bronx in the summer and pick her nose, eating ice-cream cones.

I thought I was aloof, wearing the sweater she gave me. I got another sweater. It had a blue border without any collar, shorn of all buttons but one.

"It fits me."

"Well, it suits me, Archie."

One Sunday morning we were going to breakfast and I insisted on walking, to get my Sunday morning breather like one of the Presidents of the United States. I walked all the way, the eight blocks to Coffee Dan's on the Boulevard, while Stradella followed in her car. She was watching me out the front window. The expression on her face was puzzled.

"I am the former President, on Hollywood Boulevard at crisp 9:00 A.M., a deserted Sunday morning," I said.

"My Flight Into Freedom, My Plunge Into Slavery,"
said a marquee.

10

By Stradella's bed I installed the crystal chandelier.
It hung so low I had to walk around it to get into bed.
"But there, it's hung!"

It had been transplanted from a famous film director's dining room to twinkle and tinkle for us. Naturally it had been a bargain, otherwise it would never
have been bought.

The auctioneer from whom Stradella bought it reluctantly pointed out that one of the fragile glass arms
had been broken at one of the director's great parties.
The auctioneer insinuated that perhaps a certain
romantic and immortal literary lush had hung his
wife's silk panties on it during dinner in the twenties.

I repaired the broken arm with a coat hanger but
I am sad to say, it still hung down a little limply,
which was no way, as Stradella said: "For anything
to hang in my bedroom."

Rudolph Redpaw was called in from the garage.
"Of course I can hang that right. Hanging's my
specialty."

"Your specialty, Rudy? I think everything is your
specialty."

"Pretty nearly, Stradella. You don't know what kind
of man you've got around you. I'm the son of an
Indian. When I was a kid I could sit on a fence and
masturbate at a target fourteen feet away. That was
my specialty."

"Did you score, Rudy?"

"Of course, my dear. I could hit the bull's-eye
every time. My specialty. Wow! Yee-wowww!

He made a Kabuki leap—tucking his feet up under

his seat as he floated across through the air, arms out-stretched. His face was bright red and his eyes were atwinkle. His hair was on end and his pants were abulge. Urp.

"Of all the people in the world, I think you love yourself best, Rudy."

"Of course my dear. That's my specialty. Everyone should love himself best. Love's my specialty." He laughed and asked in a quiet shout, "Want to try me?" Someone crunched into his Cadillac at the curb outside.

Stradella's landlady didn't know how to drive very well and she was completely afluster and shaking and fumbling to find her glasses which she was wearing.

"Of course, Mrs. Lester. It's all right. I assure you, I can get that fixed at no cost at all. Don't worry yourself about it a bit." Rudolph's chin was tucked very far down.

"Oh Mr. Redpaw, I want to pay for it. I'll give you my insurance card. Oh Mr. Redpaw, I'm really very sorry. I know how you feel. Oh Mr. Redpaw, I'm just all upset. You can't imagine."

"Certainly Mrs. Lester. I understand perfectly. Don't you worry. I assure you, it happens all the time. Don't you worry at all. I understand perfectly."

"Well, all right. I think your house is lovely—. Oh, lovely, Stradella."

"Do you, Mrs. Lester?"

"Oh yes, Stradella. It's lovely, just lovely. You've done so much. You've made it so perfect."

"I'm really awfully glad you like it, Mrs. Lester."

"Of course, Mrs. Lester, I will accept your insurance card—."

"Certainly. Oh certainly—. Oh Stradella, it's a doll's house. A dream house. Wait till my husband sees it. Of course he's sick this week. He's been in the hospital with another operation. They think he's going to die again. Of course I don't think he will. He hasn't died yet. But then again you don't know Louie. Oh Stradella, your house is just lovely."

"Well I tried so hard you know, Mrs. Lester. I always wanted a little house of my own. It's a personal thing with me."

"Oh, I understand perfectly. I know how you feel, Stradella. Every girl ought to have her house. And you know—it's that time—I came around to see you—our time of the month—."

"Of course you mean the rent, Mrs. Lester?"

"Yes! That's it, the rent? I'm awfully glad you thought of it, Stradella. You're such a good tenant you know, and we do so like having you here on the corner lot. I was saying to Louie the other day how much we like having you here. It's awfully nice of you to think of the rent first."

"Yes, of course, Mrs. Lester. And I was wondering if you also spoke to your husband about the option to buy the house? You remember we talked about that? I thought you'd bring me the option today. In fact, Mrs. Lester, I first thought that's why you came."

"First option? First option? Oh of course. Of course. Well I'll speak to my husband again. You know he's terribly sick, Stradella. I can't bother him about it right now."

"Say—urp—excuse me, ladies. Mrs. Lester, I understand."

"Poor man, poor dear man, he's been so busy lately. They think he's dying right now—but I already told you that. My, listen to me. Here I go repeating myself, and you were going to give me—the—I believe it was you that suggested—"

"The rent, but of course Mrs. Lester. Let me make out the check right away."

Stradella went over to the little white cupboard that opened from the wall into a little white desk, and took out her lavender check book and her lavender pen and sat down on her lavender chair.

"I meant to mail you the check, Mrs. Lester, but we've been very busy here this week preparing the house for my party. When I have it completely finished we're going to give a party to warm it. Archie doesn't think I can finish the house, but I am, and so we are. Here's the check, Mrs. Lester. Paid in full. And I hope you know that I always pay my debts and I always write good checks and I have excellent credit established all over town. So if your husband is ever worried about my paying the rent, Mrs. Lester, you'll be sure to tell him, won't you."

"Oh Stradella, but of course, poor dear man, if he doesn't die. If he does, then I'll have to tell my son. He really owns this house, you know. I just collect the rent for my son. We gave him the house for his birthday, Stradella."

"Your son, Mrs. Lester?"

"Uh-hmmm."

"Well that's very lucky for your son. He must feel like a very important and very wealthy little boy. How old is your son, Mrs. Lester?"

"Oh my son's no little boy, Stradella. My son's old enough to be your—well I should say your little brother, almost."

"My little brother, Mrs. Lester."

"Sammy's thirty, Stradella."

(Pause.) "You say your son is thirty, Mrs. Lester."

"Urup—ladies—"

"That's a very nice age Mrs. Lester, though of course I can't speak for myself—thirty after all—"

"Oh yes we know don't we, Stradella."

"But I'd be very happy to meet your son sometime Mrs. Lester. Why don't you ask your son to come around and collect the rent next time. I'm sure he wouldn't be too put out by all my pink and lavender in his house. Perhaps he could make some suggestions to improve it."

"Oh not my Sammy, Stradella. I don't think my Sammy could make any suggestions, but I'll tell him about your interest and maybe he'll drop by one afternoon. He plays a lot of tennis and perhaps he'll drop by from the court, someday."

"He plays a lot of tennis?"

"Yes, Sammy loves it. He never misses a day."

"Her son plays tennis, Archie. Did you hear her say that? He's one of the tennis set. Don't you wish you were one of the tennis set, Archie? With all that money and leisure? And a house for your birthday so you can get rent from a poor hard-working slave girl? Isn't that what you'd like, Archie? Just like my first husband? That's all he did was play tennis. Now I see he's about to get married. Where's the paper? This will interest you Mrs. Lester. Something for Sammy to remember."

"—"

" 'Johnny Jenkins, former husband of TV's Amourella (real life Stradella Fonteyn) plans on marrying Joan Creamfluff these days. He spends every day at tennis with her, and La Creamfluff has put him on payroll.' Yes, Mrs. Lester. That's what it says. I supported him three years and twelve thousand dollars poured down the drain so he could bat balls like that. I wonder how many balls I've supplied. . . ."

"Well—Oh my—I'm sure your tennis is excellent, Stradella. Well, good-by now Stradella. Bye-bye."

"Urrr—ladies—Mrs. Lester—I understand."

"Oh! You're still here. Poor man. You've been so patient."

"Well—"

"Here's my card, Mr. Menopause."

11

Creampuffs were in my head, lots of creampuffs floating, and there were flowers in the creampuffs and when I squeezed them they oozed music and my stomach contracted and growled like an angry cat with teeth and no tongue . . . until I heard the habitual music of the bread truck in the street. It was the electric music box broadcast from the loudspeaker atop the truck and it played la-de-da-de-da-da, la-de-da-de-da.

I felt good dreaming in my head about the creampuffs and when I heard the musical summons I jumped up from washing the mirrors which had been auspiciously hung on all the walls and doors so that a lone person would never want for images of himself no matter where he went through the little housey-wousey.

I hurried outside, grabbing with a perspiring talon the last coin in the bottom of my pocket, and hailing the bread truck, which stopped.

Stradella had complained as I left that the bread-man was: "Driving me out of my mind! Can't you make him stop that horrible noise? I have nightmares about it. He comes around at sunrise to sell his little cookies. Why can't he at least come a decent time?"

"Creampuffs please," I said to the breadman, pressing my dime between thumb and forefinger so that my thumb turned almost white.

"Archie, the creampuff kid," Stradella had said when I rushed out. "Just can't leave anything fattening alone."

"I'm not even dieting!" I'd called and leaped down the last stairs and into the street.

When I turned around there was Juanita. "Juanita! How are you?"

"Hello, Archie," she drawled. Juanita stepped back to get a better look not only at me, but the neighborhood. "How've you been?" She was slow.

"I've been just fine. How are you? Do you live around here? I haven't seen you for two years—two years at least, Juanita. You're looking real good."

Juanita bore up and nodded, then woke up, shook herself and sighed. "O yeah—well—I live here."

"Where, Juanita?"

"I live down that alley. We're married you know. My husband's away now. Dale. He works at Douglas."

"The airplane factory?"

"Yes, but he really does other work on the side. He's a musician really. He composes songs. Very good really. Yeah, really."

"And you live down the alley over there. Well that's swell, Juanita. How long've you been married?"

"Oh—well now—six months maybe—a year really." Juanita wore a loose-fitting sarong. "Have you seen Aramantha lately?" She turned the sarong around.

"No, I haven't. She got married, though. I saw her once."

"Uhuh—well—where are you living? Around here?" Juanita was half-asleep.

At this moment Stradella appeared on the front porch. She was hovering over me, standing a hundred yards away silently waiting and watching.

I pointed in the direction of Stradella and the house.

Juanita's face brightened up. "Oh yeah—she's on television isn't she?"

"Every night."

"Yeah sure—we watch her—really. My husband and I watch her all the time. Dale. She's certainly beautiful. Is she your girlfriend or wife?"

"Just my girlfriend," I said, though I intimated more, and finally added, half-laughingly: "But sometimes I wonder. Ha-ha." I stamped the ground.

"Are you doing any acting anymore?" asked Juanita.

"Oh no, I forgot all that. I haven't acted, I guess, since—Aramantha got married, I suppose. Around that time anyway. I just haven't gotten around to such things."

"Yeah—well, you've probably been pretty busy."

Stradella was off the porch now. She was definitely looming, and coming closer, without particular eagerness, circling her prey as she approached.

"Well this looks like a nice little confab behind the creampuff man's little oven," introduced Stradella, without defering to the speech already in progress, or smiling at Juanita or introducing herself.

Immediately I could sense the battle line set down by Stradella and for the most part observed without comment by Juanita, who was slow.

"I want to introduce you, Stradella. This is Stradella Fonteyn, Juanita—Juanita—what *is* your name now you're *married* Juanita?" I grinned.

"How do you do and I'm pleased to meet you Juanita—"

"Tombs," said Juanita.

"Tombs? Is that your name now, Juanita? Glory be!"

"Well," intervened Stradella, not acknowledging either her interruption or my interruption of her interruption. "How do you do, Juanita, and I certainly hope you're having a nice time."

"We're old friends, Stradella. We knew each other a couple of years ago, though only briefly of course. She's married."

"I see," Stradella evaluated, then resumed. "Well you'll have to come over and chat about old times with Archie someday, Juanita. I'm sure it's always a pleasure to meet an old friend in a new neighborhood. And it's been a thorough pleasure meeting you—." She extended her hand, straight and frank and official. The hand had come to pluck me. "You've got some work left in the house, Archie. I put the window cleaner in the closet. You can work there."

I looked at her, and then at Juanita, swallowed my creampuff and mumbled, "All right," and to Juanita, "See yuh," and slunk back in the house, tail between my legs.

"Where's Rita these days?" I asked Stradella. "I haven't seen her."

"Oh she's around, waiting to pounce on me from somewhere. Probably trying to buy a house in order to put me down and come around to tell me about it."

Stradella rested The Merchandise on the bed fifteen minutes after dinner before going to work.

"That cooze always has to be negative, and I'm sure there's no one else in the world she can put down but me, so I know she'll be back. Besides, when I'm doing the show she always likes to keep in touch. Never know when I might do her some good. That's what she thinks."

A little while later, when I thought all thought had gone out of that bright blond head of Stradella's, I was informed: "That's an interesting friend of yours, that Juanita. She seems friendly enough. I suppose she's always busy."

I came out of the closet. "I don't know. Maybe not. Maybe she's not busy at all. Why don't you go over and make friends with her?"

"Archie, no TV star, if she wants to keep her rating, goes looking, especially not in her own neighborhood, for friends. Where Amourella, Goddess of Love, resides, there regality reigns. It says so in my press book."

The Goddess went to sleep with her face make-up on and her hair in a puffy fluff. "Awaken me at eight so I can do my ritual of preparing The Merchandise, will you dear? This is one pussy that has to look good on TV."

And Stradella dozed off.

12

I asked Stradella about another relationship.

"Remember when I introduced you to mother, Stradella, how I'd told you I didn't have time that night to see you and then at the last minute when mother approved, I called you up at the studio and asked you? Remember that?"

"Uhmmm—yeah." She raised her head toward me. "I know how you like to talk, Archie, but get to whatever it is someday, won't you? You'll be sure to get around to what you want to talk about before you finish talking about it, won't you?"

"Yes, oh yes. Well, look. Remember how I asked you over to the restaurant and mother's boyfriend Stoney—"

"Yes I remember Stoney—."

"—parked mother's car and I parked yours? You remember then how we went inside and had steak?"

"Yeah—well, what are you driving at?"

"I just wanted to point out, Stradella, that you were sort of waiting for my beck and call then. First I told you no, you couldn't come, even when you asked to come, and then I asked you to come, and you hadn't asked me that time, and still you came anyway, which means that I was sort of in the driver's seat, just like I parked your car in the right place after the night watchman next door told me you'd parked in the wrong place, remember?"

"So what are you driving at?" she asked, with some irritation.

"So I—well—I was just trying to point out how you were so obedient to my wish—first yes—then no—without a whimper. Now it's different."

"Now it's different?" asked Stradella, confronting me with her chest. "Don't you like it?"

"Well no—I didn't say that—it's just I'm pointing out sort of how in the beginning you treated me like I was real important and how I was the boss no matter what I wanted, and you were willing, no matter what I wanted to do, and now things are different."

"Would you like to change them?"

"Well now—it's just that I—well sort of—you see I—"

"If you don't like it you know, Archie, you can leave any time you want. You can just pack up and go."

"I see. Well, no—I didn't want to do that—not exactly—you see—I just want to understand what's going on. I mean—how I was sort of more manly then and like—well—you kind of treat me as though I'm becoming mush, and I'm very intelligent you know, and I have a good memory along with nice—at least average—looks, so I couldn't really be mush all the way, though I get treated that way, sort of, don't you think?"

"Don't I think? Is that what you're asking me, Archie, don't I think? Well I don't think anything, Archie. I'm a girl of action, and I call the shots as I see them, and I act on what's got to be done at the moment, and I give you exactly what you want, so you shouldn't be too unhappy."

"Well, that is—"

"Are you unhappy, Archie? Is that it? Are you unhappy?"

"No Stradella—no—not unhappy. I just want to understand. That's all I want to do. I just wanted to bring this out so we could discuss it and be reasonable and intelligent about it rather than get mad or have an argument or be unreasonable."

"I'm not angry, Archie. Do you think I'm angry? Is that it, Archie? Do you think I'm angry?"

"No Stradella. No, that's not it—exactly."

"Well I'm not angry."

"I know that, Stradella. I know. It's just I don't want ever to end up having these sterile conversations

with you that so many people have with each other.
I want to continue relating to you. You know. And
we can only continue relating to each other if we have
conversations that are rich and meaningful and understanding. After all, I'm in the wrong so many times
myself, and sometimes even you're in the wrong, so
that it's best if we discuss things to arrive at a mutual
point of understanding, if we're ever going to stay
close."

"I don't like the way you suggest I'm angry, Archie.
I'm not angry. And as for the rest of what you've
been saying, I don't see that there's anything to discuss. I have nothing against you and all your fancy
ideas. But I think you spend too much time thinking.
And where do you get off accusing me of being
wrong? Who said I was wrong, one of your corny little
corner friends?"

"No Stradella, no. Whoever said you were wrong?
Wrong about what? I didn't say you were wrong.
I don't think you are wrong. I've never found you
to be wrong, considering your point of view."

"Don't you know it's bad when people tear you
down, Archie? That was the last thing I'd expect from
you. Heah! Here I have another little Rita growing
up right under my own roof!"

"No, but—well what about Rita, Stradella? Let's
talk about her. I mean, don't you think she represents
something in yourself that you don't like? And she
punishes you for having that whatever-it-is inside you,
and so that's why you keep her as a friend?"

"I don't know."

"Well what do you think of that? Maybe—just possibly—there might be some sort of truth in it. At
least it might be on the right track. Wouldn't you
like to think about it?"

"I don't see where it's necessary, Archie."

"Well I mean, there are all kinds of friends in the
world, and a little self-love would certainly change not

only any person's concept of himself, but also the friends he surrounded himself with, if he had either too much self-love or not enough. Don't you think so?"

"Don't bother me with these details, Archie. Turn on the television. I want to watch the G.E. Theater."

"Who's on that?"

"An old friend. Just a friend, Archie. No one you know." She paused, and then suddenly shouted. "Why are you bugging me?!! Don't bug me!"

Quickly and obediently, I turned it on. "Of course, Stradella, but then we ought to think about the fact that you once told me your mother treated you just the way Rita does, and that Rita came from Israel just like your mother, and they even look alike—a little."

"Let's not talk about it anymore, Archie. Besides, Rita isn't my friend, anyway. We aren't seeing each other these days."

"What?" I stopped breathing.

"I don't think she'll be calling again. The last time she called I just listened to that reading down until I got my fill of bawling out. Then I said I didn't thnik I had time to listen to any more of her negativity, so I hung up in her face. I don't expect ever to hear from her again. Let's watch television now. Be quiet."

My heart was beating. "You mean I've actually effected a change? Stradella, you've known Rita ten years and I came along just months ago. Have I loved you so much already the harsh scabs of old wounds like Rita are falling off? Is my love really like a balm?"

"Yes, yes Archie. Now be quiet."

"Well okay. We're going to see someone you know on the G.E. Theater?"

"Uhmmmm—yeah." The name of the program was Thirteen Men.

At the intermission commercial I turned to Stradella. "Do you suppose you'd ever have given up your friendship with Rita if I hadn't come along?"

Stradella fixed her eyes on me. "Looking for a compliment, my little love child? Is that what you're doing?"

"Oh—I didn't think of it exactly that way—no—not really Stradella. But—"

"Well, you've been the closest friend I've ever had, Archie. Bless you. You're an angel. No one has ever been as good to me as you. So God bless you. You're an angel. Now let's watch television."

At the end of the program she took off her face and started to go to bed, taking the TV with her.

"Archie, sometimes you try my patience, you know? You know what I mean Archie? Can't you see I don't want to discuss anything tonight? Can't you see that? Haven't I given you enough clues? Isn't that good enough? Or should I go further Archie, huh? Do you want me to put out a sign maybe? Girl can't talk. Don't talk to girl. No talk tonight. Is that what you want me to do? Hang out a sign and make it real obvious?"

"No Stradella—no—I wasn't thinking of that exactly. I wasn't trying to disturb you. I've forgotten it. Wow. Some things ought to be discussed."

"All right, Archie. What did you have in mind?"

"Well, I was wondering if you were ever aware of how formal sometimes—and sort of businesslike and kind of—well—not very warm certain conversations people have with you are? Oh, I know it's not your fault. I wasn't even thinking about that. It's just that some people are—I guess—kind of afraid of you. Take that conversation with Mrs. Lester the other day. It came and went so fast it was almost not even there. I almost didn't hear the conversation, it happened so briskly, like some item on the agenda. And I can't remember a word of it. Now you and I know we aren't really busy, and therefore, I think, perhaps it's our duty to kind of draw out people like Mrs. Lester who is so obviously anxious to please you and get

your approval. You know what I mean? To make
a conversation with you a rich and deep and meaningful experience. That's what I want to say. Because
you have it in you to be that way, and share that
quality with others, and make them feel good."

"Is that all you have to say now, Archie?"

"Yes Stradella—yes—I guess it is. I guess it's all
I have to say now, Stradella. I hope you don't mind."

"Mind? No, I don't mind Archie. Do you mind?
Do you mind if we watch the next program now?
It's only half-over, but I'm sure with your superior
brain and my superior brain we can match brains and
figure out what happened during the first three-
quarters of it."

"Yes—yes—I guess maybe we can."

"All right then. Agreed? Good. Agreed? I'm glad
we're agreed to watch the TV. Don't you know I have
the cramps, Archie? It's my time of the month. Pour
me a glass of blackberry wine. I'm in terrible pain.
I need absolute rest and quiet. And a glass of blackberry wine. That's the best thing for it."

I went to the cupboard, but the cupboard was bare.
"I'm sorry, Stradella."

"I'm suffering terribly Archie. Go to the liquor
store and get me some. Hurry. I don't feel well.
Right now. Please. Right away."

"Right this minute?"

"Yes, hurry, before it closes."

I went, though she didn't offer me money. I con-
sidered her state of health and decided to pay for the
wine myself. I returned in five minutes, after a trip
of five blocks, short of breath and out of pocket.

"Thank you, Archie. Thank you. You're a dear,"
she said, covering the receiver of the phone with her
hand. She sipped the wine, and went on talking, and
listening, and it sounded like what I would have
perceived to be conspiring, though with which un-

known and over what unknown I did not know. She sipped the glass of wine empty, smiled, listened, mumbled, put a fingernail in her mouth so as to touch her teeth and no more with it, and I offered to refill her glass. She held it up and paid absolutely no attention to me as I poured it. Then she smiled and made a kissing-like pout with her lips, forming the words Thank You Darling You're a Dear.

I knew I was. I settled down and turned on the television to bide my time till she chose to hang up, but she didn't choose, and she waved her hand like a wild wing fluttering and then covered up the phone and turned to me. "Turn that thing off, Archie. I can't hear a word on the phone." So I had to turn it off. I went in the bathroom and was miserable, and went in the kitchen, but I'd already washed the dishes that night, and paced through the living room till my legs were twitching before I heard the sound of the receiver being returned to the base. I returned to her base, but she rolled over and got off the bed and went in the bathroom where she locked herself for half an hour. "I'm making The Merchandise sleepable. Leave me alone," she said, without even saying thanks and that she was finished with her conversation.

When I asked her, "Who was that?" she merely said, "No one you know. Just a someone. Nothing important."

"Nothing important?" I lifted my watch to my face for a better look. "But you were talking for an hour and twenty minutes, so how could it not be important?"

"Well—it wasn't." She yawned.

I had to roll on the leatherette couch, which was cold, with only one blanket.

"I have the cramps, Archie. I'm freezing. I can't be bothered with your sniffing and sneezing all night."

13

I'd been out most of the day with my friend Samson Haibow. He was a salesman for a distillery. He'd given me a few samples. We talked about his approaching marriage which was only a week away. I came in refreshed and tingling, and perhaps just a little bit reeling.

There, on the couch, sat a man in work clothes.

"This is Mr. Walpach of the telephone company," said Stradella, and after introducing him, excused him. He got up and left.

"You didn't have to come in with your briefcase like you own the place. It's still my house, you know."

"Well, what was he doing here?"

"He was installing my new phone."

"But you've already got a phone."

"I wanted another."

"Another?"

Stradella pointed it out. "Now I've got a pink one and a white one. I needed two and now I've got them. With separate numbers. One for incoming and one for outgoing calls. Oh Archie, aren't they beautiful? Isn't it romantic? I'm not going to give anyone the new number at all."

"Not anyone?"

"No one." She clenched her fist firmly. "Except you. Now I've got two phones and an answering service."

"Who's going to call you? You need two phones to accommodate them?"

"Well, I happen to be a very busy girl, Archie, and for matters of business it's very important that my line remain open all the time."

She lay down in bed with her address book. She began dialing. "I have a million things to do. Now leave me alone. There's steak in the freezer." She pointed. "You're an angel."

I went to the kitchen and prepared the feast—though in celebration of what?—but when I brought on the feast she asked for the catsup. We chewed our way through the meat. She mouthed many an important conversation while I listened. I ventured to question the importance of her calling while chewing.

"The phone man was here all day, Archie. He kept me busy with everything and I had to keep him happy. He wasn't going to give me an extra-long cord. Then I wanted my outlets changed. Otherwise he would have been here ten minutes. Had to call the company three times to explain that my wiring needed over-hauling. My wires didn't reach into my bedroom. I need my wires in here. Now I'm all fixed up. I'm back in shape. You wouldn't want to spoil my day by complaining, would you? Can't you see I'm happy, Archie? Can't you see I needed this lift? It was something important to me. You wouldn't deny me that little pleasure now, would you?"

I tried to finish my steak which had gotten cold. "Is it good?"

"The meat's good. I don't think I cooked it right."

"It tastes fine, Archie. Bless you. Mine's just right." She dialed once more with a little plastic gimmick used like a finger for dialing. "He gave me this when he came. It's to save my nails. Isn't it pretty? Get me my lavender paint Archie."

"What for?"

"I want to paint it."

The little dialing finger was green. I got the paint and she dipped it lavender.

"I'll paint the telephone too."

"No, I don't think we can, Stradella."

"Why not?" She was smiling wryly.

"The paint won't stay on the plastic. Besides, I think it's against the law. You don't—we don't have the right. We're only renting the phone, Stradella."

She smiled. Then, while she was calling out on the out phone, the in phone rang. She said to her—I'm tempted to write Customer for the person she was talking to—Conversationeer—"Excuse me a minute, hold the line." She let the in phone ring again. "Hello? Pardon me? No I'm not!" She hung up and turned to her outgoing phone. "I'll call you later. 'Bye. Keep in touch." She blew a kiss through the wire then hung up. She threw me a laugh. "Faggots." She dialed again. The incoming phone rang once more. She hung up the outgoing phone and answered the incoming phone. "Hello? Who? What *is* this? Good-by!" She started to dial on the incoming line and the outgoing phone rang.

Stradella rang. She stared at the outgoing phone ringing in. She picked it up, hung it up, a terrific cold blast of hostility filling the air, and turned to me without seeing. "I'll be—" The other line rang once. She dialed a number. Her fingers were tapping everything. "This is forty-seven." She took up the lavender pencil and scribbled on the lavender pad. "Sixteen? Thank you. All right. No, don't bother." She hung up, picked up, and with a wet lavender finger dialed.

"Give me the number of United Air Lines. The main office."

She hung up, picked up and dialed again. She waited. "I want to speak with someone in charge please. I don't care who. Your traffic manager. Your airplane controller. Anyone. No! I don't want to buy a ticket. I want to talk to someone about an airplane. Your public relations department. Give me Marty Rubins. Oh." Her exclamation of "Oh" was a blunt thud on a soft drum. "Five o'clock? Well give me whoever's in charge right now. Very important. Greatest urgency. Yes, I'll wait." She drummed her nails on the new pink surface of her new plastic phone. Then she looked at the phone.

"This is Stradella Fonteyn calling. I'm sure you've heard of me. I've been receiving phone calls all day from passengers on one of your flights. Apparently someone has written my number on the fuselage of your airplane and everyone is calling me up. I don't appreciate this one bit and I'd like to know who's responsible for keeping your planes washed and how it got on there. It's an unlisted phone. I don't like this one bit. Besides, there were some very impolite things written on it. I want to know who's in control."

Stradella listened with one ear and rested her head on the other.

"Well, I happen to know it's true! I got one of the calls just a moment ago. My answering service has been getting them ever since the plane landed. I have better ways of spending my time, you know. What flight? Number 615. Yes, that's right. New York City! I don't think this is funny at all. Having my name plastered all over the wall of your airplane and throwing my number around like that is certainly bad company policy. What? Well will you please look into the matter? You can call me back. What did you say?" She paused, tapping one, two, three with her new dialing finger, mounting fury as a bird mounts prey. "No I won't! You find out for yourself what my number is by finding the airplane! Good-by!" She smacked the little phone down hard and turned to me somewhat seething, but that suddenly subsided. She spontaneously broke out in a grin.

"Someone's been giving me free publicity. I don't like being called up by country hicks from all over, as if those visiting firemen—"

"Those firemen couldn't stoke your furnace anyway, Stradella."

"Pardon me? Please Archie, that's no way to talk to a lady. Please be more respectful."

"More respectful?" I adopted my scholarly, nasal, abstract, scientific expression.

"Yes, more respect. That's no way to speak to a lady."

"But I thought—well—here we are in your bedroom and—well—I thought we were on intimate enough terms and knew each other well enough to—well—have a little joke."

She suddenly went through her address book, wetting her finger to flip the pages. She was dialing with the other finger and inviting someone over in mellow, luring tones. The minute she finished, she slid off the bed and stood before the mirror. She stretched. "Ah, wilderness, Stradella! Such endowments! One kiss cultivates an army!"

Then the doorbell rang.

"There, Archie, answer that."

"Certain of my desires have to go down. Certain of my intentions have to relax first."

Then I did.

Juanita and Dale, slow and tired, in luau suits, entered. "We were just watching TV," they said in unison, then stared.

"Hello, Juanita. I'm so happy to have you drop by my little house. How do you do, Dale. May I fix you a drink? What will you have?" Stradella rolled out the carpet.

When they went home, I turned to Stradella. "I didn't know you were friends with Juanita now."

"Oh yeah. I'm exhausted, Archie. Entertaining's so strenuous in your own home. Clean up for me will you?"

"How long you been friends?"

"She came over the other afternoon and brought me some flowers. I hate flowers. I told her so. They smell so much and decay and fall all over the place. But I do like plastic flowers. She likes them too, so we decided to go out and get some."

"I guess you're going to be friends now." I was half-wondering to what extent I was losing track.

"Yeah, I guess. Tomorrow I'm taking her out to Glendale—the clinic."

"What clinic is that?"

"Where I get my shots. She wants to lose weight. That's what I do to lose—get a shot every week at the clinic. What are you going to do?"

"I—I don't know."

I thought of how unplanned my life with Stradella had become, and how dependent on her, and then how planned and independent *her* life had become.

14

I hate to leap ahead, to tell the tale of awful things before the awful things were done, to plant the hate for Playbaum in the ear of friendliness for Playbaum, but, alas, I did.

"I hate him."

"Archie, you hate no one."

"Wise souls will hate also."

"You're just bored. Go play."

"I'm going to set out and provoke hate in him."

"Get yourself a playmate."

"Ride off on my silver horse to war with Samuel Playbaum!"

"Cool it, Quixote."

"Create some trouble with him, just to calm the end of all his kisses, or excite more of our own. There is a lull of kisses with us."

"I've got chapped lips."

"I've got business. I'm a man. I've got to create trouble if it won't find me out."

"You'll have enough. Why not play with your corny little corner friends? Stop trying to be such an out-cat."

"But I already am, my pussy."

"I'm going out. I don't have to listen to insulting conversation. I'll be up at Royal Court if anybody calls."

"I'm going to get him. Samuel Playbaum—X!"

What a catastrophe of manhood, that my whole life should pan out to this adjustment of my situation, because I started trouble for him. Look:

He was a big producer and he sent his car around to get her, to go "to the studio for shots." It sounded like a death wish to me. Here she was, the prime of life, the very paragon of health, and trotting off when strange men came or called up and—

But I shall not blame them. There is one thing I began to notice. Stradella Watched That Cigar. For months the smoke of it had permeated me, had gone right up my nostrils, had wrapped clouds around my head. Would you believe that I was going to write a letter read by Samuel L. P. Playbaum saying to him, straight, watch out? And still I did not get the trail of smoke, the scent that left its brand all over—Samuel Playbaum's dark gray cloud of Upmann, burning black Havana.

He received a letter from me but I little guessed he knew already everything. I said to Mr. Playbaum that I was the Friend, the Great and only True Friend of the young star he probably had heard of —there was my line of subtlety!—Stradella. Did he know her? Perhaps he'd understand then why I was concerned. Her life meant more to me than her career. Perhaps, as someone very wise, as someone who had made the scale of movie ladder-climbing, he would be the man to do it—to Discourage her, to tell her it was no good, send her back, poor girl, To Me. I mailed the letter, licked and stamped it, sent the faithful contents off. And she rewarded me.

Slap! Who the hell did I think I was bothering a truly great man with my petty larceny? She had me on the carpet for a half an hour, telling me to be more honest and respectful and not write off such letters that would hurt her.

"You are being followed," she said.

"Followed?"

"Followed. Corporate spies know everything. They know who Mr. Playbaum knows. They make their business knowing who knows who that Mr. Playbaum doesn't know yet. You've got you a shadow, Archie. Where—and how—and when—and why—you're being followed. I could guarantee it. You're recorded and reported on and taken down in detail. Someday when the goods are up and you go mad with jealousy—attempt to shoot him for what you imagine are his tick-tack-toes he's playing—you are going to find yourself exposed, and some informing youngster's going to make his fortune turning in your slightest heart throbs to the joy of Mr. Playbaum, with which he'll revenge himself and take me off forever from you. Oh—poor Archie. My poor Archie. Tender, sorrowful, Archie."

"Get lost! Get lost then! Deceiver! Wretch!"

"Don't cry. The damned don't cry."

The idea. I lived with it several days. And didn't like it much. The problem was who was my shadow? Where were friends and enemies and how did they stack up?

"You know, if I'd not written him that letter, then I might not—no, but that would not be possible. I wrote that letter, since you're caught by him. I appealed to mercy in him. Appealed to human kindness. I appealed to all of Mr. Playbaum's tenderness. And I beseeched him to forgive us, everyone, our sins, and let you go, be free, to come and live with me."

"And you don't mean that, Archie?"

"Well, I'm not naive. You don't think I'm a fool. You don't think I believe that Mr. Playbaum isn't human, do you? I don't think he's soulless, do you? I wrote kindly to him. I have seen his movies. I expect kind treatment from him."

"Those're movies he produced."

"I think he's kind."

"His money isn't."

"I think he's human."

"His business isn't."

"I think he's understanding."

"His results aren't."

"He's not one of your perverted monsters. He'll return you to me, creampuff. He won't let you die out there. That's what I sometimes pray for—creampuff. He knows you'd be happier—oh much!—away from him. He'll drop you."

"Yes, well—keep your eye out for him."

I learned then to smell the smoke. I smelled it in her Thunderbird, and in her favorite sweaters, and in her pedal pushers. Oh yes, I learned well and good and once and sure for all, to watch, to sniff, to keep track of that Havana cigar.

The faint trail of its smoke became my shadow. I was really followed now, by Samuel Playbaum's shadower.

15

We entered into the golden time of our love in the week of Samson Haibow's marriage, and perhaps it was fitting that there was a marriage at least somewhere along the line. But it was also the week of the long-planned party to warm up the long-prepared housey, and it was the golden time of our journey when we fled from the city in our love and toured.

It began, this golden time, when we sat in the living room together, side by side on the couch, and completed the telephoning of guests; for, though I didn't know who they were, as the guests were all hers, I agreed to support her suggestion that she invite almost everyone, and waited by her side as she worked at the phone, and called almost everyone, and got tentative answers from all.

"People never say what they mean. Here I invite everyone, and everyone said they'd love to come and would sure try to make it if they could possibly work out their schedule to make it. No one said they would definitely be here."

"That's the way it goes, Stradella. It's up to us to go ahead anyway and prepare for the kingdom and queendom as though a famine surrounded us, not even sure if the lowliest lackey will arrive, and he on an empty stomach, or thirsty, or whatever."

"Yeah. I guess."

"Some people even invent a language, Stradella, to heap all kinds of words on your ears without letting you know one thing they feel."

"Explain what you mean, Archie."

"Take the case of a producer's preview. You go to the theater and with him right there you're the first to glimpse his new show. Now suppose you don't like it, in fact, you think the film stank, but yet want a job from this producer someday. Some might praise the film and others might come out and damn it. But now take into account the producer himself, whom you want to impress, and get on the good side of, even though you don't know his own thoughts on his picture. Suppose he made it purposely bad, in order to write off a tax loss. You'd hate to have him think you were a fool by praising the film which he hated, and on the other hand you don't want to condemn him if he possibly labors under some dreamy delusion that his potboiler is really a prize winner. So what do you say? And this is the language of lovers in Hollywood. To the producer you say, Mr. Katz-Blatz, your film was Absolutely Astounding. It was—well—Out of this

World. I've never Seen Anything like it. The film was a positive—absolute—fantastic Departure. Notice now, Stradella, not one commitment."

"Yeah."

"You smile as you say it."

She smiled.

"You make yourself eager, anxious to please, and heap on words, but still don't praise. It's too risky to be caught liking or disliking anything, or promising to go to a party or not promising to go, when something better might come up at the last minute, or nothing at all might come along."

"Do I speak that way, Archie?"

"In Hollywood, the subtlest art of all is belonging to every movement without being responsible for any. That gives you liquid assets, and plenty of mobility to go up and down as you please."

"Can I do that, Archie?"

"No Stradella, you can't do that. You're honest."

"This party is the peak of all my dreams, Archie. Now maybe I can get launched into the world as A Person, rather than A Personality."

"Of course, Stradella, vertical motion is great and all that and most of Hollywood is just that, going up and down like a mouse on your sleeve so fast it'd make you seasick, but the real people who make it, even in Hollywood I hope, are the ones who stop all this action and start making themselves a few commitments and getting involved in some promises. Then they develop a new kind of mobility, a sort of horizontal one."

"Am I like that kind, Archie?"

"Of course not all of them develop it on their backs."

"Oh Archie—Archie—you said I was honest. Hmmm."

I heard the snuggling snickering. I'd get laid tonight. The grin, the warmth, the softness, her slight lean against me, all were promises and preludes. I was aware of the rich mellow copper of her skin, its nearness to me, limpness filled with an inner agility, a ready quickness waiting deep beneath the sleeping skin for my impassioned, bathing kisses to make her relaxed. My words had coaxed me into her favor and now she was ready to pay the tribute.

Well—so I kissed her.

It never occurred to me she purred because of her own actions, and because of her satisfaction with the completion of her house and her approaching party. It seems clear to me here, by then Stradella was no longer at all an Archiefied woman, a personal private Flum plum, such as my mouth watered after.

But none the less there I was with Stradella purring. She melted butter and slid down toward me and cooed and put her warm fingers on either side of my lips and opened her lips and branded herself, toasted against me. Then she leaned back to speak, to gasp.

"Do I talk sincerely, Archie? Do I say what I think?"

"Far from the popular Hollywood vagueness, Stradella. Far from it. Your words are definite. By their precision they're exciting, decisive, lightning bolts."

"Really? All that?"

"Thunder of the flesh. When you speak out, I shudder, Stradella. Your purifying speech tears away entire rocks of my puritan past like crags that fall into the sea. You speak a primeval language that has existed since the beginning of time and has stayed as pure and simple as all essences of things."

"Oh Archie, you mean I really talk like that? You mean that's really honest?"

"Yes, Stradella, though of course to the moralists and censors and to Hollywood in general you should apologize for not sounding vague, for speaking honestly. Of course don't let your apology be vague."

"Oh, Archie, I want your sprinkler on my lawn. Pin my pennant to your tree, and pluck me, pluck me, pluck me! Till our nest is feathered." She made it sound like a sigh, but with glee, and with a child's spontaneity, collapsed upon me, plumber, carpenter, mechanic rolled in one, and banged away upon my hammer, nuts and bolts and vices holding, and with crosscut sawed to bits.

Ladies and gentlemen, the ordeal of rendering these lines to you has been an emotional experience of more depth and dimension than I have been able to calculate, and it leaves me limp and exhausted. So I must lay down my pen for the moment to recoup my energy before we move on to a lighter hit.

She licked her lips and recanted her language. "Ummmmm! That's bedroom talk. Too strong for the living room. Got to save it. Come on. I've got plans for you!"

She was desperate to become a woman. I was so near at hand, and so near right, loving in all the right ways for all the wrong reasons, she accepted me completely. So far, she was not free.

"Stradella, have you ever gone to heaven on one ski?"

"Suppose the party fails?" she said as we crawled in her bed. "With all those second-feature people, a B-Picture party with B-Picture bores."

"I'll show you mine if you show me yours."

16

No negative bombshells, blond or otherwise, flew around us. Sex was every morning after toilet, and sometimes on toilet, in the kitchen bent over the stove, sniffing a pot and getting a poke. "Oh Archie—the party will be my monument."

The mailman daily pushed letters in through the slot, and didn't even wake us up. All the changes of address were finally straightened out.

There was a little Greek clockmaker who claimed he was Swiss who repaired the chime clock which we had on the mantelpiece. The clock decided, at midnight dong once, at one dong twice, at one-thirty dong once, and at two dong thrice.

The party was approaching. The world I was. I was delirious and backwards. When we went out I felt in. My beard bristled. My tie dangled. I was wildly tame. My underwear I wore inside out.

"Is the party really approaching?"

"We've finished. The party will be my monument. Now eat your egg."

I found the ability to primp up a peanut till it signified the whole Andes Range. I grew tired of peanuts taking the place of the Andes and wanted to put down a few real peanuts and maybe an Andes Range or two, without mixing them up, and ended up tossing the mountains to elephants and hiking around on peanuts.

The monument was approaching, the party for Stradella, and I was eating my egg. Who was she? How did her monument grow? The more I was with her, the less I knew. The more we fled, the less we flew. Into traps tripped memory, and never walked again.

How do you know a woman when all she is or ever was amounts to a collection of glances and twinkles and laughs and touches, a few words, a lot of other things, lavender, bottles, unguents, oils, a last sniff of lanolin on the shower curtain, some faded press and toenail clippings, and a certain way of opening her mouth?

How do you make this woman into a monument when all she ever stood for was clean cuticles, clean breath, hot tongue, good jokes, journeys from the bathroom to the bedroom, enflaming pictures reeking out of the clouded now shrouded sheets, a love song wrapped up in a rounded stomach, overweight and bulging breast?

How do you sigh and weep and laugh, keep your feet from freezing on the cold kitchen floor, what with the night and the empty memory of her hundred and fifty pounds and six foot one. How could you help wondering at her submissiveness to little, tiny, puny, undeserving, unattractive, impecunious me? Especially when I was so broke.

Please note it's important for the hero to deprecate himself. Actually, when I look in the mirror, there is a terribly handsome, virile, aggressive, charming, fatherly, patient, adventurous, swimming, romantic man there with his spirit like the very apple and core and seed of life itself sweeping hotly out like lava.

But now back to reality with a little surer approach.

Because I have learned that in reality I was a little, puny, tiny, undeserving, unrewarding, unattractive person, and that's why I had Stradella. Not that others didn't want her, but whom could she want, already having had all, and what want, mainly, in the beauty, virility and charm department? All she needed was a flaw, and that's where I came in because that's what her man had to be, her tragic flaw.

Her party, her monument to herself for herself, began with another party where we went to find guests for our party, which was rather a strategic move on her part, since that party was three days before her party, and all the right people were there, potted on a shelf, glazed pottery, crocked crockery.

Stradella circulated with glad-guys and I had a wonderful time. Because in all that polite pottery I met a peanut—or rather a miss—and her name was Pendant. She was aesthetically, ethereally, exhilaratedly intoxicated. Never would a sylphlike nymph like that get drunk, bombed, potted, blasted. She would get highly elated, a little bubbly, giggly, and then concede to admitting she was, yes, just possibly, ever so mildly, a wee-teensy-bitsy incandescent. I got her phone number and decided I'd really stick it in her good. Note the hostility of my attitude. But isn't that natural, considering I knew I would betray Stradella?

But Stradella was circulating with everyone in the room. She was smiling. It seemed rather automatic. She was laughing. I thought her laugh had a touch of robotery in it. She was holding her glass and saying all the right things, and listening in all the right ways, and not drinking at all, but swallowing the stuff.

Oh, she never drank anything but blackberry wine. She never smoked either, and held the cigarette in her hand as she circulated through the party. "I only smoke when I'm constipated, Archie. It gets my bowels moving." She kept her cigarettes in the sequin-covered box on the tank behind the toilet, next to the sequin-covered jar of cigarette holders which were all twisted pretzels of gold and pink and lavender plastic at least a foot long each. But why was I thinking of that?

So at the party I met Freddie Ravens, Jr. He was the son of the famous movie director. We got talking and I played The Nobody and he played The Somebody—parts that suited us well. He was only a year or two older than I and had already been written up in Life magazine. I was myself, which is always the best way to play Nobody.

Freddie was talking to a Spanish girl who was certainly talking to him because he was about to direct a picture, and that was the curse of his profession. He had to be listened to by bosoms rather than by women, and be talked to by bellies rather than by mouths.

At any rate, Freddie Ravens, Jr., finally made a very funny comment. He mentioned going to a certain high-class school once and I said I'd gone there too.

I had gone for an afternoon, to visit a friend. Since I didn't tell that to Freddie, I committed my first honest Hollywood lie. Freddie put his arm around me, said I was honest, took me into his confidence and close to his liquored breath. "Where was I? Where? Oh, yes. Well I wanted to go on with this very funny comment about this young Spanish girl with us. I met her in a whorehouse in Havana when I took a weekend off from our school."

"Oh, did you?"

"Yes, I did. Did you? You young Spanish lady!"

"Yes, that's where we met."

"But," I began, "that's impractical, here, at this party, to admit such a thing."

"What's implacable about it?"

"No, it's all really very natural—down there you have to eat everywhere—you know."

"Did you eat in the whorehouse?"

"Oh yes, we did everything there."

"Wait a minute—wait a minute, kids. That reminds me of another very funny story about her capacity."

Stradella flashed down on us. "You putting my little black boy on?"

They looked at me. "Yeah, we're putting him on."

I told Freddie and the Spanish girl my story.

She's since become a starlet or I'd reveal her name. With income and prestige and approval and holy success and hallelujahs all around her, propriety and respect and possible rake-off completely prevent my naming her. It doesn't matter. I could name a dozen just like her.

I told them I'd lived once in Cuba, with a Cuban girl, and she was very native and olive and Catholic and gentle with her brown hand soft on my arm and gave me a little baby once though I hadn't seen him twice, because she took him back after she gave him to me, and went away somewhere with her father to live in another part of the Caribbean. Weep, weep, at this point, went my voice, and my lips pouted, and my eyes became heavy, and my throat sad.

Freddie put his head on the Spanish girl's shoulder. "Oh, oh, that ought to be a script. We ought to film that. Oh—oh—"

The Spanish girl listened with her bosom.

Stradella pulled up again, flashing, and let her siren run down. "You pull your poor lost little boy act with the I'm A Sad Daddy Too twist? Poo-poor, sad-sad, boysie-woysie."

They all looked at me. "Yeah, I'm putting it on."

Rus Harren was there. He was a toilet-paper heir. Peter Winner was there, the prominent socialite wealthyite playboyite who was nearly killed racing his car a few weeks later in a spectacular hairpin turn where there didn't happen to be any hair or pins. Lance Revelentlow was supposed to be there, but for some reason Lance didn't show up and everyone was disappointed except me.

Later I realized Lance manufactured cars. When I was trying to get my rattletrap out of that sea of racers, I was disappointed. I'd always wanted to meet a guy so handsome and young and rich who was actually not spending his money, but investing it, as Lance did.

I nearly cracked the car up trying to wheedle and whittle and back it out—big old rickety rattletrap convertible that it was, with pulled-out fenders and torn-up seats—weaving in and out with delicate drunken precision between the myriads of sports cars and race cars and tiny foreign bomb jobs parked there. Mine was a shoe in a sea of splinters, a bear in a cage of chickens, a whale among eels. Oh, how I wanted to meet Lance!

"Well Archie, I invited everyone at that party to my party." She seemed very satisfied.

"Good. I had fun too. Did they all say they'd come?"

"Oh yes. Everyone said they were looking forward to it and would surely try to make it, if they could."

"I'm glad, Stradella."

"It's going to make A Person of me, show I have more than A Chest."

But I kept remembering the first seed of doubt planted in me, echoes from the party that never quite lasted and never quite ended.

One very respectable young man who was a building contractor put his head in his hand and shook it. "You and Stradella came together? You're kidding! That's an unusual pair. You really go out together? Most unusual pair I ever met. You and Stradella? I never would have thought you and Stradella had anything in common. It must be common, or is it uncommon?"

17

Sometime between the courting and the kissing I first felt the sting of that desire which was to invade our every feeling ever after Stradella rounded up some guests and labeled them her friends, captivated the captives for her celebration.

Perhaps I was actually showing my first healthy instinct in this relationship which doctors have since called Oedipal. Perhaps I was growing up, but I actually started to compete with Stradella. I made the acquaintance of Miss Judith Pendant at that playboy party. She wooed me in the kitchen and she cooed at me from the den. She made my nerve ends burn as the evening sizzled to its own end. (Does clever wording set the stage for clever lovers?) I can still see

the pile of blond hair honeycombed on her head and
the long white gown and the long-sleeved gloves.
She flowed through the door like a napkin-ad lady.
I made a try. We made a date.

Stradella didn't know. Of course not. Would I,
faithful lover, emotional spouse to the Queen, be a
talker? "Archie, your mouth is a lethal weapon,"
said Stradella when I discussed the whole playboy
party and everyone there, all their secrets and such, to
cover up that one person and my secrets about her.
"Your mouth makes my friends the weirdest couples.
Like couplets—" she laughed, "—to copulate." I merely
looked sad, sweetly abashed, and silent. A lethal
weapon perhaps, a suicide weapon, not. She could
not draw from my lips the praise I sealed behind them
for Miss Judith Pendant. And so Stradella made out
her list with a lavender pencil on lavender paper for
her day in town running errands, not suspecting my
intentions, and leaving the garden hose set. "You water
the grass now, like a good little black Japanese boy."
I would water, and I did, in my best luncheon suit.

We met at her office, my cheeks red, for Miss Pendant in Beverly Hills was secretary to Walter Slarrk,
Architect. I waited at the reception desk. I waited
in the wire chair set out for the people who waited, an
uncomfortable chair to me in my pressed suit. I held
my hand at my knee as though a hat were in it, but
to show off my youth I neglected to wear a hat, as
flowing hair's always so much more romantic.

And she came out, flowing herself and with umbrella in hand for it was just a little bit drizzly that
day. She stopped. She looked at me first, then glanced
down and commenced to draw on her gloves. "Oh yes
—oh—well—yes—my my," were her mutterings. I was
not only intended to hear them, but also to imagine
their meaning.

She was gloved and prepared and I offered my
hand to her exit. She came out into the parking lot

with me, not close, not exactly distant, but certainly not intimate. Of course I'd parked my car in the street, far from the sight of the Architect. We got to it, entered, started off. (Why was I so clandestine, even when free to park open? Was this my time of clandestine training?)

"You are a—you are a—" she began, my ladylike Judith Pendant did, meditatively—"a student aren't you?" as we drove down the street.

Archimedes Flum IV, sensing at once great danger, boomed out in a great voice to correct her before losing. "Not a student at all. I've finished. I'm an unemployed poet at the moment." That should make me, not only her equal, but her superior!

"Oh, I see," she assented and glanced down. Before I could really stamp out anything, she settled it herself. I knew I was stuck. Now I must open the wound in our relations in order to close it, if I wished favor. I must admit she thought I was too young. I must admit same without pleading guilty to same, but must present same aggressively, not defensively, for slightest slip of same and she would seal same doom in the back of her brain—my doom, her rejection—and say no more about same. She would be polite and wait out the luncheon and thank me surely and go off, never to near me again. Which is just what she did.

But what did I want? Silly dreamer, I wanted—and there are not enough words to describe my desire—I wanted salvation, the universe, the epitome, woman's love. We were nearing the restaurant and still I debated my tactics. How to prove my superior age, to put her at ease, to conquer her? But alas, we got to the restaurant too soon, one with which she was familiar and I not, one which was too expensive for me and her not. It cost me every cent I owned. I went without pennies for anything the rest of the week. Thus victory was lost at victory's expense.

Not a word of the luncheon do I recall, but as we

ate, and my mind summed up the total cost, and I chewed, and we looked around each other and behind each other but not really at each other because that had already been done in the first minute of the luncheon, I commenced dismantling Miss Pendant in my mind, removing first her magical complexion as merely the illusion of night lighting, and carrying off her hairdo as probably built on stiff fibers in the first place and therefore not very practical for running the fingers through.

When I was done with Miss Pendant she was sitting before me chewing frankly on an olive pit. I had reduced her to just Judith Pendant, a daytime secretary to an Architect. Thus did we return to her office, not a minute late for the afternoon shift, but of course, as we had nothing more to say. She got out of the car promptly, thanking me politely, and went toward her tubular tomb of an office that lay like a great worm in the center of its own parking lot, her head bent down, not even looking back once, or thinking back either, I suspect.

She had insisted I not accompany her in and I had assented. After thinking about her for several minutes, one knee cocked up on the front seat, mind stunned, I slowly turned the car and went back to Stradella. At least she was in love with me enough to make love with me and not criticize that part of our relationship. At least Stradella gave something.

So I had failed with the great blond ladylike love of the sophisticated world of the great playboy party to which all the richies came, and I met her and I even found myself believing she'd failed too, in first posing as sophisticated when she was only a secretary, and desiring me when I was not part of the playboy world either.

It is obvious now that it was all a fraud. I was a boy bum and she was a class climber, but not having any true class herself she was unable to perceive in me the same lack and so we both found each other and what disillusioned her was the utter reality of our encounter. In truth, we had too much in common to build anything in common. The truth is we knew too much about each other to bother discovering anything new in each other. She was my double.

And Stradella asked me if I had done the watering and I told her I had, and she got two tickets from her purse.

"We're going to the movies," she said. "A sneak preview: *Some Like It Hot*. I know two boys who're in it and Dorothy Loren, who got me the tickets. She did three days on it."

"— — —"

"So get out of your baggy pants and we'll go."

I realized an argument was coming on. It was the middle of the week. "Why do we fight every Wednesday Stradella?"

"Who said we do?"

"I remember, that's all. I know, Stradella."

"You're keeping track of something, is that it? Who cares whether we fight or not? Who cares when we fight? Does it matter? Really? Is it anybody's concern? Does it make things better?"

"No—no it doesn't—" I placated, already in the fight. "But I think that being aware might—being—"

"Oh my God, Archie I've more important matters to take care of. Can't you keep your studies to yourself?"

The magnificent predatory force of this female with pink knees went into action across the room and got dressed and in some sort of brooding grudge she managed to put me down several more times before departing and to humiliate me completely before Dorothy at the theater. But this is not quite right.

She did not really humiliate me because I did not feel humiliated, and if she thinks she succeeded it is only because of Dorothy's reaction to her putting me down. I did not even think of Dorothy and to me she was no more than a faceless body named Dorothy inhabiting a suit of female clothes. But when the movie was over Stradella got in Dorothy's car first and, closing the door on my face, said, "My little black boy can walk around until he feels better before going homey. My little stud has to get excited before his big mamma lets him into the warm places." She turned to Dorothy laughing quietly more at her own sense of genius for comedy than at me. The window of the car went up and she was gone.

What Stradella in all her munificent splendor had forgotten in that supreme moment of hers was that the front porch had just been painted lavender because of her coming big party and we were letting it dry undisturbed by leaving the key to the front door locked inside and using the back door through the kitchen and service porch. There was only one extant key to this squeaky entrance and I had it. So I jingled my key and kicked up my feet, fully conscious of my appearance of lightheartedness in a moment of total rejection, and thinking that it was wonderful to be rejected sometimes. I squeezed the lone key in my pants pocket and went to the Hong Kong, a bar near home, where the man I encountered was my friend Samson Haibow.

"The party's tomorrow night," I told him. "You're coming, I hope, aren't you, for sure?"

"But tomorrow's my wedding day," he said and I gasped.

"Your wha'? Getting married? Again?"

He admitted it, yes, bought me two drinks, paid up, plopped down off the stool and oozed home with me, and so we got to the back porch, more talkative than hasty. We found Stradella inside.

How it ever came to pass she got in without a key I will never know, nor did I take particular notice of the tennis socks by her dressing table, or the tennis racket behind the door. I am only mentioning these observations now as they fly back to me like missiles from some subconscious observatory in time, warning against the future where before they had failed even to ripple the present. Footprints tracked in the paint.

Perhaps I was truly innocent then, as Stradella insisted I was, and my diabolic decisions to betray her with hundreds of other women were but the youthful yearnings of one who really was innocent. How much I had to learn, such as: betrayal comes gradually and many women seldom: these are the real rock-bottom elements of a background that no longer relies on innocence. I was therefore wide-eyed and helpless standing there in the kitchen, my key in hand and friend at side, facing Stradella in her cake-swallowing negligee as she was tossing us out. I don't recall anything but drooling. God, I wanted to bathe her in my mouth, if that is a perversion not too exciting to reveal, all the while she was raging. But we were out on our ear without even gaining the living room, let alone the bedroom. "It's my house! Take your friend and get out! I don't care who you are, mister—."

In the street what impressed me so much was not my friend Samson's feeling of rejection or sense of rage that he as a stranger should be so insulted by my girl, but that Samson somehow was more conversant with the moods of a capricious and unpredictable female than I was. All he apparently wanted to do was to put me in a better frame of mind and get back to his drinking, as though he knew Stradella himself and was shielding me against her.

At the time I suspected my friend Samson himself of having had a secret affair with Stradella. But as I reread these lines, it occurs to me that he had seen the tennis racket and socks, and wished, by attracting suspicion to himself, to distract me from a far graver, more painful suspicion—namely, that Stradella at that moment was carrying on in secret with an unknown someone. What graver shock can a lover undergo than this? What more rocking disturbance to his chemistry?

And the last time Samson was mentioned by Stradella was one day when we were dusting the rafters and she was sewing the last stitches into her new dress, and we washed and rewashed the glasses, and she made telephone calls. "Are you coming to my party tonight, Archie, or are you going to your little friend's wedding?"

"Now, what do you think?"

She went back to dialing and in walked the landlady's son with a pink in his cheeks and a spark in his eye, heading straight for Stradella in the bedroom past me holding the door without even noticing apparently who I was or why I was there. For some inconceivable reason I have forgotten his name. Consult please, the earlier pages to find it. I refuse to bring it forward myself.

18

So came the night of the party. It is the party, perhaps, for which this confession is written. It was because of the party we met. It was toward the party we began almost instantaneously preparing the house to prove she was domestic, preparing the party to publicize it. And the crown of all our living was mounted on anticipation of the party. Thus is explained her almost fervent hostility toward me which never entirely healed when I ventured to predict we would neither finish the house nor get anywhere near a party. You will see the curious twist our loving took when the party became memory, but for now, the party:

A brief description will suffice, this great moment like most great moments standing primarily on its simplicity and, compared to the preparation, appearing rather inadequate.

On the inside of the front door was an honor scroll.

"To all my 23 studs who swept and brushed and hammered and sawed and screwed my little housey into more than a lick and a promise, this party is given in honor of you who are all Kings for the Knight with your little Queenie, Amourella."

The landlady's nameless son, whose face and frame have now slipped into obscurity since I wrote the last chapter, built a cocktail bar out of Rudolph Redpaw's bedboard which had been Rudolph's pet project out in the garage for some weeks. Before it he placed three stools upon which sat three whores with fat bottoms who rested their breasts on the bedboard and sipped their drinks which the landlady's son mixed.

On the floor sat a number of people who in the course of the evening dropped ninety-seven cigarettes into the fibers of our valuable hard-won carpet and left 103 burn marks. One glass was broken. I remember it well, for a sexless girl sat on it, jumped up and cracked it between her thighs. She was the only one who wore pants.

We were all extremely well behaved. There were stains of sperm and smells of crotch heat permeating the bathroom and closet, but nowhere else in the house. I vaguely remember some lady whom I think was a redhead with Stradella once when we first met, introduced as a call girl on vacation from a shampoo commercial, who made some rather vague allusions to the color of the hair in her panties matching the color of the hair under her arms, one of which she raised in laughing and teeth-sparkling splendor to show us. I recall a man whose gift for social adeptness was not too bright, who produced some pocket scissors and for

some obscure reason wanted this girl to put down her
glass and let him shave some of the hair under her arm.
I recall the late arrival of Freddie, Jr., who was our
celebrity and played the piano for an hour and a half
with the graciousness and dignity of a man who knows
the state of and amount of his income for the rest of
his life, and is pleased and comfortable, if not a little
bit disappointed by the turn of events in his life.

But most of all I recall Stradella, a face of bizarre
complexity, a mask of terrified joy painted onto another
mask of girlish delight. Serenity suddenly subjected to
the first stab of savage flame from a hot stove, a face
of yearning and trust, alternately as docile as a lamb,
easily led and responding to every word with obedi-
ence: a face disclosing the keenest insight into every
other face in that room, a knowledge of the real raw
guts that made that room tick. For the first time I
saw the naked panic, the private deep pores and scars
of a self-inflicted life that had brought on this supreme
crisis like a finished monument in a moment of rev-
elation. I saw Stradella's face on top of the body of
Juno, the Amazon, the Amourella, the Goddess of
Love, seeing in the people surrounding her the verifi-
cation of every one of her needs and the polarization
of every one of her acts. I saw in that fixed face of
Stradella the stricken image of a dozen shattered pasts
and the emergence of only this present as the in-
escapable vise of her intentionally created self. And
for all the change that was in her that night, and for
all the preparation toward it and for all the agony
during it, I saw Stradella emerging stronger, getting
wise to her own state and crawling over the silly parts
to a newer and clearer summit of personal health
and human exaltation, where with a twinkle in her
eye she was able perhaps to gain new lengths of living
freedom from the chain of a past too small for the
spirit it encircled.

It was not the turning point in Stradella's life, those

more brash spokesmen of Stradellian destiny might say. Indeed, I can not even say it was a very important day in her life. Certainly the guests at her party won't remember even half of all the things I've put down, should they come across these pages in print while browsing at some newer party. I can not even believe Stradella herself will recall half of the details I gleaned for these sheets.

And that leaves only myself as testament to the event from which all others have fled with blank response. How then is it possible, since it is not even remembered, that such a night as this could ever stamp a mark on human history? It is not conceivable. Summing everything up, before this party was, Stradella had been. After this party, Stradella became again, and very little more than the shadows of that night play across her face. The lights of that night have faded into newer repetitions.

You might be interested to know that this same Saturday for me was filled entirely with another experience.

The wedding of Samson Haibow to Astri Sveldson was at 2:00 P.M., a time when Stradella was sewing stitches in her pants and I in wedding tuxedo—which was really my same old dark suit again—was dusting off the sills.

By circuitous back-street hustling I managed to make it on wheels and, sanctimoniously smiling, with my hands hanging crossed before me and my head and imagined double chin bent down in benevolence, stood in the foyer and waited and then stood in the hallway and waited and finally stood in the patio outside and waited.

Maybe they were postponing this wedding, or maybe it was hurrying along to its appointed destiny, facts for which I have no grounds, having been taken to one side by the friend of the groom and lectured to about the use of flashbulbs inside the church and the possibility of getting a still photo of the bride and groom from the altar itself, if the church authorities would allow us to set up a ladder in front of the altar. And I was prevailed upon to hold a box of flashbulbs throughout the ceremony.

When the wedding broke and the guests came out I ran three leaps and a bound to my wheels and was away from the scene almost as soon as the groom was, sweeping his little Astri off briskly. I'd once driven her home from an argument with him and she'd asked me if I wanted to take certain liberties with her, which of course I didn't.

Now they were laying a stream of exhaust down the street and the tail of the escaping car practically touched the ground. My car was in second and tempting their fender and out the window was I, waving wildly, appearing on the surface to be wishing them well and intending to appear that way on the surface, but underneath wondering if perhaps they were going to turn left at the next corner and would I have to follow them so long out of respect, since it would hardly be polite to pass up the bridegroom, honking him, and then desert him, or should I head straight for home where I would wash the clean glasses once more and help to change the bedboard into a bar.

Later that night, minutes before the party, I was away again to the reception. Traffic was clogged. I could not find a fast street. There was no parking space nearby. I was the first guest there, and had to wait for it to begin. Pacing and standing still and drinking water and waiting were my nervous stimulants for half an hour before the pace of speed was resumed as the "glorious couple" arrived with their entourage.

The bride's parents spoke no English and later I learned they were not even her parents and not even married themselves. The man was her former stepfather, and the lady was his—excuse the substitution—friend.

The groom's father had vanished years ago because of drunkenness, and his wife who'd remained to raise Samson, was there with her new man, a little squeak of drunkenness, and his wife, who'd remained to raise no fingernails at all, and she was ensconced in a coat with a fur collar and had somehow managed to seat herself where she'd not have to move again all evening. Even her new husband used her old name: Mama Haibow. Beside her the Baptist Minister's assistant minister sat and lent his good old down-to-earth all-American godliness.

The orchestra consisted of two former buddies of Samson's and the boy who parked cars at the bar where Samson and Astri's eyes first met across the plastic neon-lighted top of a squalling snorting juke box. I remember the car-park boy gleefully smiling through every minute of his performance and I thought it was because all he could think about was that he didn't have to work tonight parking cars and that and his mind full of horn honks and motor roars was enough inspiration to make anyone a Caruso.

The highlight of the reception was the dance of the bride with her unmarried stepfather who had come all the way from Uppsala, Sweden, to Los Angeles, America, to give away in holy wedlock a little girl who probably didn't really mean so much to him anymore, but who needed and loved him with all the hope and fear of a very frightened and very trusting little person thousands of miles removed from the only trust and warmth she ever had known. And he looked rather empty of expression which I guess means that he was bored and controlling it; but when they danced I will not forget it because he bowed before her like a courtier of old and held her hand with grace and kissed it before escorting her to the center of the room. She had eyes only for him and he looked down at her like the great man he was with a genuine forgiving temperance and from him flowed a kindness I could feel as I watched them.

It was probably the moment of the first pang in her heart when she felt that twinge of pain and parting, as though she were just slightly stabbed, but in the moments that followed the wound was filled up with a deep warmth that flooded her whole being. It was his fatherly love and had come to comfort her all the days of her life. Perhaps my memory deceives me, but I know I heard a full orchestra playing a great waltz for them in that moment.

19

Would you believe it if I told you I was picked up then in a car by two young apes I never knew or saw before and driven around the corner and up in the hills and talked to? That I was the object of a friendly threat?

"You don't write no letters no more to the Playbaum Studio. You keep your nose clean. Want to lose your freedom? Just keep out of sight. You ain't got any business, buddy, sending him no letters 'bout the girls who act in his own pictures, see? Keep clear of Playbaum. You ain't ever going to meet him. You ain't ever going to say the word Stradella if you write him. You ain't ever going to bother him. He's got his own big life, little man. Whoever put it in your head to write him, get this straight: You ain't about to break in on his privacy. You got it? Keep your little nose clean, bud. What are you anyway, an over-grown midget or a stunted man, eh bud? He's got a family, Mr. Playbaum. He don't like your little letters coming registered to bother him, you see? You got it? Nose clean? Straight now? No more monkey round with big boys, got it little man?"

And that was how I heard my life was not my own and I was breathing private enterprise when I stepped out to take fresh air. It was no pretty warning. I received a true blow on the brain cells when they left me off and drove away.

I received another warning by the telephone as I shaved to go to Stradella's. "This is to let you know, you're not alone, not for a minute, pal. We've got the greatest sympathy for you. Our good friend Mr. Playbaum don't want nothing to go wrong with you. He likes your inner mechanism and he don't want any of it spilled. You just pretend like you're a good boy even when you don't know all the moves, pal. Give your friend and ours a pretty wide berth. He don't want no trouble. You don't want no crossed eyes, got it? Straight?"

Hung up. The line was dead.

And so was I, and felt like I was hung up with it. What an awful line. I pulled the window shade.

20

The burst of the bag of terrible tension that had built up for the party disappeared. Stradella was released like a bird from her cage. She swooped to wax lyrical as long as she wished, though I noticed she never asked how I liked the party but told me, "It was a real success, very popular with everyone." To her, this meant the party was miserable and she didn't need me to argue about it with her since it would finally end on these platitudes anyway.

I am extremely proud to waken all those who sleep in the back rows, to raise the curtain on a performance of a show within a show, this being a country idyll entering the scene to echo the city debacle, rural terms replacing the regulations of life and death in the city and the slow departure toward decadence.

Samson Haibow insisted I bring Stradella down to

his house for the weekend as he and his bride were
bound for a honeymoon and we would have it all to
ourselves, so immediately I prevailed on Stradella to
come, and she agreed she would until the hour of
departure when she said she'd rather not. For twenty
minutes I urged and she neighed, my tugs meeting
her boredom.

"What's going on down there?"

"Nothing," I said.

"Oh no, Archie. That sounds like a complete bore.
What kind of a house is it?"

"A cottage, by the ocean, in the country."

"Oh come on, Archie. I can't stand just you and me
together batting around a house, just us two."

"It'd be fun."

"I'm tired now, Archie. I want to go to sleep. Leave
me alone now."

"They're waiting to go on their honeymoon Stradella,
and we said we'd show up by 9:00 P.M. for the keys.
Here it is eight and you're not set and we've got an
hour and a half to drive yet."

"Whose car would we go in?"

"It's a long trip. I think we ought to take yours."

"I don't want to go, Archie. I've got my nice little
house here and my party's been a success and I'm very
content right now. I feel very peaceful. You know
what I mean, Archie? Can you appreciate that feeling
of peace, Archie?"

"You'd be mighty peaceful down there too, Stradella. Come on now and get dressed. They're waiting."

"I don't want to pack too many things. I'm tired of
packing. They're all so heavy."

"Just pick up your purse, your coat and bathing suit.
You look fine like that. Come on now. Right now. We
can go without anymore talk."

She went to the toilet first, and packed a little bag
quickly with an assortment of nighties and perfume
and oils and of course her douche outfit. We departed

an hour after we should have arrived and when we had driven an hour and a half we ordered two half-chickens in the basket. The memory of a very unusual looking woman behind the cash register, with a cigarette implanted on her lips like a permanent fixture, and a squinted birdlike stare, hawks back to me along with the recollection of chicken grease and my weird sense of comfort in just traveling with Stradella like a god sweeping her off and she quite content to be taken, and silent, though we were an hour and a half late already in delaying the honeymoon.

When we arrived the newlyweds had almost finished packing and so we weren't late in the slightest. Then a drink for the road, a wave of farewell, some last-minute instructions on the clean and dirty sheets, and how to work the shower outdoors. We were alone.

Let me tell in brief the incidents that rest in the memory like rocks once buried in the sands of detail, but now washed clean by the ebbing of years.

We spent our first night in the bed warmly pressed chest to back, and as if by the movement of the waves we could hear, at unsignaled seconds we would roll in the opposite direction and press close together like two kittens at peace asleep in a basket.

When morning came and we awoke together I importuned my lady of love but she would have none of me, and though I tried with kisses and gentle gestures she would not turn on even a sigh. I tried a newer approach.

"It's the perfect time to do it, Stradella. It's morning by the sea, and we're rested."

"I don't feel like it, Archie."

"I'll tell you what then, Stradella. I'll pay you."

"Pay me?"

"Yeah. Pay you money."

"Pay me money? You don't have any money, Archie."

"I've got enough to pay you for one."

"How much have you got?"

"Well, not very much really. Six bucks, Stradella."

"Where is it? Let me see it."

"Over there in my wallet."

"Well, get it."

I leaped from the bed to the cold floor and brought it. She set it aside on the bed table as I crawled into the blankets and against her. She made a snuggling sound that was warm. I ran my hand up her side. She ran her hand down my chest, slowly, smiling in a good-humored way with affection. I kissed her neck and she pressed it against me. I slid my lips up to her ear and down her chin and around her lips without touching them, continuing my journey up her cheek to her ear into which I fed the sweet silent token of my warm breath, and when she moved against me and I could feel her body rigid against mine, there was a terrible gnawing in my stomach as her hand ever so slightly and without direction filled itself with my stomach and slid around to my side. Tenderly and almost in slow motion I slid aside the top of her nightie and paid labial homage down her bronzed throat to the top of her breasts, one of which I cupped in my hand with reverence as I moved my lips over the nipple and wetted it trembling and circled it repeatedly as she began to draw her stomach in, then out, beckoning my hand to explore her as my lips pinked her breasts and her sighs became groans. I let my fingers travel over the open arid stomach, which is the freest access to the valley below, and on its surface obstructs no passage or to the fingertips offers no mystery except the little cave of a navel and therefore rather tends to hasten the meeting between male fingers and the curly and netted and meshed black hairs for which my fingers ecstatically had traveled and wound themselves slowly in the painful love dance of courting and entering, of penetration and death.

She who had kept her legs closed, tightly pressed to each other till this moment, put her hands to either

side of my cheeks and let her opened lips slide up my
face and over my eyes before they found my mouth
and partially surrendered, she drawing my tongue
between her teeth first and sucking it like a candy and
milking it as her hands went around to my back and
her arms ringed my throat and her legs relented just
enough for exploring, she cocking one leg up at the
knee and letting the other one lay.

But now I was being pushed off. Her hands were
removing me from her embrace, and pushing my face
away. Down my lips went over her breasts quickly,
down down wetting with my tense tongue dragging
over her stomach and veritably boring a hole in her
navel as her muscles and skin rippled once uncon-
trollably like a horse's mane, and she moaned and let
her head sag to one side over the pillow and her eyes
shut, and her free hands began to grope.

I traveled close to my face into the world of scents
immortal and set the finest jewel of a pendulum clock
trembling as it ticked back and forth and the wet
hairs parted to reveal the pink and scarlet walls of a
lava crater that undulated. And in my nose were the
mixtures of sweat and secretions of hot contained
odors pouring out of the most animal origination, and
the juices of a fruit I've never been able to purchase
at any bar anywhere or drink from any fountain but
this swirled through my lips from hers, the nectar of
Nirvana. And I was dimly aware that her lips were
drawing a line up my leg in dampened dancing, sucking the starch from the hairs in my skin and her fingertips drawing pictures over me as though laying the
faintest web of a fabric of feeling like a net, and her
mouth burning a trail of familiarity up the inside of
my leg, at which point she opened her mouth with a
groaning voluptuosity as though she had been over-
come and was stunned by the force of a feast too
overpowering any longer to withstand and she swallowed, weakly, making moans and bathing me in her

cold mouth and breath, but not stopping the movement of her lips as they traveled up, up, and then
drew again and tried to swallow as her fingers still
played like delicate little maiden gloves.

She kept swallowing and moaning in what was a
total convulsion of abdication and each gulp she made
seemed to take more and more and to be stronger and
tighter and harder in its slow, hypnotic persistence
toward the goal.

I felt we were rising to a higher and higher place
where there was less air to breathe and less desire
for breath, where our nerves were drawing thinner
and thinner, and all of our muscles were quivering to
a soundless pitch like the inaudible whistles for blind
dogs, and my body became more minute and detailed
until to the backs of my knees I could feel the position
and life of every hair and the animation of every cell.

There was a pause, as when a sweeping bird rises
to its peak. There was a freezing of motion. The bed
turned to ice. All animation stopped: it was as if a
dancer had been photographed as she attained mid-
leap and had been halted in perfect suspension and
balance between two points.

Our eyes were blown by the wind that rushed past
and our faces were erased almost entirely of expression until our heads were nonexistent—white nobs of
stone—and we were without pain in a thick envelop-
ment of motionless slow water where she had begun
it all by giving in to me and shudderingly releasing all
possession of her body and throwing it away to the
death of herself in her lover and I was pumping the
honey and butter of a new life and a new and fluid
beginning.

We watched each other with our once sightless eyes
and smiled with our entire selves in friendship and
warmth and forgiveness and indulgence, as though we
cared for each other greatly and with deep respect and

love and forgiveness again, out of the shared knowledge of the very earthly secret of ourselves, while our
bodies lay by still coupled and squeezed, aware of the
universal transcendence that our knowing gave up
over our bodies, until the last natural spasm ended
and subsided and the last natural squeeze came forward and withdrew.

We were without recourse.

Two minutes we were silent.

Then.

Dawn.

"Well—that's it. Let's get going," said Stradella. My
body fell off hers. She sat up. She took the money
and laughingly threw me a side glance. I put my
hand out to touch her.

"Let's try that again," I said, feeling sure I was
ready to begin all over.

She got up and went to the bathroom. "I've got to
wash out the little Archies. I'll bet I've got a million
little Archies running around inside me. I've got to
wash them all out and not leave any in there so they'll
be lonely. I have to go take care of all my little
Archies."

"Oh, come on, Stradella. Let's try one more just for
the fun of it, in another position."

"You don't have the money, Archie. Don't you know
you're all broke now and don't have another penny
and you'll have to borrow from me all weekend and
can't you be a good little boy like others are? Don't
you know when to be grateful for what you've got
and not beg for more when you've run out of money
and can't pay for it?"

"You mean you're actually going to take that
money?" I asked.

"Of course I am. You made a business agreement.
You promised a certain amount and now you've got to
stick to it."

"But didn't you just plain enjoy what we did, Stradella? Is the money that important you must take it, after all that pleasure, my last dime?"

"But that's what you agreed to Archie and that's a pleasure too. It's kind of fun to earn money doing your pleasure and know you're getting real money for it and not just the same old one more lick and a promise."

"You mean you're really going to take money, like a whore?"

"Who says it's like a whore Archie? It's natural, and it didn't take anything away from what we enjoyed and it did add to my own good feeling that I was actually accomplishing something."

"You know, Stradella, I think that you are going to find every time you couple with a man, if this is your attitude, that the very reason you couple for, which is to bring you closer to someone and closer toward marriage and a lot of children, will be the very thing that drives you farther apart and makes it harder and harder for you ever to have any closeness at all with a man or marriage again or children. I think, with that outlook, as time goes by you'll get more and more men closer and closer more and more often, but every time you do, the closeness and intimacy of your act will become more distant until finally it'll not exist at all."

"You think I want to get laid to be close to a man?" she asked, genuinely interested in this conversation.

"Yes, I think so."

"I don't know," she said. "I really don't. Maybe you just get laid to relax muscles, to get rid of the pimples, to charge up the battery."

"Is that what you think it's for, Stradella? That and that only?"

She thought a minute, then, "Yeah. Yeah, that's what it's for. That and that only. All your other ideas are just silly, Archie. That's what it's for, just to keep your complexion clean."

"Then I say the real whores of the world, if that's their attitude Stradella, are really not whores at all, and the women who do it for the other reasons are probably the best whores because they don't stop at pimples and battery charges but let it be whoring all the way to the last little ounce of every feeling they've got, that there's nothing more whore-naked in the world than a mother of ten kids who's faithful to her husband. She's the real whore, the supreme and ever-lasting and unceasing twenty-four hour one from every direction and position—with body and words and family and business until she's just one great internal-external transparent eternal fuck, the mother, wife, mistress, friend, partner rolled up faithful to the fellow in all positions."

"You're very crude to use that word, Archie, and I think you ought to act more respectful to a lady and not speak that way to her while she's on the toilet. And furthermore I resent being referred to as a whore. That's no way to address a dignified person who is a real, true, refined, kind and considerate well-mannered lady."

"Which proves my point!" I shouted.

She wiped herself and got up, pulling the handle and letting her skirt drop. She came across the room at me flashing her simple peasant-girl smile. As she passed she rotated her hips and brushed her hand across the front of my pants. "I'll show you mine if you'll show me yours," she said in the voice of a little girl in the third grade at school trading dolls.

We lay on the sand at the beach and went shopping. In a third-rate dime store we picked up two mugs of coffee, two pairs of slippers and two sacks of candy. We picked up some gift paper that cost more than the gifts and we wrapped them and hid them around the house for the Haibows. We bought ourselves two great-sized sombreros, mine of pink and white rings, and wore them. Stradella kept track of how much I'd borrowed and owed her since naturally it was I who was to pay for all this. So I appreciated the thrift at least.

She earned more in one week than I earned in three months, but I was becoming a man because she was becoming a merchant and the little boy blues had to be paid for since now they were boring her.

I recall we made the bed up with fresh sheets and when we drove back to town, she hummed. Yes, hummed songs, and sang some, and purred like a pastoral kitten with the deepest sounds of reflection I had ever heard coming from her throat, of the stillest section of the long flowing river of love, where it runs the most silent and deep, and I knew more than she did what a profound effect this weekend had made on her. But no more.

So we went to the grocery and the city returned to us. She burned the dinner and I slept on the couch watching TV while she made notes and the telephone rang.

21

Shortly thereafter, finding my company comforting on out-of-town jaunts, Stradella agreed to accompany mother, her devoted Stoney, Stonewall Jackson Smith, and me to the desert where but three scraps of memory linger. They are pictures:

Stradella sitting at the table in the hotel with mother wielding a knife and fork like a monarch, Stradella looking very much like mother's little girl as I looked like her little boy and Stoney like her satellite. It is true I worshiped mother and the way I expressed such a monumental emotion was to be contemptuous and vituperative.

But there was the worldly success of Stradella Fonteyn, sitting with one hand in her lap and her head bent down just slightly in the way good children of successful parents are prone to sit. My love for Stradella was in fact homage to mother, a monarch in the same worldly success who had never, to my existing knowledge, had to do anything for the acquisition of what Stradella had gotten only through suffering and sacrifice. How little I knew then of mother.

But all that was soon to become known, for the discovery of Stradella was my introduction to the person who was really mother, not my dream. So much for the slightly incestuous glimpse of Stradella sitting demurely at table with the rest of us children for mother.

Second picture is a piece of pure pulchritude. Perhaps it is a little bit comic. Perhaps it is no more than pretty. I don't believe it's symbolic of anything, but then it might portend profound depths, but if so, count me out. Amuse yourself with it, is all I ask. It is a picture of Stradella in her pink brief panties and pink brief bra and her sunglasses of white bone shaped like two hands cupped around her eyes and her huge new sombrero that measured four feet in diameter, stretched out in a deck chair, in the middle of the desert with not a car, a road, a house, a river, a hotel, a stray dog or a group of tumbleweeds within miles.

And seated next to her in this picture, on the very small traveling bag she used, a full three heads below her, was me, reading the book of her own poems to her. Since you now fully visualize this still color slide, let me surprise you by putting it in motion for a moment before turning the leaves to new scenes in my scrapbook. I get up and try to lie on top of her. She brushes me off like a fly. Then, reconsidering, she lifts one leg and allows me to run my lips up her thigh. Then she decides to change her mind again, looks around as though embarrassed by such action in the absence of a public place, stands up, makes me hold a blanket before her, so that neither of us can see her, and proceeds to change behind it. Finished, she comes out, we fold up the blanket and chair and walk off into the sunset across the desert five miles in a straight line, getting sand and little fossils in our toes, until we have disappeared as tiny dots among the sage. Before we go on, as an expert might observe, that lifting the leg bit of hers I think is rather a good summary of her entire bit, don't you?

But the third picture is again back to mother. We all shared the same hotel suite and mother got the bedroom. The rest of us slept in a row of cots set up in the living room. But I thought it rather odd that we should be lined up, Stoney nearest mother's door, Stradella next, then my little brother, then my sisters, then mother's beloved dog who took the chair, before finally, and lastly, me on the couch. I felt a little odd, being at the end of that long line, looking over the dog to keep one eye on my angel sleeping by Stoney. Those are the three pictures.

When we returned home, Stoney drove mother's big car with all the kids while Stradella and I went in her Thunderbird. I had a feeling of being bound to mother as we raced across the desert to catch up with mother's big car, and passed it, and got caught behind trucks and raced across the desert again and caught up with mother, and passed her, back and forth like a darting little flea, finding neither accomplishment nor success nor even a rewarding relaxation because of this. I was helplessly bound to an inferior-sized car whose sole virtue was its superior speed, while that very virtue robbed it of the heavy steady stability of mother's machine.

As we drove, I was educated into the sex practices

of many Hollywood stars, Stradella recounting to me their special pleasures. For instance, a certain Mr. X, "likes to have beautiful girls take a dump and urinate on him in the tub. He does it at parties. All the time. I saw him do it once at somebody's house."

"Oh, yes?" I asked. "Doesn't he get it all in his beard and really messy?"

"Oh, yes," she said. "But he loves it. You should have seen him beg the girls to do it."

"Really?"

"Three of them. For an hour he begged, and he almost trembled he was so anxious. He finally offered them money. Then they did it at once."

"Were you one of them?"

"I? No, of course not. Do you think I'd do a thing like that? Who needs it? I don't need that sort of thing to keep going. That's for the glad-time girls. I've been asked for years and I've never put a price on it yet. You ought to know that about me, Archie. I'm surprised at you."

"So, what about—" I paused.

"I know another star who can only make love with three women at a time. Isn't that weird? Isn't that really a bit sick?" She made a quizzical expression. I saw it genuinely puzzled her. "But of course he really can pay. I guess that's why. Is that why I guess it, Archie? Because he's rich?"

But I was followed. There was no doubt of it. Not the universe of out-of-town trips could adjust the shadow. He was on my tail.

I felt it when I went out shopping, felt it when job hunting, saw it in the way that people looked at me and then their eyes trailed off behind me and went vague, like I was in the way of some express train moving down behind me from some awful source.

And they reacted kindly, looked at me with new perspective. I went to the Guild when we got home, to get a circus job. They wanted clowns that week. I asked to see the top man. He talked nicely to me.

"Yes, your credits seem in order. You look like the right clown for the job. You like to clown, eh, Mr. Flum?"

The man was nice to me and made his conversation friendly. I was going to be a member of his circus troupe quite soon.

And then the telephone. It rang.

"Excuse me," he said, picked it up and listened. "That's right—yes—uh—huh—yes—." And he turned around as he spoke, looking at me, picking up my form, the honest application blank, and turning his back to me as he went on talking with the caller, going blank himself. At last, then, he replaced the black receiver and said, sighing, "Well, I guess—uh—mister—uh—yes—well, then, we'll call you. Take a little time to think it over. We'll be getting someone to—uh—get in touch with you."

He smiled and excused himself. He had a lot of work to do, would not put too much hope in getting me the job, so many other applications, you know. I was pretty young to be a true clown, anyway. He had his eye out for a more experienced man.

Would I leave this clowning photo with him, though? He wanted it, just so he could remember me. Yes, there was evidently something—Yes? I had a million copies of the photo, had a million of them. I could spare the picture. Well then, fine, he would expect to hear big things of me one day, but as for this, well—maybe I was really not too interested anyway. He didn't think I would think much of it, as clowning.

No. No certainly. Good night. Of course. It was not day.

22

Stradella decided that week I should travel. There was my father whom I could visit since he'd asked me and she wished me to get money from him so I agreed to go and bought my tickets and got ready. Me, the robot. But the night of departure she dallied and lounged in the markets and did not get home until it was too late for her to take me to the airport, so I begged her to drive me to the bus, which made her howl like a cat and go to the toilet, and I waited, until at the last second she hurriedly drove me, let me off, and then vanished into the night without even waiting for the bus to arrive. I was on my way to the north with doubt in the south and unrest in my heart.

My father, to whom I had never been close, stayed distant in the same house and, with the urging of Stradella ringing in my ears, I finally nerved myself to the only means of attack that were possible if I was ever to get any money. One could only be an unpaying guest in a house so long before asking for something.

He sat me down for a drink and to face him and after three minutes and with the drinks nearly gone—conversation impossible as we knew each other too well for trifles but not well enough for serious matters —I leveled a voice that teetered on short cords and tried my best for the manhood that was long overdue. The slaughter of the father was to me, you see, the start; symbolic conquest of his basic resource: my victory.

"I want some money, Dad."

"I don't have any. What do you want money for, anyhow?" he replied and was ready so fast with his answer I could have sworn he expected it.

"I'm broke and in debt and my car's done in. It's

no good and I have to drive a long way to get anywhere in L.A."

"I can't help you out."

I looked my father straight in the eye. There was
freezing in my stomach. There was a fluttering in the
nerves of my arms. It came out like the first speech
of my life.

"I don't care whether you can or not. You're going
to help me out because I've got to have this money or
die, and you're going to die before me if my hand and
will have anything to say about it."

My father seemed to cease breathing. The ice cube
rattled in his glass. His face whitened and he sat up
straighter.

I looked. I just looked at him. In thirty seconds three
hours elapsed, but even thirty seconds is a long time,
and I waited that long, closer to death than manhood.

"How much do you need?" he asked.

I set my figure at half what I'd needed and pacified
myself with a hope that someday when I was a real
man I'd do better.

He got up and stormed into the kitchen where he
poured himself a new drink and bitched to his new
wife in tones loud and long enough for me to hear,
that I was a selfish and demanding son, come to rob
him.

He came back three drinks farther ahead of the one
drink that finally reached the glass, and in his chair
brought his eyes to my face, and said like the bull in
the *corrida* relinquishing his last shiver in the struggle
of survival, "All right you can have it. But I'll expect
you to pay me back at the rate of five dollars a week
and sign over your car and whatever you've got in
possessions to me and have your mother co-sign for
the security."

He got up and left the room for one more drink
before I could reply to that, as though it were a fore-

gone conclusion that I would naturally comply with whatever he said, or else a foregone conclusion I perhaps would show him the superficial and one-sided fairness of his scheme for repayment; so he left as if he were racing for the toilet.

When I stood at the plane depot with him next day, he bought me a second and extra-large drink, which was my reward for whipping him and my badge of graduation, I thought. We shook hands and I departed after one last question, born of my state of relief and feeling of being relieved, and because I wished to end on a human note with him after the grand rape of a few bucks.

"Have you ever dreamed all your life, Dad, of the one and only great woman of your life, and then met her?"

He looked at me like a man struck somehow by a blow to the body gut. It took him a one-beat to recover. "Your mother was like that," he said hollowly.

Now, thinking of mother, I try to understand my love for Stradella.

In L.A. I waited two hours at the bus stop after I'd called Stradella from the airport and been told at least to take the bus if I couldn't afford a cab.

When I was a boy of eleven every Saturday I attended the matinee movie. The theater was seven miles from home. The show was over at four, when I called mother to come pick me up. She said she'd be right there. The evening performance was at seven and I remained, shivering through the dusk in the moonlight, a little boy in a T-shirt, overalls and cap, as the crystal frost fell, waiting for mother whom I telephoned again with the theater manager's nickel. It was past 9:00 P.M. when she answered the phone in surprise.

"Didn't I pick you up? Aren't you out in back playing? My God!"

In an hour she finally came to save me; this made in all a total of six hours I'd been forgotten, remembered, re-forgotten and re-remembered.

With Stradella it had only taken two hours. But the similarity! Think of the similarity! It exposes my infantilism. Even the words "came to save me." What prisoners of the flesh we are, even in our words.

Her first question was about money.

"Yes, I got some."

"Let's see it," she said.

"He promised to send me a check."

"You didn't bring it with you?"

"No, he told me to write for it in a few days after I'd thought it over, and I was already so exhausted just getting him to agree to it that I said okay."

"You're going to phone him tonight," she said.

"But I—the letter—."

She picked up the phone. "I want to place a call north to—what town does he live in, Archie?—and reverse the charges!"

I objected. I tried to persuade her that she didn't understand the psychological implications, and that, above all, she didn't understand the delicate techniques of my Dad. Never mind. All of a sudden, there was my Dad accepting the reverse charges, and saying: "Yes, Archie, what can I do for you?"

"Er—uh—well, Dad—you see, Dad, I—I've thought it over about the money and I really do need it, and really do want it and would like to—uh—have you get it in the mail as soon as possible. You see—"

"Just a minute, Archie. This connection's bad—" he said.

"How much is he going to send you?" asked Stradella.

I told her.

"Double it. Tell him right now you want double." She ran her palm up the inside of my thigh. I wavered.

"Uh Dad—could you maybe make that check out for —uh—whatever it is I asked for and double it?"

"Double it? I'm broke now, Archie! This connection's terrible."

"But there's a rush—."

"All right. You'll get your check in the mail in three days. Good night, Archie."

I was so relaxed I panted. "Okay Dad. Gee—yeah Dad—gosh—well I mean thanks and okay and—"

But Stradella squeezed my leg with a disciplinary nonono, and my Dad hung up and all of a sudden the money was of no importance, even though I was rich, and crowned king, because it hurled me into a lovely world of transcendence that excelled even Stradella. I was an equal to Dad.

She led me into the bedroom and pushed me back on the bed like I was a cumbersome intrusion and only my loins dripping over the edge of the bed mattered to her, and she proved this by getting down on her knees before me—Money Bummy—and taking down my dress pants and burying that beautiful head of natural brown hair into the heat and reality of my groins.

This was truly the only time I ever got any money from my father, and all because of Stradella, who knew him better than I without ever having met him. The fact is, after a lifetime of planning and careful study, I had never even succeeded in getting a word out of him. How clearly I saw what an anemic, emotional misfit I was in this world of hope and fortune and men and women like my Dad and Stradella who invariably occupied the driver's seat—especially after Stradella got the money out of me.

This was also the only time Stradella ever undertook overtly to satisfy me in sex without requiring or apparently even desiring herself to be pleased. I was not suspicious, but only surprised by this, until the surprise all wore off and I just contented myself with suspicion. Remember it. Remember this place in the chapter. Like fire to wood I'll return to suspicion, but let me turn over a few kindling sticks first.

23

Friend, if I could tell you all the things left out, the bonbons and the honey pies, the cream a thousand conversations turned, you would be here for hours.

But we owe this single homage to our solar tart. Our harlot tart. What she did not give straight to me, she led me on to find in others. Thus, perhaps, she could be honored just for leading me to the Playbaum land, into The Hollywood Opera.

"You know what they're trying to do to me? Listen, Archie, put that down and listen. Everything—I'm finished. I can't make it anymore. They've put me on their income tax."

My sole and flat reply was, "Who has?"

"Don't do that. Stop doing that. Don't do that anymore. You put that down and listen. Listen—" she said.

"—"

"They write me up. They put down everything I've earned. They put down how much on me they spend for their income tax. Oh, Archie, I need sympathy!"

"Perhaps a public accountant—"

"When're you going to pay attention? All's I need's some understanding."

"I'm understanding. All's?"

"Mr. Playbaum's going to turn me in. I know it. I can feel it. This isn't any of your business anyway. You just go back to what you were doing. Oh—Archie —that feels so soft."

"I'm not bothering you am I?"

"His accountants said my tax bill was so high he'd better send me out to stud farm. No, not quite so slowly, Archie, pay more attention to what you're doing."

"I'm trying very hard, Stradella."

"They say I've got to add up and my bill's tremendous. You listening? Archie, pay attention! Archie, I'm not just a piece of real estate, am I?"

"Stradella," I said, and I stood up, and I think I truly quivered. Yes, perhaps I trembled visibly. "You are the Promised Land," I said.

She melted into feathers, blankets, cushions, like a soap flakes ad.

"He said he wants to put me on the pension plan. Can you imagine? Me and Social Security!"

"—"

"Now, I'm a woman who needs it. I told him so. Emphatically. He said to me a hundred and eighty million people—I don't know what else—and I told him I can't stand the figures. He told me the game's a game and I said, no—it doesn't matter what I said. I don't deserve that. No, no Archie. You love me?"

"—"

"Don't answer. Just keep chewing."

"What about the public, Stradella?"

"Yes, the public. I said that to him. He didn't pay attention. Archie, I'm no box of cereal. I'm a—I'm a —Live Commodity!"

"Stradella, you're like oysters," I said, and I smiled, and I looked at her full up with adoration, red to one ear from the other, beaming.

I know a description of myself attentive to her is not necessary. Maybe several adjectives are not required either. Still, the point is, being that way toward her, I can not deny it here.

"You think that I deserve to be sent to the stud farm, Archie?"

My only answer was to swallow, and to look up,

and to grin, and sigh, and—and—but the world moved on.

"You're a nobody. You're a midget, Archie. You think too small. You don't have big plans. You're never going anywhere. You're all the time discussing."

"Well, here's for bigger midgets."

"You're a fool, not a clown."

"Clown."

"You're not funny. You're sad. You're no clown."

"Clown."

"How did you dare try to get in the clown union?"

"Clown."

"Mr. Playbaum nearly died."

"Clown."

"I'm ashamed. You should remember other people's feelings, Archie. How does the press feel—how can Stiff O'Toole and all the other columnists expect to write you up—and me—The Goddess of Love, when you're a—and not even funny. Higher. Not so fast. Don't bite!"

"I thought I was original. I thought I was a clown who was a clown."

"I need a man who'll behave. Big—brave—strong—straight—behaved."

"Stradella," I said, and I looked at her, and in my voice was softness, and I was with all my concentration filled with thoughts of tenderness, and feeling them, and aiming them, toward her.

The subject of this story's passion. From this world of womanhood and upward everywhere, the key to all was passion, and the center, feeling, and it trembled when you touched it and it moved no matter when you saw it, and was always there, and secret, and sublime. My ideal state and reason, passion, was my ticket everywhere, my yearning everything.

"Looked up by the great, looked up to by the small, I can't just go out with a tiny, little, talkative, meaning-less—"

"Yes," I said, and said the famous joke. "But I've been sick, Stradella."

"Be somebody, Archie."

"Personified."

"Like Mr. Playbaum."

"Smiling."

"Mr. Playbaum's left me, Archie."

"Archie—"

"Mr. Playbaum's dropped me."

"Me—"

"Do you love me, Archie?"

"Stradella, now, sweet—"

"Quit me then! Leave me Archie! I don't need your love. I don't want your love. Love sells you out, betrays you, turns you in, enslaves you, sends you to the tax man, then the stud farm. I'm the victim of it —of all kinds of love. I don't want love. I want lovers, Archie!" she cried and ran out.

24

There was only one final trip before the last tripless spiral was entered like a tailspin that pulled down everyone around us in the avalanche.

Stradella journeyed for the weekend, and I did four weeks of dirty laundry at the laundromat.

"Dorothy and I are going with another girl on her boyfriend's yacht for the weekend," Stradella told me, as she floated in her bubble bath.

"Just the four of you?" I asked.

"Sure. Just the four of us. Sure," she said, and leaned her head back against the pillow. Remember the pillow. Remember the line she used when she leaned on it! The smallest gestures open the largest doors!

I looked down at the rug from where I sat on the carpeted toilet.

She said, "Did you think there'd be more? An orgy, maybe?"

I looked at her. "Maybe," I said.

She went on her weekend Friday night while I was in exile because of her temper tantrum. She'd intended to go Saturday morning but because of a last-minute phone call packed quickly and told me to get out.

Saturday I watered, painted the red bricks of the garden purple, trimmed the hedge a bit, vacuumed the walls, and went out to the bookstore where I ran my eyes on hero writers, feeling somewhat inflated and boasting to myself of me since there was no one else there. I noticed the attractiveness of the girl selling old volumes, picked my nose, and met my best friend and his wife, Russell and Gussie Sellman.

"We just got a book for a dime in this antique sale and look what it's got on the inside!" Gussie exclaimed. Written in ink on the old book was the signature of John Quincy Adams later verified by scholars as authentic, and evaluated for Russell and Gussie at a great price.

Hurriedly I combed the rest of the old books on the dime shelf hoping to find a Lincoln. I parted for home, for a can of cold something before the night shift of nothing.

Looking through the bathroom for a match to light my cigarette—for there Stradella kept her holders—a sudden idea of fiendhood possessed me. Like a vulture's shadow creeping up a wall in moonlight it stole on me. I could feel the pace of my thinking slow down, the heat of my actions cool, my arms and fingers glide from quick-sharp to slow-motion. My eyes, now glued like buttons in a monster's head utterly unlike my soft pools which housed so many crocodile tears before when they dreamed of Stradella, zeroed

in on the little cupboard door at the head of the bathtub, from the handle of which hung the pillow against
which Stradella rested her head while in the bubble
bath. This was the nook Rudolph Redpaw and I had
made. I looked at the little cupboard several seconds.
My heart was thumping and my body temperature
changed. The everyday noises of the afternoon ball
game on the TV next door and the occasional distant
car horns and the children's Saturday screaming at
games faded from hearing. Even the old hag lady
who'd been the first guest in our house so long ago
on our first entrance into it, whose husband was
watching the ball game, ceased haggling through her
hallways at her shell of a spouse from over her dishes
next door. I was standing alone in the quiet house. All
I could hear was the mantel clock, the one that had
been sold to us by the Greeks, which we'd repainted
with gold leaf that night the young man who reminded
Stradella of me had told jokes in a Jewish dialect and
helped us. But I was alone in the quiet house. I was,
I think, afraid.

But there was a monster like a vulture in me, and
he made me reach out my hand. My fingers furled
around the knob on the cupboard. It cracked in the
wood and squeaked as I opened it. I let the little door
down all the way. And my head leaned forward and
peered in. Yes? I looked very carefully. I felt as if I
had a fever. My heart pounded. I fumbled around
among the boxes of Kleenex and Kotex and the hot
water bottle and enema injector. It was gone. The
little pink plastic travel kit with the rubber bag and
hose and nozzle and the jelly and the parachute.

I closed the door. I ran through the house. I searched
every drawer in the bedroom. Gone. I looked on the
shelves and in fur-coat pockets. Everywhere. I looked
under the bed. It was gone. But must I repeat it?

I went down a dozen streets and my veins were

draining so fast from the top of my head to the soles of my feet, I could have been on two streets at once going opposite ways and both running and walking and passing myself without recognition, until I came to the bookstore just closing like a campfire in the desert night.

I began the laundry at two that Sunday and tried my best to read while I waited and tried my best to stop my mind roaming and ran home every half-hour from three until five looking for Stradella. I searched the house again twice, no luck. At last I folded up the laundry, most tedious of all washday tasks, most unsatisfying, and most time consuming. There was Stradella when I walked in. She was opening her mail, stretched out on her bed. She was talking on the telephone.

I smiled falsely but cordially, perhaps even elaborately. I sat for two minutes so my calmness might be established and an aura of casual spontaneity created.

She hung up the phone. "How's you, my little black boy?"

I drawled out some elaborate foolishness.

"Did you fold the little white laundry?" she asked.

I emitted a vague, unemotional reply.

"Well, I'm glad you had a nice weekend," she concluded.

"Did you?" I asked.

"Wonderful," her face lit up.

"What happened?"

"We went on Mona's boyfriend's yacht and met these movie people and they came along. Clear to Ensenada. Boy, what a big yacht!"

"All the way?"

"And there weren't enough sleeping bunks and we had to double up. So I ended off in an upper beside Robert Barron, the director. You know him? Have you ever had to sleep on a boat, Archie? I got such hot pants rocking in that cot and I guess being beside the director didn't help much. I was so hot I nearly died. The ocean turns me on."

"So what did you do?"

She could have told me how much I was needed. She could have intimated with a laugh that I was truly missed, or my loving was wanted, that there—but alas, what she did say:

"Well we couldn't do anything on the boat because of all the people around and so when we landed in Mexico we all went to a hotel but they just had one room for six people."

"So—"

"We didn't do anything. There was no privacy. Not five minutes alone all weekend. But he bought me the most beautiful cashmere sweater, with a fur collar. It cost thirty dollars. Money means nothing. He told me: Buy what you want and I'll pay for it. So I got the sweater and an ice-cream cone too. How do you like it?"

"Oh, it's fine," I said when she displayed it. "Here, I'll unpack your bag." I inched my way closer and carefully, calculating my actions for surprise attack, opened the bag without cultivating suspicion. I even flashed a smile as I did it, though all the time my brain ticked like a timepiece. The phone rang and she answered it at that instant and in the next I was sweeping my hand through the bag and then victoriously, but with the already calculated expression of puzzlement and boyish hurt and surprise on my face, held the douche bag up for her.

Stradella, talking to old Rita, looked once at it, paused mid-phone, looked at my face and laughed to Rita.

"Archie's just found my douche bag in the suitcase. Now he'll think I went to a Hollywood orgy. What? Yeah a great time. Who? Oh, yes. And his brother too. I met them both. So we had a—what? Oh, he tried. She was caught by the curse. I had them both on my tail. . . . Aw, look at Archie my great big little black white boy about to cry. Is he hurt, my boy? The awning about to drop? The crocodiles going to fall?"

When she hung up and got bed-set I thought we'd be "bound-bound," to relieve the vacation rocking, but she was tired and not willing. The phone rang and for ten minutes she whispered and mumbled with someone, and all I caught from my living-room exile where she'd banished me to fix a picture frame were a few, "No I can't," and "I just took a bath," and "I'm too tired for anything tonight," phrases.

Stradella and I never talked again of that weekend though a week later she mentioned the guy she had rocked with came over and moped around, fully boring her, while I was out somewhere. I gathered her design was to make me feel special.

"I finally got tired just sitting here staring at the walls with him since he didn't have any ideas. So I went out and worked in the garden but when I asked him to help he went home. Now what kind of bores are these take my time up? Who they think they are, King Farouk or something?"

But suspicion was edging me cornerwards. Something was making it come out.

25

I began to dig at Stradella while she sewed.

"I guess you're pretty tired of me by now."

"What?"

"I guess you're getting to wish I wasn't around so often, I imagine, huh Stradella?"

She stuck her finger with the needle. "What do you mean?" She eyed me, tentatively, a certain jealousy flickering in her. She suspected me of having somebody else.

"Have you thought of finding any other boyfriends yet, or what?"

"Archie, I'm busy sewing. You want me to stick myself again?"

The pretty picture of Jaguar Jack popped into my head like a post card.

"He looks just like me, Stradella. My friend Juanita introduced you on my weekend away at my Dad's, eh? I wouldn't have known but for that picture you had taken at the picnic where my old friend Juanita did her pimping."

"Archie, that's no way to talk about your friends. Juanita likes you."

"Well damn her hide for a deed so foul! Showing Jaguar Jack with his arm around my Goddess. Did you sleep with him, or what?"

"No. He wasn't circumcised. Who needs to put up with that jazz?"

"I wonder how you know he isn't unless he's tried and you have? Yeah—yeah sure. And now I remember how you treated me back home from my trip to Dad's, getting no pleasure out of your thirst. Of course! Was it guilt? Payment back for pleasure sneaked?"

"So I can't even sew my torn clothes in peace and quiet! I have to listen to the Grand Inquisition! Change the channel, Archie. Your commercial needs work."

"You don't need to feel guilty, if you want to start with some other guy, Stradella. I know how it is, and one tires. I can see. In fact if you've already started it's all right only don't think I'm going to mind or be hurt. I won't because it's nothing to me and there are plenty of chances for us all. As a matter of fact I expect it and haven't felt bad 'bout it 'tall. Only tell me though, so I can go look and get things started a bit for myself."

"Yeah I have. Last week with some stud and this weekend with several. You knew that, didn't you

Archie? That I would? You know everything. I never
lied to you or asked you to be faithful to me. I never
promised to be faithful to you. I never married you
or gave you any hopes, did I? You don't think I'm
betraying you now? I know you've been a good boy
and kind to me but I am bored pretty easily and after
all you don't have really much to offer a girl like me.
You've got to expect I'm going to get what I can when
and where. A girl's got to think of her future. I'm
interested in many things, Archie, and one of them is
this house, and you, and you've been a part of it all
and helped to make a lovely pretty home for me and
put confidence in me again for the first time. You're
a blessed and a beloved angel, Archie, who was sent
to me for the divine purpose of keeping me company
in my loneliness, and I'll always be grateful. But the
finger moves on and once it's pointed I have to follow
it. I wish you'd come to church with me some Sunday.
Juanita's converted me to going and I'm starting to
study the lesson books they sell about Jesus after the
lecture. It's a movie theater in Beverly Hills. I wish
you'd come with me. God is love. I'm like a river,
Archie, and I flow with the times, and I'm like a cloud
and I blow with the winds, and I work deeper chan-
nels in the earth and wrap folds of warmth like cotton
around the earth and I can't help what becomes of me
or our relationship. Jesus saves it. You were probably
out yourself and got laid last night and that's why
you're making me say this."

I went to my mother's house for the night. I should
have knocked when I entered. Stoney stood up suddenly and mopped his mouth with his necktie and
pulled at his buttons and passed one hand through his
thinning scalp, grinning all over with his usual warm
greeting, "Hi there, fella, what's the good word, boy?"

I entered the room and greeted mother, neatly com-
posed but smirking slightly where she sat beside Mr.
Smith.

The next day Stoney was gone. Going to explore for toothpaste in mother's bathroom, I passed the bedroom door and saw a strange man chasing her around the bed, and mother still in her nightgown. He was tall and very fat and had a belt as well as suspenders, a watch fob in his pocket, and smoked a cigar. He wore a flat-top western hat.

Mother told me he was rich. "The man's a miner after gold." She showed me a memento he'd given her. "This statue is one of three in the world. Mr. O'Malley sent the others to President Eisenhower and Sir Winston Churchill."

"They're his friends?"

"I don't know, but he's very rich. Mr. Wilson begged to give me his money and his policy. It was sizable, Archie. Would have made your old mother a millionaire. His two children even met me and said they'd rather I took him than they keep him on credit. Naturally I turned the man down, Archie. I'm not a common woman after all. Too bad, though. He died a week later, talking to me on the telephone, begging me to let him sign over all his money. Oh, I've missed some real opportunities in my time, but I'm not a common woman. You can't say that about your old mother. A common woman wouldn't do such things."

"Or get such offers?"

Now you know why the discovery of Stradella was my introduction to the person who was really mother?

26

The first of the week I was told to find work. The second of the week I was told to find a new home. The third of the week I was told again.

"I'm tired. That's all. I just don't need you anymore. Understand? All through. Finished. Now get out!"

"You been sleeping around with more guys? Is that it? You want to take on a new boy?"

"Get out! Go on! Get out!"

She'd been pounding in picture hooks to hang herself in framed photos from an old article out of Life magazine. She hurled the hammer at me as I skirted down the front path. It hit me in the rear end. A hammer on a fleeing bottom doesn't hurt too much, but it makes an impression.

"Get out and stay out and don't come back! And clean your fingernails and get out of those baggy pants sometime. You're not a clown in the circus in my house!"

The same night I met Erma, who was most fond of me the same night. She called me her brother and took me home to see her cat. It smelled terrible in her apartment but she insisted I was marvelous and that I had a great mind. She seldom emptied the cat box because it was so dirty and the cat hung from the curtains and hissed at us, but she told me again I was the greatest person she'd ever met and I decided to cash in, at least to try to tolerate the smell and stay.

"Let's make love," I suggested after three kisses and two hugs in a row were rejected.

"I don't want you for that purpose. I like you. Let's be friends."

"You don't like to love friends."

"I don't like to love you. That's repulsive to me. You're too nice for that. You're the finest person I've ever known. I wouldn't want to do that with you—ruin this with that when you're too good for that sort of thing."

Now this last statement put me rather in a headspin. I didn't feel about myself quite the way she did. As a matter of fact, I was convinced I wasn't too good for anything she was complaining about and holding out against. Later, I thought, later lady. You're going to make love tonight whether you know it or not, and I proceeded to crawl all over her, which was easy for me, being twice her size. She clawed and resisted and put me down with words and told me I had no right and no business and I was just like her father and when was I going to stop; we didn't know each other.

Now that comment about her father almost threw me. I decided some things just can't be said right, at least to decent people. But I draped myself around her. I pretended more or less like I was the coat and she was the rack. Suddenly she stood up and marched to the door and opened it.

"All right. Get out. Go!"

Do you notice the similarity to my recent scene with Stradella? I have taken great pains to make them say the same thing.

I rose from the couch steaming red and my necktie asunder, breathing hard, and walking slowly. At her side I put one arm around her.

"Let go, you beast—dirty thing. I thought you were better than that."

When she called me a beast I decided that's what she'd intended to say from the beginning, and all at once I could smell the stink in her apartment and I didn't care whether her cat would fall out the window or not, because I was wishing so hard she would open it, and maybe jump out herself, to give this place a better smell.

I looked with blazed eyes like a man flamed by wine. She stopped talking and then closed the door. I had not gone out.

"All right," she said, and walked to the edge of the bed and stepped out of her dress which was apparently all she wore and lay down on it and spread her legs apart. "All right, come and do it," she said, and wet one finger and rubbed it between her legs.

I went home, seeing even to this day that girl's twinkling eyes and sparkling teeth as she wet her finger and laughed. A laughing virgin is a virgin for sure.

I found a house in the ads and a job the same day. My job was an appeal to my romantic nature. I became a clown at the Pierrot Restaurant on La Cienega Boulevard where at noon until midnight five days a week I would open doors and call cabs for the traffic that brought hungry stomachs to a Pierrot meal. I would wear a base paint of clown white and a number six black on my brows and lashes and number nine red on my cheeks. The costume would be fire red like long underwear with larger than real fluffy buttons down the chest and a long sock cap with a bell for a tassel and shoes like little elves wear. It would help me eke out a more or less decent living.

My house was behind a garage that was behind a large house and it was no bigger than a trailer. In the large house lived a little old lady—like out of a witch's tale, eh? In her living room were nine open Bibles, each on a stand. She owned the property, around which she'd put up a steel fence with gates and locks and keys. Her face was red and tattered by many creases and puff spots. Her hairdo was modern and elaborate. Her figure was youthful but her complexion was condemning. It revealed a fantastic worrier.

I took the house behind the garage behind the house, and she acted like a cocker spaniel in the flurry of vivacity that followed. She asked me my religion and I launched into three minutes on God whom I loved and prayed to and daily entrusted with my destiny and good fortune, praise the saints who knew Him! She was glad to rent the house and hoped I didn't have whisky on the premises.

"Never touch the stuff," I said.

"You don't smoke either in bed or your rooms do you?"

"Never touch the things," I said.

"Well I'm very glad to learn that. You must be a very fine person. But we shall see."

I thanked her for the keys and toward my new quarters wandered. *But we shall see.*

"Oh pardon me, Mr. Flum," she called out the back door. "You don't have women in either, do you? I can't have that on my—"

"No madam, no, I never—" I assured her.

She went in.

My house was two rooms. It should have been one. Each room was half the size of the other, and after the kitchen, which was a third the size of the closet and didn't permit of French bread or stiff noodles or other long objects in it, and the bathroom which was a fourth the size of the kitchen with the washbasin over the toilet and the half-tub tilted and partly built into the wall, and the closet which was an eighth the size of the bathroom in which one shoe fitted sideways and an overcoat folded over, were taken out of the two rooms, I could enter my house by the front door and look out the back yard with an unobstructed view. It was here that I took up residence and I was proud to call my place a home.

Stradella announced she would like to see it. We arrived in her car next day and she encountered my landlady immediately.

"I'm Stradella Fonteyn. I'm sure you can help Archie out by painting the floors in his house. I noticed you have a painter working in your garage. Does he always work there? Rotten yellow is a disgusting color for a floor. Archie'd rather have it white and I'm sure you wouldn't mind."

The landlady, Mrs. Cider, knocked at my door shortly after. "Oh Mr. Flum—you don't mind if I call you Archie?—your girlfriend or whatever that woman is doesn't plan on spending the night here, does she?"

"No, no. No, ma'am. Never. I can promise you she won't be sleeping here at all. I told you I never—"

"Yes I know—all right—" she said and went away.

Then shortly after she came back. "Say Mr. Flum, I mean Archie, you're not—well you know—that is—I mean you don't have men in—."

"No ma'am. Never. I guarantee I never—not that, ma'am, for sure!"

I believe she went away as unsatisfied as she'd approached. But I suddenly realized I was being interrogated. It would take me several weeks to find out that my noble red-flannel clown self was not so low as to need this for its life.

Mrs. Cider confessed to me she was a friend of the Lord since her husband left her and that she had one boyfriend since, and he'd left her just as the man whom she'd known as father deserted her mother when she was young. Now on Saturday evenings she went dancing at the church where she had met a retired symphony flutist who had a crippled foot and could not dance, and probably could not run away either.

I heard them one Sunday morning as I fumbled with keys at the gate. They were in the back room of her large house moaning and wailing in a very unchurch-like fashion, singing hymns to passion rather than to the Lord. I couldn't get that damned gate to open, so I just leaped over the fence and went down the drive-way cursing the trash cans I stumbled over, and wondering about man's ways.

My car was in its death throes. My feet were my travel. I saw Stradella shopping one afternoon in a junk shop but didn't go in to greet her. Shopping never intrigued me since I usually ended up paying.

I went to her house instead. On the door was a note, pinned in the paint. "Baby, dropped by, love Ace."

I took out and penciled an addition in lower case: "me too, love, archie."

One afternoon, the clowning having gone well and my lunch break approaching, the familiar old Thunderbird cruised up. She was there. She had come for me, at last.

"I want to go for a ride," she said.

"What, with me? Like this?" I asked. "But I want to eat."

"Get in," she said.

We rode across town. She began the talk. "I'm going to become a whore," she said. "All my life I've been asked. Yesterday in the market I met a producer who told me I could have a thousand dollars from him anytime. I want an ice cream. Let's stop here. Will you buy me an ice cream, Archie? So I think I'm going to sell it. All these years I've never put a price on it. Now I'm going to. What good's a life where you've got the name and not the game? Ever since I was twelve years old people called me a showpiece and asked my price but I always said that I had none. Priceless. Yeah—that was me, and now I don't care anymore since they never did. I'm going to cash in while the cashing in's good."

We were back in front of the Pierrot and I was popping out and back to work.

Mother and Stoney came down to my house and Stoney said it was "an all right mighty fine place for a boy now, Arch. A good place for headquarters for our future man of the world.'"

Mother looked around and laughed. "I'm sure glad the girls can't see this. Wouldn't they die laughing. And your little brother would be humiliated! Archie, you're always surprising. We never know when or where you'll go next. Isn't Archie silly, Stoney?"

I attempted to make tea but the gas stove was weak and the pilot light kept flickering so the water would never boil. Stoney suggested we all go out "for a beer some place to celebrate Archie's being a man now with a place of his own, a real bachelor." And I said I was sorry the stove stalled but we'd have to see about getting that fixed. I was sure going to have everything working real soon.

Mother had to pick up the girls and my little brother from some Young America Club which had pictures in the *Los Angeles Times* once a year after the annual ball and bazaar. They were society bound, my sisters and brother, because mother'd "learned my mistake in you, Archie. Now I'll raise the rest of them right." Besides her big car was low on gas and not working too well these days. She'd just spent a repair bill equivalent to six weeks of my salary on her car. So she didn't want to go out for a beer. Besides I couldn't dress up for it.

"How much is the rent for your matchbox, Archie?" she asked, as I stood at the window of her car.

"It's a one-week wage," I said, "per month. Just like Dad told me. Rent, one week on four. Remember?" I looked eager.

"Your father has lots of silly notions," she said.

Stoney was silent and she told him to drive off. He looked at me sadly before putting it in gear. The window rolled up electrically, cutting off my nose. They vanished.

I heard the leaves rustle and went up to the bookstore around the corner from Stradella's. They were closing. As I passed a little house on the way there was a baby white kitten frolicking. And for some crazy reason he followed me. I don't know what he expected. He kept up.

I turned into the bookstore and asked for the book, *White Fang*.

"We don't have it," they said. "We're closing now."

"Oh yes—of course."

Another attendant suddenly leaped. "Look out for your cat!"

"My cat!" I exclaimed. He was up on the used-book shelf doing a somersault and jumping. They went to grab him and somebody with a fly swatter bore down on him, so I swooped the cat up and glanced down. "He'll be okay now—say look! Here's the book, *White Fang*. He was standing on it! I'll be darned. He's not my cat you know but I think I'll keep him and I'll call him White Fang. Why not?"

"Sure, why not," said the attendant and wrapped up the book. "Here's the book. It's two dollars."

"Two dollars?" I asked.

He didn't take the cigarette out of his mouth but let it dangle there, twining smoke up.

"Two dollars, no kidding?" I said.

He looked down and unwrapped the book. "Without wrapping, one fifty," he said.

"But—but—" I went.

He walked back and replaced it on the shelf.

Another attendant rattled the door, holding it open.

The little cat's name became White Fang and when that proved too long, I tried Friend, which stuck.

27

A little fellow. . . . Friend. . . . Let me tell you what I told him. . . .

Realistically, it must be obvious I am no more of a hero than any other man, and to some men I have been very much of a hero, and to others, very much of a sick little creature like a dog.

The frightening fact is that I have wanted to be a hero, and this has led me into the company of more than one superior person—superior of course when compared with me.

There you have what I am, which brings terrible punishment upon my own head and at my own bequest—associating with my betters.

How it inflames my emotions and awakens my diseases that sleep like little thieves in the secondary veins of my body. I grow dependent on illness—the superior illness. At night I crave and—no, insist on seeking out my superior company.

When they reject me I pursue them, but as a shadow always. I'm afraid to be discovered.

Being shabby, I once accorded my feeling of being controlled by my little thieves to the natural consequence of wanting to be a gentleman. Being shabby, wouldn't the aspirant gentleman beggar feel more inferior than the beggar who didn't aspire?

Now I've discovered it's not inferiority at all.

It's a mania: In search of seclusion to amplify perversion, I've shunned good company that was offered to me as a miser shuns partners who seek him. My friends were my enemies. I clung more affectionately to their shadow than I did to their presence—as a child clings to his mother's breast and scorns milk.

That's the image you must never forget if you would remember my profile. I was hating my friends since they hated me and they expressed it by shunning my company. Then I realized I was hating my friends and that's why they hated me.

I'd hated first, they said.

But I went on shunning their company, anyway.

Spying rather than vying was the only reward I savored. What man can love himself, loving cats, when he sees himself as a dog, and certainly less than he'd want to be?

The more I craved my friends the more I hated my friends for being craved and the much more I hated myself for sinking to such depths of having to crave them at all. Dogs! those superior people.

When finally I faced the issue with my heart and permitted myself freedom in the full range of my emotional keys, and fell in love with my superior—fell in love—in love—please hear me out!

When I fell, I found out she was no superior at

all, but very much of an equal, ordinary, sick little
creature like a dog, like myself.

This was the pill of poison! This was the beginning
of the terror. We were equal! We were the same, man
or woman, un-different.

I needed encouragement. She needed indulgence.
We had each other. Anxiety was our go-between. How
could she encourage me, needing so badly someone
to indulge her? How could I indulge her, needing
encouragement?

We suffered together.

Apart, we'd have been without misery but had the
misery of loneliness.

I thought the only solution was growth and the
awareness of change, but perhaps I grew not at all in
that escape from the prison of myself to the broader
confinement of her. I suppose I only changed. Bitter it
was to see myself, a player who changes his masks
without improving their expressions, needing solutions
tonight for problems that destroyed me yesterday.

Woe, woe, misery, misery, woe!

More of me is revealed in one word from that
second to last sentence than by anything in that sentence itself. That word explains me with accuracy.
I was *Needing*.

Some children need. Others just do. To my credit
it is, needy child I was, that at least I needed great
things, all be them not fulfilled. Not to a gram, not a
one, were they filled, and they were not filled for the
very reason I was a needy child and the needers are
never the receivers because they're not the fulfillers.

Excuse the wittiness—a cover-up for feelings of
great fear and insecurity; and self-contempt too, and
other things. Excuse the apology contained in the last
sentence. It is merely a further substantiation of the
very fact it expresses.

If the beginning of cure is the recollection of ill,

even back to the primordial birth of its malice, I
shall shock you. I remember back. I remember only
too clearly something I needed from food to love.
I shall whisper now what that was, what was many
times told me with scoffs, though by rights such a
word as I'll tell should be shouted.

(I needed the breast of milk.)

Kept waiting for meals, due to my mother's dislike
of motherhood, one day, on receiving the nipple in
my mouth, I clamped down on it too suddenly, or too
tightly, as you will, and not only with my lips but
actually down with my baby gums.

This hurt my mother.

I thought I loved her though. Quick to withdraw
her breast, she went, when she discovered I'd caused
a slight bleeding, and slapped my cheeks three times
with the very breast itself which had started to feed
me.

. . . So I've remembered and now that memory and
that memory only must feed me.

My head is a storehouse for such bitter droplets
and yet my stomach growls with hunger. I can't stuff
my head in my intestines. I've tried. But the will to
the superior life, the revolt with present life, the contempt for past life, nullify all three passages to hope.
I can not crack the cipher but live in it, and in the
cipher alone, I can no more than vegetate.

Granted, a vital cipher am I. No more charming a
cipher to be wished for, nor funny, nor diverting, has
ever moved in my circle.

The fact remains, until it gives me pain, I am always
a cipher the same.

Affectionately I'm called a clown, of course. Dis-
paragingly I certainly am, of course. What brings
up the grin from the bottom of my bowels?

. . . My dirty mitt.

People think it looks funny, my standing there

researching myself, and surviving on my own pile of sod, grin on face, tear in eye, miserable, lonely, an aristocrat of the heart, and of poverty.

People don't give me credit for knowing where I came from.

By the way, there it is again, that word, changing form but supporting the pattern. *Give.* I'm so trapped in my own self, it seems, even my words give away what I am, and my secret, most when I'm least of all speaking and no one at all even listens. So? So. I want others to give me something.

When I was still alive, my Father corrected me for dirty nails and report cards that ran downhill. Likewise, table manners never seemed quite correct in his house. Talk was either too loud or too quiet. He was completely dissatisfied.

"You're a dumb cluck! Think! Learn to think! Brainpower and how to use it. You're stupid. You don't think. You're dumb!"

One day in the back yard I did think. "I can think," I thought. "This is my first thought."

I will never forget that moment as I strolled across the back lawn, and the governess read, taking the sunshine in her crisp white uniform of crinkly folds, and the servants worked, the maid on the staircase shining the bannister, Obadiah in the kitchen brewing soup, humming, the gardener weeding and the chauffeur painting the door. My Father withdrew. A dumb cluck he had called me, and he stopped. There was spittle on his lip, a gray glare in his eye. This was the man who spoke of his Father, the great man and pioneer, drinking hot tea and passing iced pee.

To the end of my days I would see him. I would struggle in my own little way. I would use the weapons of authority to attack it. I would use power to quell it. I would use wit to end it.

Yet invariably I would align myself with the superior, and this only by acknowledging I was inferior.

But I would reject the fate of the inferior and think to myself, "The best reason for this is superior."

But if I discovered I was superior, then, even to myself superior, I would discover this thinking was exhausting and these thoughts were much too much, and thinking too much is the same as no thoughts at all, because of the death of imbalance, and so I'd be unequal again and forced once more into the shadows, but this time of my own inferiors.

How do I cure my own inequality?

Am I unequal with others or are all my unbalanced sides equal?

The more I live in the present the more I'll rebuild the past and so model new youth for the future.

But I think whatever happens shall isolate me, and in the end I shall end as all ends.

I know I have flaws and I know heroically I want to be flawless, which heroic fate is my gravest flaw.

You can not accept what I am, for then I'll know what you accept. I'll detect it. And then in quick order I'll improve it.

With my wit even myself I'll outwit, pouring the liquid of life, mixing the drinks of nature with the natures of drinkers.

You can see such a mind as I have performed and displayed here before you would not be capable of love.

Strange though, but recently I discovered it was capable of hate, and discovering this, now I've come to despise even me.

This, the tongue that's recounted you this, the drivel from the first punctured moment, is perhaps my one ticket to tomorrow.

My shouts shall rattle the walls. The walls shall crumble to the river. And the river of drool shall wash, and it shall wash away even the riddle.

In the past easily I would fit into the most impossible situations merely because of their impossibility. I would give myself over freely even to the most searing frustrations, just in order to burn out frustration, and clean it out of me.

In the passion of discovering new selves, I created by the cremation of old selves. Thus, my story. . . .

How nice it is to know I hang no longer on the past, pursuing impossible happiness, when I can stand up in the present and find happiness flourishing so beautifully in my yesterdays, every one, of my past. Certainly there is no lovelier day than that which shall never again be.

I think sometimes I need you, Friend. I need you now for the yesterdays when I had no need and you gave me, as you give me—but wait! Just look:

The dawn, in gold and yellow streaks, breaks with a hasty ray across the the morning sky, and lets the lurking birds put out the frosty night as blossoms shake off dew and shadows grow to shapes, as if in a single moment all that once was winter now is spring and new. The lurking birds chirp carefree tendrils gaily. Happiness pursues me, king of melancholy.

Yesterday dawns. Once more the new sun shines. In memory. As all that I have here.

I see my motive for going down was aimed at coming up. My past was all planned for the future. That goes without saying. The ugly becomes beauty's creator. And so many other trite things.

I recall I sought to hold such qualities as beauty and all my diseases, but I was selfish, and that selfishness kept them from others, and kept the cure from others, and the freedom from others, too.

If some people are most exacting, and here dazzled, saying this man's got wit, or that man's too much, and stagger, and can not find flawless what I say, nor even say that the corrupt becomes flawless when shown, then I must bow, and must weep, and must suffer the failure of my memories to restore youth, and let my flaws pass unknown.

I'll only warn you once: Don't want to play ball so bad you can hardly play ball at all.

Sums me up?

No such thing, Friend.

This action shall show what we sing. . . .

28

One afternoon at Pierrot's a station-wagon load of children drove up and I opened the door. The kids piled out like a landslide, and there was one who took a good look at me and commenced to howl, the sounds rising from her little round mouth like bubbles, and all the other children stopped and stared.

The mother tried to calm the child. Then another mother's baby began to scream, and then two other children were visibly terrified. They all cried on the curb and I tried to calm them down by smiling kindly and saying, "That's all right, I won't hurt you." But the more I smiled the more they screamed and clung to each other and got the rest of the kids wailing. I wanted to be funny like any good clown but my inspiration was frightened by their fear. Such a noise on the curb it was, the maitre d' came out, summoning the waiter who followed him to bring out the manager.

My smile was genuine but the make-up of paint was a tragicomic lip twist and when I moved it to smile I frowned, and the more I looked pleasant the more my face scowled.

The maitre d' asked me the trouble and I tried to explain but all I could do in the noise and confusion was shout, and the more I shouted the more he was upset. One of the mothers now began to shout and

over the wails I heard: "He's frightened the babies,"
and "make him go away."

There was hysteria on the block and a crowd gathering, including the managers of other nearby restaurants. My knees were weak and my heart was faint. I
saw the maitre d' at last pushing toward me through
the bobbing babbling heads of little girls and holding
out one hand as if to get me out of the way, and escort
me at the same time.

Into the kitchen we went by the back door and he
asked me to stay there and don't move. He vanished.

I stood by the dishwashers and leaned on one hand
and then stood by the salad chef and finally sat at the
waiters' table, my hands hanging down between my
legs, and one knee twitching as though not comfortable in that position. I watched the salad chef dicing
the celery. He looked up at me in his white hat, his
hands working automatically. I looked down again at
the floor. The soup chef spilled some bouillon pouring
from one tureen to the other and it sizzled as it
spattered on the steak grill. He cursed through the
rising steam. The kitchen maids were perspiring as
they mopped off the shiny steel counters with white
damp cloths, one of them flopping out steaks on a
wood block and placing papers between them as she
piled them up on a plate.

"Mr. Flum," said the manager, leaning into the
kitchen from the restaurant. "Come in my office one
minute, please, will you?"

I took a bath that night but could not remove all
the white base or rouge which had worked its way in
my pores. I'd rubbed my face so hard it was red
and I developed my first skin rash at that time, which
comes back again every time my employment is
severed.

Friend enjoyed my bath-taking project and walked
around on the rim of the small tub, purring and

staring down at me in the water. When he passed behind me I leaned back and rubbed his side with my head until he squeezed on past. Finally he stopped and gazed down at my toes which were flirting like little fish. His interest became so rapt I reached over and picked him up and carefully set him down in the water. He wished I hadn't done that, but then when he looked around at me, asked "Why not?" and when I smiled and nodded, he sat down. After a few more moments he tried scratching one ear with his hind leg and when that failed, because of the spray, he contented himself quietly to wait for my favor. So I pulled out the plug and stepped out as he leaped. We dried off together.

My door rattled. "Open up! Archie, what's wrong?"

I let in Stradella and she sprawled on her back in the largest chair, absolutely bushed.

"What's wrong with you?" I asked, my heart pounding.

"My mother and brother are here."

"Your who?"

"My mother and brother and you've got to help me, Archie. They're too much for me. I can't do it all alone, I tell you. I've got to have help. They're exhausting. I can't fight the whole world alone. I'm not made for it. You've got to help me, Archie."

I consented and dressed. They were brought in and introduced—Dinky Funtberg, her brother, and Maggie, her mother; Maggie had stopped on her way up the driveway to fish something out of Mrs. Cider's trash can, a garter belt with one hook missing.

Stradella said she'd leave Dinky with me and we were to come home at 7:00 P.M. for dinner and not before. "Can he stay with you?" she asked me.

"But where?" I said, as she left.

So Dinky established himself comfortably, crossed his hands on his stomach, and from time to time emitted a contented fiend's glare that I never, never forgot.

"So how well you know my sister?" he asked.

"Pretty well I guess. We're quite old friends and do a lot for each other. Your sister's a wonderful girl, you know, and I certainly think a great deal of her. She's the queen of the world here, you know, in some ways."

Dinky did not respond to my effusions—he was too proud for that. His superior and somehow secretive expression convinced me that he knew more than I— but still I went on rattling even though I knew he could say things that would turn a fireman off.

Which reminds me of a few more things I would like to say about Dinky, this space offering me the chance. He was tall like his sister and, like his mother, hunch-backed. He was so slender it didn't matter which way he was facing, he always seemed a profile, and like most profiles I've seen that are cut out with scissors at the side show, a shadow. On Dinky's head was a beany, a cap like an insult, too small to fit and too large to ignore. It would neither stay on nor fall off, but just sat there creating suspense by the brimful. He spoke in baby talk, except that he whined, and whenever he spoke he seemed almost to be sneezing. His nose ran. It usually ran at a faster rate than his conversation, so fast his hand seldom bothered to catch up with it, though once in a while he passed his necktie across it.

Dinky was an unforgettable person, and people who only saw him once remembered him forever after, even if they didn't want to. It was hard not to remember Dinky.

Getting back to the conversation in my house, I asked him how long he intended to stay.

"I don't know, a few months, maybe more. Bella invited us out here. It's her trip. I think I'll stay till her money runs out or I get good and tired of this place."

"Did she pay your way?"

"She paid my Dad, but when he got the money he decided he wouldn't come across with it, so the old lady and I came second class. We surprised her."

"—"

"I've got an invention I'll sell first, then I can give a few orders myself and buy the whole town of Los Angeles, tell everyone what to do when I want, after I sell it, make a fortune to make their heads swim."

"What's your invention?" I asked.

"An anti-gravitational canceler. I turn it on and it eliminates gravity."

"I see. And does it work?"

"Not yet. I'm only working in theory now. I've got the paper work to get down before I build it. You'll see. It will make a fortune."

"I think so."

"You don't?"

"I do."

"Oh, I thought you said different."

"No, I said it sounds marvelous."

"I thought you said different. Just wait and see first. You'll be wishing you knew me."

"But I do, don't I, sort of?"

"Not well enough for that. I don't know if I can trust you. You're a friend of my sister's. She's no good."

"No good?"

"I don't think my sister's a virgin. Have you slept with my sister?"

"Have I? Why, we're good friends Dinky, really."

"Don't call me Dinky. I don't like that name."

"What should I call you?"

"I don't care. Not Dinky. That's not my real name. Make some other name up."

"—"

"My father always said she was no good. My sister's a whore. She's always been one."

"_"

"She was born one, I think. She's a bum. We kicked her out. That's why she's here and not home where she belongs and married to some nice guy from our town."

"But she—"

"Everything she ever got we could have given her if she hadn't left. She's a whore, though. Dad says so. So he won't help her out. I want to meet some girls. Do you know any?"

Before I record any further, if there seems to be any mystery, let me merely point out that I was mystified too at the time. Dinky dropped quite a few clues in that conversation, though I was too much taken by too many things, then, and only now as I've written it down, and that from memory, and then gone back for a re-reading, have I even noticed myself for the first time how really jam packed with clues his conversation was.

For instance, he reveals the thick cloud surrounding his memory, thus: "I don't think my sister's a virgin." He reveals the traumatic experience of his life, thus: "Don't call me Dinky." And he reveals the masochistic nature that emerged from the trauma, thus: "That's not my real name. Make some other name up." A few minutes later he rings in a couple more of players with his fate, father and sister, emerging with decided conviction in only one sentence, thus: "She's always been one." If I were a writer of fiction I could not ring in a more intriguing suspense getter than the character of Dinky, bristling as he does with questions that would make me understand Stradella. How little aware I was then of the answers he was giving me in every gesture and word. But then I'd not dreamed of the questions.

That night Stradella held a conference with me.

"Can you find him any girlfriends, Archie? He's as hot as a candle, got off the plane panting."

"I don't know any, Stradella."

"He's twenty-seven years old and a virgin. I think I'll call up Valencia."

"Who's she?"

"A call girl I know on Havenhurst. She works the Nest, that bar up the street, and maybe for not too much she'll toss him."

"You kidding?"

Toss, by the way, is West Coast trade talk for Trick, by the way, being something a more delicate ear shall become accustomed to in time, if the present rain of Stradella's reign continues.

"But of course," said Stradella. "You've got to talk cool to a whore. You can't tell them right out, you know. They've got temperament." She was dialing. "Valencia? Stradella." Voice lowered, as befitted the occasion. "How're you? How's the business world? Yeah, got your flag up? Good." Reshifting on the bed, she continued. "Say, look Val, my brother's in town. Just got off the plane and I don't know what to do. He's been looking around all day asking me where are the beautiful Hollywood babes he's heard about. Yeah." A friendly chuckle here. "We draw them from all over to get laid don't we? Well, naturally I thought of you and if maybe you weren't doing anything tonight you might be able to take him out for a while. Have an ice cream or something. He won't drink. Yeah. A baby. How old? Twenty-seven. Oh, fine. I'd be glad to pay you for your time if you—favor? Gee that's real nice Val, real nice. I thought maybe you would, after going out or something—what? So you want I should have to deflower him myself? How would that look in the family album, his own sister? What would my other brothers say?"

When Stradella hung up, she looked weary and ironic and sighed across the bedroom at me. "He tried to crawl in bed with me last night, his first day in from the country. I got mad. Can you imagine that? Is he

all right? Is he, Archie? Am I supposed to do everything for him? Is that what I should do, be a good
host and help him out every way? Is that what they
expect of me, huh?"

"I don't know, Stradella. What do you think?"

"He kept insisting and made me feel guilty. I don't
feel like feeling guilty. He treated me awful and
because I wouldn't, he swore at me. That's not right
is it Archie, to swear at your own sister?"

"I don't think so, Stradella. I haven't. I don't think
I've been rude even when you've turned me down."

She was bored by my turn of talk so she got up and
went to the bathroom. I followed. She shut the door.

"Not when they're here, Archie. There's some time
you just can't spend with me, understand? Tomorrow
he's going to Disneyland so maybe that will calm him
down."

I recall a twinge of resentment as I saw Dinky, his
hair combed and full of cologne, driving off in Stradella's car to his date. Also a laugh of relief was mine
when he got back a half-hour later and announced
the girl had ice cream with him and no more. She'd
told him she was sick and had gone in. "She's just
trash," said Dinky, hanging up his beany.

We took a walk, Dinky and I, spouting off theories
about life at each other. Stradella had urged me to
"take him off my hands for a while."

The exact feeling I got from that walk, when all is
now settled, is hard to express. I can still see him
arguing with two girls in a car parked by the curb as
to why he couldn't pick them up if he wanted. I can
still see him wanting to peek in an apartment window
where a beautiful lady who'd just walked her dog away
from a tree ahead of us had gone. I can still see him
gawking at Googies, the principal coffee stop for all-
nighters, and at Schwab's, the principal drugstore for
last-minute all-nighters, and wanting to know why all
this had to be and why it was as it was, arguing at me

for proof constantly, which more than curried my theoretical bent and polished my glasses for me in the hot breath of his steaming close brandishments, to gargle at great suppositions. But most of all I remember we walked for three hours and that insurmountable fact hung heavy on me each minute and has not been forgotten nor will ever be forgotten with all the passage of years.

We drove in my car up in the hills next day, which, judging from my car, is an accomplishment in itself. He pulled out his field glasses when we parked at my favorite spot on the Italian Cypress Road overlooking everything.

"Where's Stradella's house? Where's our place?" he asked, hoisting the glasses to his eyes and standing in front of me.

With luck I finally found it in the field glasses and there was Stradella on the front lawn, hose in hand. What a thrill to perceive such detail at such a distance! But there was some fellow in a dress suit talking to her. Finally she set down the hose and went in the house with the fellow.

Not bothering to be polite nor caring whether he got his fair share at the glasses for a look or not, I brusquely commanded Dinky, get in the car with me, or be left.

I wandered casually into the living room after a mad drive down the hill.

"Archie and Dinky my brother, Jack Jeffers. He fixed my toaster and just returned it. Isn't that nice of him, Archie?"

I was noticing the Jaguar at the curb outside. "Indeed. Indeed," I said.

"Well—" the man who looked like me put his hand on her shoulder. "When will I see you again, Stradella?"

"Let me think it over, Jack. I'm so busy," she said, and walked him out to the car, leaving us in the house

—that infernal Dinky and me. She was gone a half an hour by the gold leaf Greek clock ticking strictly on the mantelpiece. I was inwardly pacing and outwardly yawning. Dinky droned on about engineering inventions until all gravity everywhere was canceled, when finally Stradella returned.

Later:

"Did you have an affair with this guy Ace, Stradella?"

"Ace? Ace who?" she asked.

"Ace of the note on your door."

"Ace? Oh, that Ace! Let me see—" she thought now. "No, I don't think I did. We just met a few days ago."

"How long were you sleeping with just me?"

"I was faithful to you, Archie, longer than anyone. Five and a half months if you want to know. That's three months longer than I was to any of my husbands. You were an angel to me and don't ever forget it but I can't repay you and I'm not going to try because I don't owe you anything at all."

"Yes, I know."

"So don't bug me with any more questions. This is not the third degree or something."

"I don't, Stradella. I know that."

"Take Dinky out and get girls or something, but leave me alone. Just go away."

She always, like mother, reclined on her bed during these important scenes.

"Get out and leave me alone, can't you see I want peace? I want quiet! Now get out! I'm tired!"

Suddenly she screamed and kicked her legs and waved her arms as she lay on the bed so that for all my trying I couldn't avoid imagining her except as an overgrown infant in a bassinet angrily waving its limbs for some sort of attention or food. She screamed so loudly I feared for the neighbors next door, the old hag washing dishes while her shell of a mate watched the TV. I left without a word, tiptoeing away as if from my own shadow, impressed by the scene she was making.

That night I went back to her house to apologize. I cracked. I often cracked. The boy inside the man could only take so much and when he'd taken it, he cracked. I went to Stradella's hoping to be received welcomely. I knew I'd feel completely freed then.

And there, as we'd sit talking, and her eye'd look straight in mine and show just kindness, and my eye'd look straight in hers, "cow-eyed" as she described it, something would happen. I'd know It, know I was loved, acknowledged and accepted, that I was believed in on my own terms.

I cried. I sat there facing her, and cried. I can not help it I cried, and I am not ashamed because the tears came so naturally.

"Why are you crying, Archie?"

"Don't pay any attention to it," I said. "Just a passing rainstorm."

But she knew that it was something deeper, got up and walked around the room on little errands. "Archie is just a poor child of fantasy. He's just a child of fantasy."

And so I was, you see, for when I cracked and went to see her, I found her "gone out" lights were on. She wasn't home at all.

I became an expert on every light in her house. I knew which lights she turned on for sex. I knew which lights she turned on for going out, and always they were my beacons, the signs I'd come to go by, for every day it became harder to ask her any questions at all.

Because she wasn't home, because she'd lied and been tired in order to go out, I'd not been able to make up. I went home. And Friend had made urine on the floor.

I rubbed his nose in it in a fit of intense and awful

rage. I held him by the paws and smashed him with my hand a half a dozen times across the face. I was incensed. I'd done this twice before to him when he'd gone outside of his sandbox—when Stradella'd gone outside her promised province.

I socked him till he howled, then I held him in my arms and wanted with a frenzied fury to hurt him more. I could not help myself. I tossed him through the bedroom and then into the living room against the cabinet.

Then I made his dinner for him, as he cowered in the corner with one ear turned back.

I wrote a little note about all this, which I still have. It says: "He's eaten, and is lying in my lap now purring and he has been kissing me—and I've been kissing him. I love my cat. Is that so hard for you to believe? There he goes kissing me again. It tickles. Oh—I love it though, for he is purring, and it is a love kiss. Yes. I'm stroking him with my free hand. He actually is pressing his head on my arm. He actually is pressing it, not simply resting it."

It was then I thought about one thing she had said when Jack Jeffers, whom I knew as Jaguar Jack, left. "I felt funny with both you and him there." I'd thought nothing of it, but the suspicion took seed. It could not have been planted in more fertile soil.

She was Jack's girl now, but still using me without being my girl. She was a believer in fidelity and free love where contradictions couldn't possibly happen: Because she was nobody's girl.

That night I reconstructed her evening, and looked at my watch every ten minutes wondering whether she was out with Jack now and if so, was she doing it with him. Doing it with him! Look! I don't even need to mention what "it" is, so well am I understood. A dozen times I must have walked around the block of her house in stomach-tense anticipation of her return, hiding in the shadows of the trees across the street as I looked weeping at her house with the "gone out" lights on. And a dozen times I looked in the bars, for had not Juanita mentioned them recently? And was not Jack's presence her doing?

Then I remembered she'd said she was going to see the Tombs' new house maybe tonight. It was about a mile away with Juanita and Dale painting and dusting and fixing it up with curtains to make it in every little way another housey-wousey, except that she was pregnant which was really going to put some powder in the cannon. Stradella was going to make curtains.

So I rushed to the Tombs' house and found Jaguar Jack's car parked in their driveway. I looked in their house. No one at home. I looked in his car to find his address. I went to his house. No one at home. I went back to Stradella's. No one at home. I went back to the Tombs' house. No one at home, but the Jaguar was now missing. I went to Jack's house. No one at home. I went back to Stradella's in time to hear the toilet flush and see the bathroom light flick off, but no Jaguar there, and no sound of anyone. But Stradella was inside, and I wasn't. I heard her blow her nose, and then silence.

I went back to Jack's house. No one at home, so he must have been off to someone else's house, cheating on the cheated and the cheater, as I'd say for literature. He could take out my Stradella and not only hurt me taking her, but then turn around from her to cheat with another, thus hurting all over again.

She telephoned next morning, laughed and said, "I'm sitting on the toilet thinking about you. You're probably the only person in the world I can talk to on the toilet. That's real funny isn't it?"

"You're happy today," I said.

She got angry and hung up.

And I learned they had all been out, junking the curtains of the new housey-wousey. Juanita and Dale, Stradella and Jack, to a bar I'd searched that evening myself, where I'd not seen them at all. So where had they been? Not even the shadows know.

29

One afternoon Stradella and Dinky came knocking around to my house and we went to find a round bed for Stradella that would properly suit her new mood. Why she wanted me along I never could imagine.

We saw one, and she asked the store manager if she could lie down and try it.

"Oh boy," she said, before all customers. "This round stuff really turns me on. Come on Archie, let's see how you fit."

Later we went to an Ice Cream Parlor where Dinky held his camera up in the waitress' face and took her picture. She jumped back.

"I've just taken your picture, that's all. Don't worry. Give me your address and name and phone number. Don't be afraid, Miss. I'll go out with you tonight and next week you can have the negative."

I'm glad to say she did not want the negative next week nor the date that night and so the great lover finished his ice cream and spilled a drop of it on the camera that hung around his neck.

On the way home we took the long route, jammed in her car, and went out to the airport. Stradella suddenly pointed: "Look at that. There's Ma."

There was Maggie, with two bags apparently stuffed with paper, making her way across an intersection, when a car stopped to let her pass and she leaned toward it and asked it, "What?"

The car apparently wanted to drive off, but she stood in its way, so it couldn't.

The traffic clustered up behind the car and horns began to beep. Maggie leaned in another direction

and some things fell from her arm and she became
absorbed in picking up the scraps of paper and old
prunes she'd spilled on the pavement, leaning forward
so that the backs of her legs showed.

"Let's get out of here," said Stradella.

Three weeks later I was driving them to the beach
in my jalopy and they'd forgotten all about it. Maggie
went to the toilet in the Men's and got lost shortly
after. She wandered away and we didn't see her again.
"Maybe Ma walked in the sea."

Dinky ambled off with a fellow named Lanny whose
interest in inventions apparently excelled his own.
Lanny also had a Pearl White feeling and a Gilbert
and Sullivan fascination, so he was good for Dinky
and helped him broaden his scope. Lanny Hotstroke
was his name. "Birds of a feather—flap their wings
together. Rhythm, uh Archie?"

I brought Stradella back home by myself. She got
out of the car and said, "Thank you very much,
Archie." She turned and started in, then changed her
mind as I was about to go. "Park it right here," she
said, and led me by the hand straight into the bedroom, where she undressed me.

"Look at that," she said, standing back after I was
stark naked. "It might not be a new bed but it's got
a new plastic cover to keep from soiling my bedspread
and it makes me hot. Lie down."

I did and she played with me as though I were a doll
she could coddle. Completely nude, she knelt on the
plastic spread over me. She leaned down, and my eyes
were filled with the length of her. She clasped me in
her palms as though I were a sausage, and rubbed herself against me with a steady rhythm and then a
furious pace.

She made strained expressions with her face. "Don't
look at me! Don't look at me!" she panted, seeming
to know what I saw. "Close your eyes. Don't watch!
Don't you know it's not polite?"

And I realized I was no part of this scene at all,

and so quietly I set myself to the duty, as I lay there on my back, of keeping as strong and ready a soldier as I could, and praying for her pleasure, and quietly waiting without thought of myself, for all of this to come to an end.

"Why didn't you want me to do it the way you've always liked, Stradella?" I asked.

"I don't know," she said with a voice that was off in other lands when we sat putting oil on the TV set's wheels later.

"Didn't you want me to?" an obvious lead-in uttered by me and intended to solicit through pauper-eyed innocence.

"I don't—like that way anymore," she said.

"Isn't it good?"

"It's all right."

"Doesn't it work anymore?"

She said, "It never worked, Archie. It never really worked at all."

"You mean," I said, "all this has been—show?" I thought back doubtfully over our entire relationship.

"And today you saw the star, not the part," she said.

"But—but why? Tell me," I said.

"Hmm," she said, musing. "Nothing to tell. A certain big star once tried it on me. That's all. I told him not to, but he did. I told him I'd had enough and was tired. He said he'd like to and I should just go to sleep. So he did, and I went. And I dreamed and dreamed. Such beautiful dreams, and I never knew them again till I met you. I didn't open my eyes for hours, even when I woke up."

"Was that the first time anyone ever did that for you?"

She paused and looked off and assented with a "Hmm." She seemed to be relaxed in a way I'd never seen, as if the resistance to me was gone, and the voice could pour out easily, unfettered by the hostility with which she'd expressed things in the past.

"Was it, really?" I asked, full of eagerness.

"No," she said, her voice anciently quiet. "My father made me do things to him when I was nine." For a moment we only looked at each other. So this was the inner door. Finally, I had reached the last compartment.

"He did it to me every day, but he had a beard and mustache and I didn't like it too well because he scratched my thighs. You see, Archie? But he taught me that men like it that way and I liked to let men do it that way because that made men like me and—so."

I was stunned. "Is that all he did?" I asked, disappointed.

"Hmmm."

"What else did he do, Stradella?" I asked, building up a resentment to this man who'd preceded me.

"Nothing much. He made me try him a few times. I was only nine and had a little—I was small you know. I didn't have a very big mouth. So he made me—we—I never minded that too much because I could—hmm—why do you want to know all this? I didn't mind how it tasted anyway. He used to come all the time that way. We did it once when mother and Dinky walked in. Yeah, I remember their faces. Real surprised like. And Dinky always saying, 'I wanta come wif,' instead of saying 'wif you,' like you are supposed to. His jaw just dropped off when he saw us. And Ma—she's a foreigner you know—Ma's Jewish. Pa got mad and made Dinky take his clothes off for a whipping. When he finished he showed me how great he was, and he was great too, by showing me Dinky's little tiny thing. It wasn't much, I know that."

We waited in silence a moment. "So that's all?"

"No. Yeah. I guess. What's it matter? Ma stopped sleeping with Pa after that and so we slept together all the time, until I was sixteen and won the beauty contest. You don't want to know about all this, do you? Then I ran away and worked in the factory and I met this man who was my boss's boss. He took me bicycle

riding and wanted to put his finger in me all the time—
while I—you know. They all like that, don't they?
That wasn't much though until I met his wife. I think
he told her about us. She invited me out to their house
and after a while I got to like her better than him
because she was nice to me and she understood how
I wanted to better myself with nice clothes. So we
went bicycle riding after a while and left him home."

"Did she want to sleep with you too?"

"Archie, what do you think I am, corrupted or
something? How dare you suggest that. You don't
understand."

"So then what?"

"My parents got me to come home but I did model
work in New York when I could and one day this
fellow I had known, and turned down, followed me
home. Pa was a sailor but he was on shore leave that
week. I remember him. Hmmm! Izzy Krantz. He
followed me into the house and pulled a gun. He held
me and Dinky and Pa at gun point and made me
undress and let him bang me. I was seventeen so it
wasn't so bad, but I've never felt right about guns
after that. Pa didn't like it one bit though. I guess he
was cold. We used to love listening. 'Batman' was
he'd forget about the gun and just try to come when
he could, and then Pa'd overpower him. That was
something to see. Yeah—really something. There I
was lying on top of the radio-phonograph console.
It was a new one. Yeah, I remember, and the top
was cold. We used to love listening. 'Batman' was
my favorite program. We only had three rooms in
our place and nine of us living there so 'Batman' was
everyone's favorite. We lived over a store. And Ma'd
just walked in and was wringing her hands in the
corner. Then there's Izzy with his pants down and his
gun held against my head. I was afraid the gun would
go off when he came so I worked real hard to make
him forget it—the gun. I wanted to get out of its way,

you know? Can you appreciate that, Archie? I must've done all right because pretty soon he shuddered like you do when—and then the gun just fell on the floor. Like that. Pa and Dinky grabbed him. What a scene. And he didn't wake up till the police came. He got twenty years for rape and assault. I didn't mind what they gave him but—gosh—what Pa and Dinky got from him—and only they said it was only rape. Do you think it was? I mean I went out with him several times before that. Pa never slept with me again. As a matter of fact, you know, I think he kicked me out after that—yeah, right after, and then I came out here to California. That's significant isn't it? I haven't seen any of them since, till Ma and Dinky showed up."

"And how do you feel about that?"

"I don't know. I don't think sex is the big deal everybody makes it. What do you care? You got enough. And you always talk about sex. I just do it. In fact, I think sex—yeah—I think sex is a bore."

"What about how you felt when your Dad didn't come out here?"

"When, now? So he didn't come out when I invited him, and sent him the ticket I worked hard to buy. So if he had he would have been around here every morning at seven for a plate of eggs like he was on the ship or something. I'm glad he didn't come. I get tired of people imposing!"

I played inquisitor grandly, and I was pretty proud of my achievement.

Stradella sent me home after that with a tender pat on the cheek. When I tried to kiss her she said she was not interested. "We're friends now. Didn't you say once we'd be friends? Isn't that what you once wanted, Archie? All right, the passion's spent now, the old cooze is dry, there's no more for little black boy. You know my secrets and there's no more to show. We'll just be friends for the rest, okay? You can respect me and I can love you, as I always will. But you'll get yourself a nice little girlfriend some-

where and bang her all you want while I'll sit on bar
stools, take diet pills, put on heavier make-up to hide
the truth from hot little boys like you who want Boy
Scout knives, and we can see each other once in a
while."

As I drove away I remember her face framed like
a moon in one of the little side windows of the house,
watching me go. It touched me so deeply because
I knew in that day she had given me her soul and in
order to get it I'd lost her as a woman, never to regain
her again.

How many times would my memory reach back?
I recall the night at mother's some talk came up and
I was late leaving. The phone rang and Stradella was
livid. The steak was cold. The pie was burnt. The
vegetables were soggy. I was late! When I got to
her house minutes later, eager to be the good man,
I found the meat still frozen in the freezer. The pie
was still baking in the oven. The vegetables were not
even cut in the cooler. So the future became the
present in Stradella's need of my company.

I recall waxing poetic one night at the wall desk in
her living room. I wrote, "The soul of man lies in
between the bowels and the brain—to some a monument, to others a ligament." Then I wrote, "There is
good when good and bad are not, and there is bad
when bad and good you've got." I followed that with,
"Look at yourself in the mirror until you see the glass
is a window," and "Someday men will stand again
among the stones of men and think of death and
dreams no more and weep not till they know they're
there."

At this point Stradella called me from the bedroom
to come change her ice pack. I told her to change it
herself, I was creating. She threw the ice pack at me
and threw me out of the house, told me don't return,
I was through. In an hour she let me in so I could rub
her back.

Another time she told me I would have to change

my clothes and dress up because if I was not going to leave, she at least wanted me presentable when she went out with the most important love in her life. The person turned out, I found out after dressing up to meet him, to be me. And we ate in front of the TV set at Dale and Juanita's where their cat kept obstructing our view in order to watch the TV herself.

Another time Stradella had me meet a woman she was going to school with and told me the lady was going to live with her. Then she began a business course. She was really going to cash in on innocence. She got a ninety-two on her test.

Another time she told me about the offer made her to play the game "No Touch." Mr. Playbaum, the producer, who owned a house on the same street as mother, one night had a shooting at his house. I heard it and later saw the police come but there was never any mention of it in the papers. When Stradella worked in his picture I met him and he was unable to remember Stradella's name, after he'd been so long with her when they first met for that interview, and so he just called her Girlie. Or was it my presence that made him forget? Or did my presence make him cover up carefully?

The offer he'd made her was to swim nude in his pool at a party he was going to give. She should try to lure men in the water and get them undressed and seduced right there before the eyes of guests, waiters, wives and possibly even children. "It'll be a good education for them, that's for sure," said Stradella. The object was that if she succeeded, their wives might divorce them, their children might hate them, and any other form of personal trouble and internal dissension might come upon them as a result of their public display of weakness. He, of course, Mr. Playbaum, would deny any connection with Stradella's actions, but she would have a contract for the lead in his next film plus ten thousand dollars, which was what I earned in five years.

The reason for his desire to have this done is that the reflected weakness of others would diminish the obvious weakness of himself and so make it more possible for him to gain power over them. He wanted a position of authority in the brotherhood of producers. This was how she was going to get her next lead and a party thrown in her honor.

I had a dream about it that night. The door dog at the party barked:

"Fun and blackmail, come one and all, dip in the pool, dip in the girlie, have hors d'oeuvres and whore's curves, drink Double Cross Scotch on the rocks and eat Blackmail Potato Chips. Teach your children to sink or swim. Learn the crawl and to crawl with the butterfly stroke. Learn the last stroke. Lose your inhibitions. Lose your wife. Why keep your feet on dry land when you can leap in and dive to the bottom? But hold your breath, and don't be surprised if your ears pop. That cesspool is rather deep. When you touch bottom you might come up to find you've gone deaf. Others have done it. Come to a party in honor of the new star in the new film. Leave your hat in the hallway. Leave your career in the ash tray. March into the room trimly dressed in your single-breasted suit and leading with your double-breasted chin. Naked but for shoes and tight socks, you in your pale white skin and short hairs will know the hangdog reality of holding your hat for a tail, trudging out. Ask no questions and have a good time. Laugh it up at the Diners' Club. There'll be photographers to record every drip who drops in the tank and gets tanked—photographs of every smile that fades. They won't get in your way and won't ask permission to flash at your splash. Oh you'll be a long time remembered—the life of the party, the guy who really plunged in, the guy who couldn't dry off, the guy still wet behind the ears. Everything is paid for, and if you doubt it, you'll get a bill later. The drips who dunk will leave the pool dripped dry. Stradella the Siren will go off at all hours. She'll even blow your own horn for you, but watch out pops how it toots ever after. We think her whistle is watertight!"

My landlady discovered Friend. I am convinced she did something to him while I was out with Stradella because ever after my best little white friend in the world was docile. She announced that I was evicted, Friend too. "Cats are not allowed in God's house." For seven weeks I argued this.

One day Stradella and I met for tennis. She was two hours late. We played thirty minutes and I beat her three times. "I never missed so many balls at once!"

One day I spent all I had for new shoes and pants. I went to see her at once. She admired me no end, and then asked me why I so subserviently solicited her opinion. "Who's going to wear the pants, Archie?"

One day I was driving in Beverly Hills and passed her car going the opposite direction. By the time I'd turned around she was three blocks away. In my old jalopy I raced, but never found her, even after searching for an hour wherever I thought she'd have gone. But what would I have said? I told her later. She said, "Do you know where you're going? Around in circles still, eh?"

One day she passed me in her car on Sunset Boulevard, toward Beverly Hills. She honked. There was some well-dressed woman riding with her. "I'm going to be a real lady someday, even if I have to be someone else to be one."

One day we made an appointment to go shopping. She'd bought a house in the hills and was anxious to show it to me. We went, but darkness prevented our seeing it. "Oh well. It's only a house. I've made twenty-three thousand dollars in nine weeks," she said. "I'm going to own my own home and really have things so I'll have my own security when this body starts to give out. No retreads yet, just a few blowouts, Archie."

No doubt if it's houses she wants to buy now she'll get rich enough suing me, after I've planted this book in her hands.

One day she invited me to invite her to a show and we saw "The Drunkard" three days before it closed in its twenty-eighth year. She'd just found three gray hairs in her natural auburn and refused to dye them —point of character—but told me all about it. A new starlet was there with her regulation reputation which was for a fifty-inch bust and it was preceding her amply to verify the rumors. Stradella and I talked it over like two stricken politicians in caucus. We agreed. "Add syrup and feed the army," said Stradella.

One day Stradella came to my house, the day I was planning to move. The landlady had commenced entering my rooms all the time and leaving little notes on things and doing I don't know what that tranquil-lized little kitten Friend so: notes like, "unholy dust," and "sinful sheets." Argument or no about the kingdom of cats in heaven, I was certainly crowded on earth, and before Friend became too mopey, I moved.

Stradella's horn honked. I recognized her, though I'd been asleep in the chair. I had not seen her for months. It was like someone returning from one dream into another one. I would have recognized anywhere that voice for which she'd been taking lessons with a blind man when I first met her, oh so long ago in another youth. Not a nasal whang of it had changed.

She said, "I just wanted to see how you're doing, Archie. We're both moving out the same time. I don't suppose you want to help me. My furniture's being delivered at my new housey day after tomorrow. I've got a million and one things to do. But it's my own place. It's costing me thirty-five thousand dollars and I can't afford it but it's beautiful. Will you help me fix it up? I've got a list made out—."

"I know, you told me," I said. "Sure, Stradella. I'll help."

"Did I? How much time can you spare?"

"You're getting absent-minded," I said. "How can you move in if you can't afford it?" I was noticing from the side of my eye the traffic had to go around, her car's rear end jutting out some.

"I went into partnership with the builder, Archie. That's how I moved in. If you can't buy it, join it. It's easy when you know how."

"Okay, so good luck, Stradella," I said. "You'll do it again."

"I put up the interest, he puts up the principal Archie, see? It's easy. I've got business sense."

There was traffic blocked up in the street in front of my landlady's house now because she was jutting out, and they honked. Two cars faced each other, a Rolls and a Thunderbird, honking their horns and blinking at each other, each too big to pass the other, while Stradella jutted out. It was getting cool. It was dusk, I remember. Then the man in the new Thunderbird suddenly leaned out his window. The new Thunderbird, you know, is much larger than her model. Stradella's was the original baby. The man shouted to me across the dim, almost gray street as somebody else beeped a horn.

"Hey you! You there! Sonny!" I could see he was well-dressed and his car was shiny. (Did I start to say tinny?) I was going to ask Stradella to pull forward so he'd pass. He asked, "Is that Miss Stradella Fonteyn?"

"Yes, it is," I answered.

"Well, tell her Wallace Brenner wants to say hello."

"Certainly."

She was looking up at me standing beside her little car. A man from the Rolls Royce leaned out his window.

"Stradella?" he called and took his hand off his horn. "Hey kid! Tell her Josh Edwards says the same, baby! Dig me, sweetheart?"

"Okay, yeah sure," I said.

Some other horns were honking now, and so Stradella put her hand on the gear, squeezed and rubbed the knob. "I've got to get going. My public, dah-ling," she drawled satirically.

Stradella backed out. She turned left. She drove away followed by a train of honking cars and winking headlights, the Rolls Royce among others, and several following who were just home-bound people in garage-scuffed family cars, and a bunch of youngsters in roadsters. The home-bound people didn't care a darn about all this but they were part of it anyway because they just happened to be there (and that's the tragic fate of their entire dominated, denominated history).

If you fail to picture the scene as I've given it, pretend it's the final footage of a Hollywood movie, and for the ending as the powdered lovers part, see a long shot from a great height, your camera encompassing the street at night as Stradella backs out, turns left, and drives off at the head of a line. The line is long and clattery with noise of every description and the inevitable bored salesman sitting in one car with his hat shoved back and his shoulder slumped forward and only one hand on the wheel, not even bothering to resist but just waiting, boredom incarnate. Keep your eyes on this screen as the horns fade and the train of lights vanishes. The bride of the city returns to her lair.

Then when the cars and blinking lights are gone, look very very carefully down at the silent sidewalk screen where they spoke the very last perfumed words. If you can see him there now—I refer to Archibald Archimedes Flum IV—but of course you can't. He's gone.

30

An Encyclopedia Of The West:

In California, the Golden State, whose symbol is the bear, whose flower is the poppy, I lie. The state originated in myth and was first mapped as an Island. Its name was taken from a popular Spanish romance.

And that was how it originated.

Since earliest American times, men have come over the High Sierras on foot, in wagons, on trains, in the air, and by boat to its Pacific shores, mostly to Los Angeles, and Hollywood, where the Terrific Runs In The Pacific.

They were seeking their fortune. They still come and they still are.

Now me—and it's tragic—I was born there, seeking nothing.

At the rate of One Thousand people per day, the Population of the state increased. Doctors sent old people out west to die, and Patients to sunbathe. Others came to find stories and write and many came to work.

Or for other reasons.

I was born there, for no reason.

California played the historic role of being neutral during the Civil War and volunteering troops for Both Sides—North and South armies alike.

Today California supplies Every Side with atomic and hydrogen bombs, missiles and airplanes. It manufactures its own automobiles and grows its own food, from cattle and sheep to lettuce and oranges.

The highest and lowest geographical spots in the United States are in Southern California, within view of each other. It has the most pictorial mountain range and seacoast in America, the most fertile valley, and Death Valley, plus a dried-up Sea, and some blue water lakes, like Tahoe, and Arrowhead, and another one called Lake Sherwood.

The natural harbor of San Francisco is the most outstanding in the world and the United States Navy is centered in San Diego. The Golden Gate Bridge and the Redwood Forest are among the world's great wonders.

Los Angeles is now, by area, the largest city in the world, the most densely crowded with automobiles, and among cities, the newest, for in 1900 it was little more than a Town. This destines it, at some future time, to the opportunity of being perhaps even the most modern of cities.

It was the motion picture that first immortalized Los Angeles. Movies were first to move.

Hollywood originated in myth and has been mapped as an island inside Los Angeles ever since. Today the reach of Hollywood extends throughout the world and what is actually Hollywood appears little more than disappointing. The mode of mind that is Hollywoodian crops up in as far-distant places as Moscow and Tokyo, as well as on the home ground, however.

I don't.

What Hollywood is, has been imported. What it became, was exported. The very foundations were built on far-distant influences. If anything originated in Hollywood it could only give thanks to strangers. The native was almost unheard.

I fulfilled my destiny that way. A silent man is someone worth listening to.

Mutual among those in Hollywood, pursuit of fortune was the aim. The pursuit, of course, was the entertainment business and the pursuit itself was entertaining.

People were more highly paid for even the lowliest work in the Industry than anywhere else in the World. What they would do to become part of it seldom was exaggerated, except by themselves.

Exaggeration was the life, all right!

From the boy who wanted to sweep stages to the girl who would bathe in spotlights, competition continued on very wide ranges of cultural and noncultivated languages. The competition had a more than International flavor—a Nonational flavor would express it better. The hybrid life had so many times been mutated it could almost, in some ways, be suspected of defying life itself.

Come from some outer space—from New York or Paris or Johannesburg—men and women seemed subliminally engaged in the struggle to find themselves human. They were strangers in this new land (the newness was all about—above the surface) and they too were alienated and alienating.

There were more religious colonies and sects in Los Angeles, practicing broader and stranger Concepts, and more psychiatrists in just one section of Los Angeles, than anywhere else on Earth.

And now Stradella:

I knew little from where she came. She brought her youth at nineteen and a Forty-one Inch Bust, one hundred and fifty pounds in a sublime bronze skin, and six-feet-one of height with which to rise as far as instinctive shrewdness could lead her.

As you will see, I loved her.

Few know the meaning of love. Fewer still experience it.

Circles surround it. Seasons evade it. Bats ignore it and owls consider it.

Hawks would destroy it. Eagles protect it. Butterflies hover over it and beetles bungle under it. Dogs bark at it. Cats raise their backs.

Lines underscore it and water submerges it. Men talk about it forever.

Who knows what love is?

Not the fox. He hunts.

Not the bear. He prowls.

Not the animals of all the kingdoms. They none speak the language.

Youth approaches it. Age reflects it.

Intelligence bears it. Wisdom evades it.

And fools defend it while asses despise it.

No one speaks of it. Those who have known it forget it. Those who would have nothing to do with it remember it.

And of those who are in it—alas!

Ask a drowning man for a match, a baby to feed itself, a genius to outwit himself, a saint to prove himself sinner—all would be wiser than to ask love to speak.

Love is the heart of the world. Wherever you happen to find it, notice the path nearby, leading fools to folly and angels to glory, the sun to shine and the moon to weep.

The very world we walk in goes around it.

Of all things moving it's the fastest and never gets to the point.

The invisible hollow that leads to delight—the most we have in nothing and the least in everything, the indescribable around which living hums, the torment of one, the felicity of two, the strife of three, that's love.

Let yourself be a boy and caress it, a man and clutch it, a veteran and crush it, no X will mark the spot, no breath breathe from its center. That's love.

The secret—the secret—its secret—alas! I never knew when I was there and now that I'm gone, what's in knowing?

Talking of love, I touch everything. And yet even a sentence is too much.

As the parrot said—the parrot was on excellent terms with himself—"Love is never on good terms with itself. Each man has but half a love," the parrot said. "Love's a fig's end."

Where did you learn such jargon?

Love's hardly discussed anymore. It's quite out of vogue this season. One never hears it mentioned in the best of circles, except in the lowest of company, or loneliest of places.

Always a secret, even when known, my advice is Don't listen to parrots, or love. Choose your bird before the stuffing. My bet's on the dove.

When I saw her for the last time it was as though a thousand million pollen blossoms bristled in my skin. My cells expanded. Every pore took up the color of electric lights. I flashed on like a neon bouquet. Every hair was crackling with the fire.

A friend described me as a connoisseur of love, much as though when Woman passed me, no matter where or what I was at, the nostrils quivered, commenced to dilate, as though the Woman carried in one hand at shoulder height the finest glass of champagne wine and I, poor lush, the Desert Island Kid, had thirst—but the sure thirst and sublime thirst of the Connoisseur, the man who Knows by Sipping, tasting more than slurping.

And Woman for me was Stradella, because she taught me Woman. She was my nectarol, my phantasmagopic, the opium in my veins, the virgin in my colon, the vinegar in my liver, the sulphur in my lungs.

To look at her for three straight minutes was for me to play with mortality.

I ran the joy of every minute injuring me by the slightest gesture of goodness toward her, because she absorbed it in such a way I could not be kind to her without being kind to myself.

When I saw her the last time my every sense was sated and my every query answered. I knew Stradella and through Stradella, knew me.

In the years to come, in Odile and Odette and Irmadoon, in Luana and eventually Vedra, in Eurydouchka and finally Katherine Amedia Rhumthum, in Zipper, in Minervane, and in Yin-Lou, plus all the others deeply cherished, and even Delphinia, I saw the flowering and the maturing of the seed planted in Stradella, of the bearing of fruit first tasted with her.

There was innocence before her and there was knowledge after her. On her pivoted a razor-thin moment when there changed a whole tide.

She was a rich, completed history for me. It had not ended, not through a thousand women, though it stopped. It had never begun, not through the few first girls, though it started. It had always been going, and would always.

I was to taste it, then, and know then as I was tasting it, that this was she. And in all of my life I would forever taste it, sublimely varied, nuance to nuance, a sampler of great wines, and in the women who followed would not bury the memory of Stradella, but enrich it, reinforce it, and deepen the shadows and shades of the sublime women who was my woman of which there were fifty women, or seventy.

Not even these words, once aimed at forming and killing our love by crystallizing it in petrification, have done their job, but have enlivened her.

They have heaped on the fire the passion of coals from my ignorance and my desire.

As long as I'm Man I'll desire Woman. She to me was that Woman. Stradella, the infinite, incarnated in every woman who has ever followed her and was in every girl come before her—but in her, Stradella, for me, attained, with me, and only me, the height of our realization: the hour of truth when we Are.

She would never be the same with another man. She would never be the same again. I saw myself in eulogy:

"He may live long, he may do much. But here is the summit. He never can exceed what he does this day."

She might have become the old hag of some bartender somewhere, the whore on the corner, the queen of a Maidenform Ad. I don't know. I have lost her.

She is gone, and yet somewhere. We have not forgotten each other, and against all the world, that is our bulwark, for eternity. We have been sealed up in the last castle of the heart, where we have already died and been killed, and our destinies are buried in our own memories, together.

To me she was a moment men seek in all moments, seldom know for any, but dream of.

Now she is gone, and I have known her—a secret no one but we ever shared—and will never return— because I am gone too. And I would not return now, not if you paid me. That time is Never again. I have no regret for it. That time is Eternity, and for Always. It is past you say. Yet it is Now. Almost all is joy. The rest is gratitude.

And a little bit of humility.

Where Stradella succeeded was in perseverance, for she did not find fortune where she looked, nor how she looked, nor in her looks. She found it where she was tossed, which was into retirement from show business, and a business that well profited from her unnaturally natural shrewdness.

Of course she was tossed elsewhere from time to time.

Stradella lived. She worked in Los Angeles, hard and daily. Her day off began after dinner and ended by ten in the morning. Ceaselessly she pressed and reached for the always elusive fortune that only broke off by little pieces at a time, and did not necessarily turn to dust in her hands. She invested it in California —and farming lettuce profits, turned the newness over in its furrows.

Jean Harlow was the first big platinum blonde in Hollywood, but others of the species followed, like Mae West, Marilyn Monroe, and, finally, of course, Jasmin Tulip. who proved you don't even have to keep blond in order to be the top blonde, the bronze blonde.

And there were the Vamps of a Former Day—
Hannah Minervane for one, mother of a great producer ultimately, who played the Little Girl Vamp,
the star of Gigglette, a Diaparade.

Below this embankment of beauties there was an
entire sea of aspirants.

They arrived in Hollywood with their forgotten
names changed and sometimes found work for a
while in offices, or cafes.

Their conventional jobs didn't pay well.

They were outside the Industry. Out there living
seemed as plodding and real as it was Back Home in
Anywhere, U.S.A.

So they began by making The Rounds, these aspirants. Who will forget the rounds made by Ariadne
Berlin, for one, who came to be a big star finally, in
the thirties, dancing through many a musical.

The Rounds, that means they dressed up for the
sole purpose of appearing undressed.

They carried their folio of photographs and handed
out the best to anyone who'd take them and read
what was on the back. They had their photos dupli-
cated into hundreds of copies for agents and casting
directors.

On the back of the photo was their often skimpy
list of credits, and their Phone Number. That phone
number provided their experience.

"Oh! How different it was in the olden days—golden
days—boldened days—stolen days."

Sometimes they met the Right people quickly. Invariably they met more than one right person, and
invariably they'd meet many of the Wrong People
First.

People were right or wrong in so far as they helped
the Career. Stradella—Stradella—at her height—at her
brief height—she Was Hollywood. Then she just Was.
And now she Has Been. Brief Candle.

An aspirant's personal aspect was of little worth on

the market, all be that aspect oftentimes considerable. What mattered was Contacts!

In Hollywood the first rule was Purpose.

Ambition was an armor.

Sometimes it protected talent. Sometimes it even put talent to work.

But many times it merely concealed talent's absence, the void, which doesn't really matter, since those who did judge judged and were judged not by that, by talent, but by the quality of the armor itself.

The Gimmick, as they called it, a bristling word—the gimmick, then, was that Projection Was The Weapon.

Valor without armor perished. It died—oh most ignobly!

Stradella's weapon was her chest, her hair, and her height. She used it through many a duel, wrapped in dignity and mink, which were torn off, invariably, leaving her naked and best-selling. She appeared in thirty-odd films, her own TV series, and countless magazine articles that lead to the insides of locker doors.

"But gosh—!"

She embellished herself with the right clothes, a few personal mannerisms that seemed feminine from eighty miles off—and quite often gaudy or sham on closer inspection. She knew this though. What did that matter? The box office and money were more than eighty miles off.

Spend one day at the Hollywood Ranch Market, which never closes, or the Arrow Market in West Hollywood on Sunday, where the many Stradellas buy groceries—their wheat germ and yogurt and No-Cal, or at the numerous health-food stores—lichee nuts, garbanzos, raisins, and organically laid eggs, if you please.

They don't dress like each other, and if they have anything in common appearance, it's that they don't dress like anyone else.

"I don't know, but I truly came to love one."

High heels (white), pedal pushers (pink), sunglasses (sequin covered), purses (vast and bottomless, oh most inevitably LARGE), with as much of their back showing, and their bust, no jewelry and hardly any make-up and most probably no lipstick at all, or else very light lilac, was what they often dressed like.

I saw my first bronze blonde on horseback. I was at the Pony Ride. I was eleven months. I pointed and smiled and burst out clapping my hands. I had not made a sound, not so much as a moan, in my entire life. From that Pony Ride onward I never stopped. I found what had until then been missing, the bronze blonde key to my blooming.

Later memory grasped at that Shopping Center image—one of the buttons in the back of the pedal pushers, or the zipper on the side, it stuck out in a funny way, or was partly open. Memory said lots of things. The heart never whispered. And so was memory revolted.

Only the heart survived.

By their haste and sloppiness, they rejected you. And they knew it! Who could I be to matter? you said. Their time off was Away from The Show, they said. They were out Shopping and not being shopped. It was none of Anyone's business even to Look. Just try Talking sometime!

And so, trudgingly, you go back to watching TV, or writing your memoirs, the saga of a sad clown.

But the Stradellas got started—hat check or cigarette sales on The Strip if they were lucky. A spot doing commercials on a local TV station live late at night for a recapping tire company or a used-car lot, until they were Seen, and picked up.

Meanwhile there was the beach, and the inevitable interview, or maybe, if they were lucky, both together —someone's pool.

It's a serious business and it never stops. There was no time to laugh. Their gaiety might be at the expense of their next producer.

Or next friend. . . .

She lived at the Studio Club first, but they locked their doors at night, and after she'd been in one or Maybe Even two little-theater productions, her naïveté gave way where the doors would, and into an apartment with another girl she set up shop, a base, with phones, wired for love, if she was making enough.

Otherwise the answering service got her calls—"Miss Stradella Fonteyn's Residence!"—crystal paradise in the very syllables, and the message was put in her box.

What did she like? What most?

What got her ahead.

Why?

Back home there was a sick mother who turned into an old hag, or a father who died in an automobile accident, or a little brother and sister whose hungry stomachs made her miss school in order to work. Back home there was Memory and some hardship and not too much Experience. I will better myself. I'll go to Hollywood. I'll Show Them. I'll prove . . .

But most of all she'd show herself, and sometimes she'd see herself, walking on a leash her pink-dyed poodle in his golden gilt collar, his little black and undyeable nose sniffing the sidewalk chewing gum.

She sometimes got old and ended up working hard, sometimes getting married, and sometimes turning into an old hag or dying in an automobile accident, or just raising hungry little children who kept her from getting her Big Break.

But occasionally she Became immortal—if only she gave up, and lost enough, and finally was squashed enough, so that nothing else but the Immortal remained.

To be rich—
And famous—
And powerful—
The gold-seeker's eternal dream!
All alone.

It meant sometimes boiling her own skin in some-body else's pot, if you know the idea. Which hell could be worse?

It was the Exchange that became Myth, and when she learned That, she was Launched.

Stradella Fonteyn was listed in the Studio Directory. It's published four times a year by the Academy of Motion Picture Arts and Sciences, ten dollars a copy, in one volume originally, then in two volumes, then three volumes, and finally countless, I guess.

Here were the photos of Every Actor in the In-dustry: Male Lead, Ingénue, Child, Character, West-ern, Heavy, Comic. All the categories were there, and photos of the oldest and biggest stars, and the youngest strugglers who couldn't get their first part.

Female Lead, that's where Stradella was.

"Just look at her face! Don't you think she'd be great in the picture, Sam?"

Answer: "Who looks at the faces. . . ."

There were four hundred and twenty-eight Female Leads listed in her last issue. Maybe twenty-eight were Stradella, or maybe the Other Four Hundred. Maybe Stradella was going to Hollywood, or maybe she died there in Cedars of Lebanon from an "overdose," or maybe she was on tour in a Tijuana dance hall, cabaret or "play" house, when the Truth hit.

Her service was getting the calls. "I'm sorry, sir, Miss Fonteyn is on location in Mexico. May I have her agent contact you?" She could have been in a cat-house, it would have been the same.

"Thank you, no, I'll just try another number. Let's see . . . what other girl won a beauty prize this year?

Maybe we ought to discover someone, Sam. Who hasn't been discovered lately? We need a real Live Stradella."

There's the mother of three children in Illinois, the wife of an airplane mechanic, who won the Miss Tangerine Beauty Contest. She was exposed in the press as no Miss but a Ma, and those weren't tangerines either. They were grapefruits.

Conviction? Stripped of her prize and shipped to Hollywood for guest appearances in three jungle pictures. Convinced.

There's the girl who went into mourning at the death of her lover, the Don Juan of Hollywood, and threw off her black veil three months later when her swainless publicity was waning. She shot her new Romeo in the Juliet, right with a pistol in bed. She was held by the police a few days before being allowed to put on the Black Veil again. Her unfortunate amour had Succumbed to her wounds.

"Well, that's show business."

There's the girl who was rumored drowned in the Pacific when her car was found unlocked on the beach with a photo of her on the seat that was terrific.

She was picked up by a truck driver a week later, wandering near-naked in the desert—the Painted Desert—and claiming she was kidnaped and—You Know. Look at the wrist burns made by the Rope on page one! On the front of her body and the newspaper, great bruises. Photos flashed, near-naked. But the contract she signed shortly after was well dressed.

There's the girl who killed herself four times last year—she was appearing in a suicide film—and was finally stabbed by her boyfriend this year—he had the lead in a murder picture—and unfortunately perished, after recovering just long enough to give a farewell interview from her bed and explain to the world she regretted it.

She overacted, warning all little girls against it.

There's the star who bought the old mansion on the busiest street in Beverly Hills and had it painted violet. On the Fourth of July every year she had it especially whitewashed—Red, White, and Blue.

She did a lot of troop shows.

There's the girl who had her navel removed and showed it on TV—or rather—the absence of it. She later became the Mahjarini of Cooze-bah-har, or Hooze-cah-bar, or some-such-thing.

There was the girl who wore her dresses open in the back to below the base of her spine, tapering V-like down to a nice slit for Victory. She was featured walking away in countless magazine photos. She walked away from a lot of films, too.

A girl remarkably resembling the star of a number of movies went to a party given by the star and tossed her in the pool. The girl's attempt to get her picture in the papers backfired because she resembled the star so much the editors called even her pictures only more pictures of the star.

There's the sexpot who repented and Joined A Monastery, attended by photographers. She had a dispute with the Father-in-Charge about bringing her Chihuahua, but a little monk volunteered to take care of everything. (See CINDERWINNER.)

There's the newlywed actress who had the major (or colonel) operation that big year—something on her glands or the box office or something—and then, that following year returned to the hospital for a memorial service and to will her remains to science, "if and when," as she so delicately said so poetically, in an elaborate dedication in which a new wing was opened.

"Maybe we ought to discover Someone New, Sam."

How about the girl who claims to be a virgin—has medical testimony to prove it? She's right too: Those doctors who brought testimony Know. She says she'll be Queen of Hollywood, but she won't give Herself to Anyone—except, of course, "the finest, most honest, gentleman on earth." Her phrase.

"You said it, Sam!"

The Hollywood Opera. . . .

31

I went to Stradella's, to show her my newest clothes. "A fine figure," she said. "You're becoming a regular dandy. You switching?" We stayed together until midnight and then, when I tried to make love and she refused, a fellow named Ace showed up. So at that hour she put me out and he gave every evidence of remaining.

Therefore I remained, but on the outside. I stood by a tree, across the street from her house. There were some people sitting on the front porch there smoking cigarettes in the dark. They saw me and I saw them.

Pretty soon they went into their house, and well I could understand this, owing to the hour. Stradella's porch light went out. The inside lights didn't go out or on and Ace didn't come out or get in as far as I could imagine, judging from the lights. What was he, queer?

I noticed at one point the neighbors were inside their living room now. They were still smoking in the dark. Their cigarettes were pointed toward me. What right had they? I thought that odd. Were they watching for something? Were they waiting for something? Perhaps they had called the police, I thought, and if so I had better get out of there.

I walked away fast and broke out in a sweat and a trot. I traveled one block. A police car pulled over and shined a spot light on me.

They were two officers who searched me, examined

my driver's license, asked me where I was going and
where I'd come from. Had I been standing for three
hours, since midnight, in the shadows in one place
behind a tree down the street? Of course I admitted
it all. They asked me why.

"I suppose it's because those people who phoned
you were feeling I was spying on them. Is that it?
If they felt that why didn't they put out their cigarettes, pull down their shades and go to bed?" I asked,
hating their little dots of cigarette light that had
pointed so broodingly like silence poised safely to
observe death.

I later saw the policemen talk to them. How I
hated that calm indulgence, the philosophy of the un-
touched. Do I seem to rave? It was the hour, the nerve,
and the spectacle of public display being questioned
so bluntly to the mocking laughter of every apartment
window.

"Why were you doing it, buddy? Just answer my
question," the cop said.

"Because I had a fight with my girlfriend and she's
got another guy in her house and I was waiting for
him to go home."

"What's her name?" they asked.

"I can't tell you that," I said. "She's no part of this.
I don't want to bring in her name. That wouldn't be
fair or honorable, do you think?" I asked.

"You're right," said the cop. "It wouldn't, so what
is it?"

"Why do you keep asking me that, officer?" I asked.

"What is her name and address, buddy?" said the
other cop. "We've got our records to keep."

"You mean I'm going to be arrested?" I asked.

"Not if we get the full record and it all checks out,"
said the cop.

"I don't understand. I thought you just said we
wouldn't have to involve her," I said.

"We won't if you just tell us where we can find her

so we can ask her a few questions so we won't involve her."

"But that's involving her," I said.

"Hurry up Flum, Archimedes. It's late and we're supposed to make our coffee break. Just give us her address or we'll take you along with us."

"To coffee?" I said.

"To the station, Flum. Now who is she?" asked one. The other wrote it all down because I told it all and he put my name at the top.

"You won't bother her now that I've told you, will you?" I asked.

"No, we won't," they said, and they drove off to her house and rang her doorbell to bother her. I watched. I stood behind another tree and observed it all. They waited ten minutes. Stradella finally put on the porch light and answered the door—in her nightie! She'd been dressed when Ace got there. The lights hadn't changed for three hours, but Stradella had. How could this happen to me? I was faked out by the lights. She had not flicked on one bulb different or flicked off one different and yet now she was discussing with two police officers my presence for three hours behind a tree in her neighborhood, and was completely different. I was there behind another tree in her neighborhood to see the proof of it. Funny I should have to spy on those checking on my spying.

Suddenly I ran home fast because I realized if Stradella called up on the phone and asked me I wanted to deny it all. I'd reply with my head under the pillow and sleepy, as though I'd just been awakened.

She never called though. Was I disappointed! She never even mentioned it until curiosity seduced me and I asked. All she did was halfway laugh. "Yeah, funny, wasn't it. Funny." Her voice was quiet and reflective sometimes beyond my expectations and eventually beyond my understanding. Does dust return to dust like this, from rain to earth to rain again,

from sea to salt to sea, from innocence to knowing to
ignorance again?

32

Two days later I went to her house and was pain-
fully, if ironically, polite. I said nothing.

"Archie, you've got to help. Look at that."

She pointed the front door screen out. There was a
hole in the bottom of it.

"What happened?"

"Dinky threw a salt shaker last night. He and Ma
got back kinda late. I want to move them out, Archie,
but I know they're going to be angry so I want you
to help move them so they won't resist and when they
get back all will be done."

"Where to?"

"A hotel."

She found one. We moved them. We went back
and sat down and waited and when at mealtime they
walked in, Maggie and Dinky, Stradella had a big
dinner waiting.

Maggie had numerous paper bags in her shopper
and perpetually stored them away in back drawers
and shelves where perpetually Stradella unearthed
them, some full of orange peels and hard crusts of
sandwiches, others with nylons or soiled panties.

Maggie put down her burdens and stored them in
several places laboriously while Dinky found a chair
from which he could hunch forward and leer at me
and then at Stradella when she came in with hot
plates, until his napkin was tucked in his neck and his
beany hung up for him.

We all ate silently and without a word, after which
the plates were removed by Stradella—her own servi-
tude and desire to give rather than receive in itself a

suspicious thing, which only Maggie eventually understood. Then we looked at each other.

Was it my place to speak, or Stradella's? I was sure it could all be said quietly and with logic, for after all, in a house with one bed it was hardly wise for unamorous guests to remain more than a few days. Therefore I suspected there would be no bad feelings at all, but rather a smile and shrug of relief, for now even Dinky and Maggie would have privacy. With privacy comes freedom, with freedom, mastery. But it was not my place to make the announcement as this was Stradella's house and her family.

She went into her bedroom and Dinky followed. I waited with Maggie who was involved in wiping the catsup off her lips and dress front.

"Get out! I don't want you in here! Get out!" Stradella screamed.

"What do you mean?" came the obsessed and mad voice of her brother.

"Let go! How dare you! You're hurting me! Let go!" cried Stradella.

I leaped to the bedroom to find Dinky on top of her, twisting her arm back. "Let go of her!" I shouted and pulled him off.

He turned on me with livid little dots for eyes and spittle falling from his mouth. He turned back to her.

Stradella was up and behind me, arms raised and a ruler in one hand. "Get out! I don't want you around here!"

"Oh my God! Oh my God! I knew it! I knew it! Put that down! You'll kill my baby!" cried Maggie wringing her hands in the living room and then all at once, as she got to the bedroom, jumping Stradella from behind and trying to pull her over but succeeding only in a few wild slaps.

"Let go of me! Ma, now lay off!" yelled Stradella and I drew her mother back to the living room forcefully.

"You no good whore! You tramp! You bum with your phony friends!" cried Dinky racing to the living room after his mother, and hurling insults at Stradella as he fumbled and picked up the fire poker. He waved it. "I'll kill you. Trash like you should be dead and I'll do it!"

"Put that down, kid, or you'll never get up off this floor!" I said in the deepest voice I could command, and marched straight at him.

"Make him quit, Archie! Make him get out! Throw them both out! Get out, you thieves! You parasites! Leave me alone! I'm tired! Get out!" Stradella pounded the floor with her feet.

"You were always like that! You're no good. You're cheap. You're common. I knew this would happen. I knew it. Oh God. You're not even good enough to love your own brother," bawled Maggie.

"I'll—get—you—" wallowed Dinky in his own passion and raised the poker over his head and with all the strength of a deranged ape quivered and shook and turned red in every muscle as he bent the poker in half.

"Now get out! Go on! Get out of my life forever! Get going!" bleated Stradella.

Dinky lunged. I intercepted with a left fist into his chest over which he cringed with an "Oof!" and a blast of spittle. He swung at me. The poker toppled floor-ward.

Suddenly Maggie was on top of my back and little knives were in my cheeks. They turned out to be her nails.

Stradella hit her twice with a pillow that broke. It was a pillow she'd made herself. The house was fogged with floating feathers.

I realized all at once I had Dinky's wrist and he was turning. I twisted his wrist and had him. He bent backwards but could not get his arm free from behind. Shoved by Maggie who was being hit by Stradella's feather-flying pillow, we all catapulted to the front yard where I saw Juanita and Dale running up.

I let go of Dinky, and Stradella was running back in the house, locking the door with fidgeting fingers. Then she shut every window in the place, feathers flying out of them, nervously whining some kind of gibberish to herself.

Dinky made a lunge at her screen door and went through it to collide with the front door.

"Oh, come on, Dinky let's go now!" I called.

"She's no good and never has been!" wailed Maggie. "She always hurt my baby. She treats him awful. Bring us out here with no money then kick us out in the street like no good! Where we go? And she so fine with all her money and ways."

"I've got a hotel for you. Come on," I said.

"May I help?" asked Dale getting next to me now.

So we got the two Funtbergs in Dale's car, leaving Juanita with Stradella, and headed for the hotel. We stopped at a red light. All at once Dinky leaped out. He started running back.

"My baby! Look how you torture him! You no good! You bums! You're no good!" Maggie was out of the car running after him..

"Head for Stradella's!" I told Dale.

We waited on the front porch when Dinky, followed by his puffing mother, reeled up some minutes later.

"All right, now come, Dinky. At least you can see the place. Look at the hotel once, see how you like it, find out where it is and walk back here to Stradella's if you want, but come on first to the hotel so I can get my part done and go home. I've got to get up in the morning. I'm tired and it's late."

We got to the hotel but Dinky refused to go in and started taking off again. His old mother flapped flat-footedly after him for twenty feet, then paused in her sweat-soaked housedress, the same as she'd worn every day of her stay, and turned to go into the hotel breathing hard.

"He's a disturbed baby, mixed up, and don't know his mind," she muttered repeatedly as we led her inside. She sighed at the counter and laid her bundles down on it. "So you're a friend of Stradella's?" she said to the old woman back of the desk. The old woman, halfway extending the room key to us, paused at this and looked at me.

I smiled to pacify her.

We led Maggie up to her room. "Is this Stradella's new house?"

"It's a hotel, Maggie."

"What hotel? We're not at Stradella's anymore?"

"No, Maggie, but you can rest here and wash here whenever you're tired or want to."

"No more Stradella?"

"You can go visit her, Maggie."

"Why doesn't my boy leave her alone? This is a nice place."

"You've got a bed to sleep in now, not the cot."

When we left, we met Rudolph Redpaw on the steps of the hotel outside. He was as usual controlled with his chin tucked down and his hair standing up.

"Good evening, Archie. How are you? This is my new wife, I'd like to present Archimedes Flum," he introduced me to a little tiny lady who had the largest and longest crop of red hair I've ever seen.

"So you're married again, Rudolph."

He laughed. "You know me. That's my specialty! This is my twelfth time Archie. Always in love or never alive. That's my motto!" He was as crimson as Mrs. Redpaw's red hair, and they walked into the hotel, bowing "Good night, Archie," as they went.

"He helped us fix up the house, you remember him Dale?" I said as we went to the car.

Dinky was pacing back and forth on the lawn and in his hand were some pebbles.

We convinced him that now was no time to argue. He'd lost, and if he persisted I'd personally call the police and have him jailed since he was obviously insane, unable to control his senses, and homicidal. I wasn't going to leave Stradella till he'd gone back to the hotel for good.

So we got him to ride back to the hotel. He said good night. He went in like a good boy.

Stradella admitted us after we'd explained for five minutes that Dinky and Maggie were gone.

We had tea and tried to calm down. Stradella was being told how to knit a blouse by Juanita.

The phone rang and Stradella hung up after a bored, "Yeah, okay." She looked at us. "Ma says Dinky's on the run again. He doesn't like his room and says the bed's too small. He wants to sleep with me. Ma said I should let him tonight. Gosh, doesn't he ever run down though? He's been running around like a madman ever since he got here."

When Dinky hailed in sight we greeted him on the porch, Dale and I, each with a hammer and hatchet in hand. He slowed down at first, and then came forward slowly. "You can come in for a minute to talk Dinky, first, but you'll have to leave when we tell you and if you try anything at all I promise you'll be so quickly wiped out no one will know who you were. Understand?" I said. I believe I was angry and enjoyed dramatizing the moment.

He nodded.

"All right, what do you want?" asked Stradella.

"I want you to pay for my invention. I want you to pay the hotel room. I want a hundred dollars a week allowance and two new suits of clothes and your car."

"Is that all?" asked Stradella.

"And I want to decide whom you'll go out wif."

"All right Dinky, all right. Now can I go to bed? Is that it?"

He agreed that was it and walked out. I locked the

door after him and turned to Stradella. Some seconds
passed before she spoke.

"See how they get it out of you? They sure know
who they can hit up or not."

"You're not going to do that of course, are you?"

"Me?"

"Yes, Stradella, you. What has he done for you
and what do you owe him? You've got absolutely
nothing in common with each other, not even a name."

"I know. I know."

"So naturally you're not going to, are you?"

"Well—maybe."

"But your car."

"No, not that. I thought I'd buy him a new one.
Mine's getting old."

"You thought you'd what?"

"I'll get him a couple of suits. He needs them. And
some allowance. He can't get along without that.
Naturally I'll pay the hotel bill. It's not that much,
and only common courtesy, since I moved them there.
They might not really like the place."

"I see. And you intend to do this for real?"

"Um. Probably," she said, half-preoccupiedly, half-
bored.

It was some months before suspicion took root in
this matter, but if on the surface family fidelity seems
to be the only motive of such passion, look again and
perhaps you will find deeper and more personal re-
lationships involving, no doubt, a slight trace of
brotherly blackmail. What was the family skeleton to
which these people reacted so capriciously, plucking
it out and regarding with horrified exultation, then
tossing it about like a burning cinder and blaming
each other for its terrible aspect, then together carefully burying it again in the family closet with mystic
rites as though it were some cherished relic?

I must confess I wondered as I went home, and the
next day too when, as I drove through a strange part

of town, I saw Maggie seated on a bus-stop bench, miles from her hotel and Stradella's place, staring off into space.

33

"That's right," Dinky said. "I've got a message for you!" He was knocking at my door and shouting through the window. "Maybe it would interest you. I've got the message from a friend of yours, from Samuel L. P. Playbaum."

I opened up.

He came in like the king cat and he sat down all puffed up, and didn't take his beany off.

"So—all right—what's the message?" I said.

He looked at me funny. "Aren't you going to give me breakfast?"

"I don't think it's necessary."

"All right," he said. "Lunch?"

"Look, Dinky, what's your message, or get out."

He looked at me. "You ever know a lady Playbaum?"

"—"

"Ever know a certain Hannah Playbaum?"

"—"

"Her middle name was Minervane?"

"—"

"I'm going to Europe with her."

" . "

"She calls me—I'm—you're awful talkative, Flum. Me, I'm becoming an important person. Do you know what my old man did to me when? He trained me with his fist. You see this eye? It's bigger? That's because he taught me how to look at things. When I didn't he would beat me, see? He got me, see?"

" . "

"I've really—I made up my mind though. I knew I came out here to do some big thing—something. You know? I'm going to kill myself."

"No kidding."

"I've been planning it. I've worked the scheme. This theory is—but no one wants to listen to it."

"—"

"Okay. I've worked out the details so I know it's right. No one has the right to say it's wrong."

"—"

"It's simple. I set up my death to look like someone else's set it up for my murder. Death is my revenge. Someone whom I hated murdered me. I'm the living proof. Everyone accepts my testimony. Murdered by my enemy. Well, I'm not one to bear a grudge. They all know I express my feelings. So, I die as the expression of a feeling that I never lived to express."

"—"

"I'll do it."

"—"

"My death is going to be big testimony. Bigger than my life. I'll have the last word who my friends and enemies are."

"—"

"You'll see. You'll read about me."

"—"

"I've been thrown out of more homes and mistreated by more people than by any other person—Hollywood. Let go of me."

"—"

"I don't like your looking at me. You're nobody. I've been through what life is. Every day. People don't surprise me. A nut if you think you can stand there—"

"All right, Dinky. Now then, what's the message you brought me from Playbaum?"

"Ha! You mean you listened? Ha! You mean you believed? Ha! You're the first. Nobody listened to me. No one! Ha! Well, ha! Well, ha!"

"So, Playbaum—"

"I don't have a message. No. He never even heard of me. You think I'm stupid? That's the only message I've got and no Mr. Playbaum had to tell me to bring it to you. He's never even heard of me."

"Then I'll have to ask you to leave."

"Don't be polite about it. You remember what I told you? You're the one who listened. Ha! Well, you'll see! Ha!"

I put Dinky out and heard his shouting in the garden. Mrs. Cider caught him tramping through her patch.

"Look out!" he cried. "I'll commit—"

"You go right ahead! You'll hear from me, young man!"

"They'll say you drove me to it! My old man—he'll prove it!"

"Leave my clover, young man!" Mrs. Cider raised her hoe. "You—you—jazz musician!" She drove him from the ground and set her chin to hoeing. There she raked his little beany in the weeds and bad grass.

34

The streets around Stradella's grew more than familiar to me. I walked them every night, from the house where I was born three blocks away to the alley beneath the new building next door. Stradella had cut off our relationship again, as she "no longer had any use" for me. The street lights winked through the tree leaves and I in black shoes—for the shadow—with rubber soles—for the silence—in my black sweater and overalls, developed a route of stations behind large trees or bushes or the occasional large cars fortunately parked near her house.

Some nights I arrived only moments before a man would drive up in a sport car, knock, and take her out. Other nights I would prowl for perhaps an hour, jockeying myself into a perfect position for learning whether she was home or not.

My technique is practically a manual. I declined ever to pass directly in front of her house. To avoid this, I would approach on foot from a distant street, keeping always to the side where shadows, or lack of light, or absence of people made for greater anonymity. I would invariably smoke a pipe, pretending to use it as a means of expressing my utter innocence, should such a necessity ever arise.

For instance, the person happening by sees me stationed behind the big tree diagonally across from Stradella's, with its view of Stradella's two living room windows, two side windows, and half her bedroom windows. This person does not know that I have seen him first, and sprung suddenly into my more conspicuous, therefore more innocent role. I step to the middle of the sidewalk and begin to examine and pat my pipe. I bend over it industriously, thus hiding my face, and wangle one finger into the bowl. I try desperately to dislodge from its insides some imaginary piece of dirt or tobacco. When the person approaches, I automatically, without looking up, step aside and wait until he is gone. If that takes too long, and so as not to cause suspicion in any persons whom I have not seen in the countless dozens of lighted and darkened windows about, I stroll away, sometimes to go around the block again in order to arrive right back at the same spot.

But there are other tricks—the dissipation of suspicion before it has been aroused being the primary aim of the technique.

For example, familiarity can awaken curiosity.

Therefore, since I habituated the neighborhood after dark, ease in an after-dinner constitutional or midnight before-bed walk, were the basic impressions I sought to leave. Of course, since all this took place so close to Stradella's house, it might be too obvious. After all, I was known to have lived there. Now if I were seen approaching the house, looking as if at the same time I were avoiding it, my cause would be guessed at once and Stradella notified.

I needed to devise a costume that was totally different from the kind I had formerly worn while living there. I realized that a rich man looks less suspicious than a poor man. Also, if his best suit is black, as mine was, and indicative of his fortune by the quality of its cloth and smartness of its cut, its very blackness is also a disguise that makes him a brother to the shadows he cultivates.

Thus it was my wont to wear the clothes of Sunday, to put on a clean white shirt with a dark tie, a dark vest over that, and set out, pipe in mouth. Also, I carried, on some occasions, an umbrella cane. This latter was optional. Since such an object was of little use in Los Angeles, it labeled me as a nonconformist. With it and my shiny black shoes, I was a character. In this kind of secret work it is sometimes an advantage to be a stand-out in the group. However, for the most part, my pipe was sufficient.

I did contemplate various other strolling excuses. The most obvious was the acquisition of a dog. They are fine animals for providing an utterly uncomplicated response. A man with a dog on a leash at any hour of the night could be an object of pity, or more likely, of humor, and the laughter he generates guarantees him absolute oblivion. I did not, however, acquire a dog, as it would have tied me down if, perchance, I was called upon to run, should Stradella ever unexpectedly arrive.

My neatest formula was the elegant dark suit,

rubber soles on the dark shoes, and the dark overcoat, a must. It was behind the upturned collars of the latter I could make my quickest facial disappearance.

There were three different approaches to Stradella's by street. To be thoroughly safe, I began by parking my jalopy in the middle of a block at least six blocks away and preferably between two other cars.

At this time I was not usually informed whether Stradella was home or not. Sometimes one or two quick passes by her house in my car would yield the desired information. My knowledge of her lighting system was a great help to me in making rapid conclusions.

But even if I knew she was home, there was absolutely no guarantee she would remain home, and there was always the danger she might see my car if it were parked too near.

Jalopy disposed of, I began my foot parade, a flight from lava love, a journey in a jungle down dense, denuded, pompeian streets, slushy city sewers of passion. I walked among my many selves and watched my whole life pass, changed most of all by the change I saw.

There were two couples who constantly walked the streets of that neighborhood. The first couple consisted of two men who ambled slowly arm in arm, and I guess no more need be said of their danger to me since, far from observing my clandestine crises, I'm sure they were more anxious to conceal their own.

The second couple was a man and wife. They walked their dog at all hours of the night. I used to see them frequently between 9:00 P.M. and 4:00 A.M. But no matter when I saw them, they were always dressed the same. He wore pajamas and slippers and she wore a nightie and slippers. They were covered up with overcoats. I am proud to conclude that either because of their rather embarrassing nocturnal garb or my own extremely sly maneuvering, and despite all my adventures, they never once identified me or showed any appearance of recognition.

Approaching the house casually by moonlight and street light, it was permissible to pass people anywhere within a radius of one block. After that point caution intervened and it was necessary to put on a show of assurance. I was kept busy memorizing the position of every automobile, checking, as I passed, to make sure they were empty. A young lover parked in some car might not accept as normal the sudden appearance of a man in dress suit frantically dodging behind his fender. I also had to be on the constant lookout for possible neighborhood gossips loitering along the street as they exchanged small talk. When I was satisfied that there were no threats, I would proceed, somewhat chagrined at the perfect functioning of every street light, and desperately praying they would all go out. But if I caught sight of just one neighbor sitting on his porch pipe-smoking, or calling in the cat, or moving his car, and I was convinced he had not seen me, I would immediately beat a hasty retreat by the same route. If I had been seen, I would simply walk casually by, glancing up ever so disinterestedly at the house whose details I then proceeded to memorize.

If I had not been seen, and my retreat had come off successfully, I would take a long leisurely walk around the block in the opposite direction, so as not to repeat my original approach to the house within the memory span, by which I mean the suspicion span, of my invisible neighbors.

When I was again within visual penetration of the house, but beyond the range of the aforementioned neighbor's vision, my pace would slow to a walk and I would begin to take notice of my surroundings.

A charming sight were the lovers in one of the automobiles, she very young, he, a mature man. They parked in the shadows, I noting all as I passed—they were lying on a bed in the back seat—and they noting me, or my shadow at least, and cowering guiltily. I made a mental note never to use that side of the block when their car was there, or they would suspect me of spying on them and perhaps even trump up charges against which I would be defenseless, for of course I was determined not to implicate Stradella or to divulge the true nature of my behavior. At the same time courtesy bade me give them a wide berth because it was perfectly plain that the young girl was not allowed out and that her middle-aged lover was a forbidden fruit. Actually they couldn't accuse me publicly without getting themselves in trouble.

Next, safely behind a tree, and out of the neighbor's view, I would study the house of my prey with microscopic scrutiny.

The neighbors having innocently left the stage, I was free to advance. First, a casual walk by her house on the opposite side of the street. This was fairly safe. The only risk was in her looking out. That side of the street was as well lit as any, and too accursedly well lit for me. It was as easy to survey her place from here as from anywhere else. I would note the dim lights in the living room, the drawn curtains, the closed windows. She was home but not in the living room. I would notice the bright pink light in the bedroom—her bedside lamp was on. The chandelier was off. The sex light was off. Conclusion: she was at home, on the bed, or in the bed, going over bills or possibly telephoning. The presence of a lover would have been revealed by the shining of the kitchen light, or even the living room lights, the kitchen light on to get ice cream after sex, the latter neglected in a hasty bounce to the bedroom before sex.

So feeling certain this time she was quite alone, I'd approach again, up the sidewalk that led directly beneath her window, though actually it was immaterial whether she was alone or accompanied in bed at those times. If, as I approached, I noted the awful haggling neighbors who lived next door had turned off their TV and their house was dark, then I also knew it would be safe, on coming down the alley to the garage of the new building next door, to climb over the fence behind their house and walk right across their front porch in order to penetrate closer to Stradella's open window.

As I passed beneath Stradella's bedroom window I was exactly underneath the street lamp. But there was a range of about three feet where, from Stradella's bedroom, the sidewalk could not be seen. This was precisely under the window and precisely next to the building and precisely where I would stop. But it was also the most visible spot in the neighborhood. Not only that, there was a long shadow cast by another street lamp which became directly visible from Stradella's bed. All she needed to do was glance out the window to her right. This she might do on some sudden impulse, or perhaps simply as she hopped off the bed.

Therefore, desiring to stand in that place, I had to pull my pipe trick and, to compensate for the shadow, hunch over like a deformed man. The reasoning for this was sound. If Stradella did look and even if she regarded the shadow as human at all, she would never identify it with me. As for the neighbors, all of whom knew me, I would not be very recognizable, and the pipe distraction, aside from its rapport with an old hunchback's character, would explain my presence to anyone.

Now the purpose of this pause was to listen. From where I stood, I could see nothing, but I could hear almost everything. Was she telephoning? Was she rattling papers and paying bills? Was she with someone?

If I heard her conversing, and could not determine whether it was by phone or in person, and then finally figured out that it was by phone, I had a secondary act.

Knowing Stradella's efficiency and perpetual attention to the correct manner of handling her telephones, I was practically always sure my secondary act would be successful.

I would have to walk at least three blocks away, at a very rapid rate, secrecy being unimportant at such times. I would find a telephone and drop a dime in, and call her, dialing first the outgoing number. After the connection is made there are about two seconds' pause before the first ring. If the line is busy, there is an immediate busy signal. If I did not get a busy signal I would then call her incoming phone, and more than likely get a completely different result.

Then and only then would I be satisfied that Stradella had been called by someone and was now engaged in conversation. I never knew her to call out on the in-phone but once, or to let anyone call in on the out-phone, except me, which was a source of great personal joy and confidence that I never tired of treasuring.

My subsequent act was to return to the ear post and, to the best of my ability, listen in. Eventually, I developed such skill in spotting trouble zones that if I wanted I could have gone directly up on her back lawn, into the semi-obscurity of moonlight and shadows, lean against the open window and not only hear everything perfectly, but see as well.

The only risk of this position was that I might be seen by unseen persons in unlighted windows, or—worse—the highly improbable double approach: that passers-by might come from both directions at once, whereas I could only look one way at a time.

The second danger was lessened by the existence of an even darker escape behind Stradella's back door. The disadvantage was my sudden emergence in her front yard might surprise any neighbors looking in that direction. I therefore practiced extreme caution (save for once), and chose to relinquish my lawn post on the slightest threat, before being forced into this risky exit.

Be it also known that there is a rhythm to everything, even spying. The voyeur, the detective and the undercover agent have one thing in common. That is their capacity to grasp a few strange details quickly and to quit the scene without breaking their rhythm. Quit the scene they must in order to make their movements look as casual as possible.

Within earshot of the telephone conversation, I would try to figure out how long it was going to last, and how long it had been going on. If I heard nothing more interesting than conversation about the weather, I would make a quick exit and look around for a casual two minutes in order to make sure I was safe before returning to the sound. Actually, it might be only one minute, or perhaps, three; the timing of my absences was the real test of my skill.

Were there a neighbor in his yard, and planning to be there a while, my actions were limited. If Stradella was inside the house for no more than ten minutes after a night on the town, and her date still inside with her, I was safe. But if he remained there more than ten minutes, my danger increased, and I had to be either at the listening post under the street light by the bedroom window, or else in the back yard by the open window—don't ask me why—especially if the kitchen light had already gone on, and more especially if it had gone off again—but please don't question my motives.

What was to be done when, as I casually circled her house knowing that she was not home, a strange car came along?

The danger there was that I might be seen in the glare of the headlights. Because of this, it would be necessary for me to figure out where the car would park, if it were really Stradella's date bringing Stradella home. Obviously, I could not allow myself to be near the place where the car parked.

These crucial moments occurred more often than I like to remember. I had to turn my back and walk rapidly away two or three blocks.

And all because I did not have a car Stradella wouldn't recognize, which I could have parked right by the sidewalk near her bedroom window.

Returning quickly, after having taken into account the presence of her date's car, and the state of the lights in the house, I would then be faced with a choice.

If the kitchen light was on and the bedroom light off, I had time. She would be making coffee for the next few minutes. Stradella never had sex while the pot was boiling. If the living room light was on and the bedroom light as well, that usually meant the bathroom light was also on—and now, beware, for doom is coming surely and swiftly.

My heart would commence to pound. I, frightened and eager at the same time, made haste.

Five minutes.

Quickly around five blocks in order to make a casual approach from the opposite side, to find myself once more under her window. Now I had a moment to reorganize my energy. I would tune my ears, listening for clues that would tell me what was going on inside. Now it was time to move into the second position.

As I said, if they had just arrived, the windows of the living room would remain open until she had taken her coat off, which gave me time to get into position beneath her windows. I could thus hear better. In the meantime, those living room windows would be letting in cold air, and would soon be closed by Stradella. And if she glanced out, I would be seen. Therefore, as I approached that highly perilous position in order to be able to hear everything—even the awful augury of silence—I had to decide whether I should turn and retreat to avoid being seen, or whether I still had time to pass under the windows, and if so, how much.

Having that bit of information measured, I then walked four blocks and came back to within a few feet of where I'd been before, but this time by another, the third, and last, approach.

You see, after every pass at the bull, so to speak, I chose to clear out of the vicinity entirely and enter again from a new way, fresh as a stranger, so as to be able to evaluate the situation more accurately, and appear more innocent to any eye watching me.

There is one rule I neglected to mention. I never walked past the front door of Stradella's house. The exact state of living room conversation was of no interest to me. Also, with Stradella's unpredictable personality, I could never know for sure when she might suddenly get the urge to throw the door open. I therefore hesitated to be there. The kitchen, which was on the same side of the house, presented the same problem, as I could never be sure when she'd leave the living room to enter it in order to escape her date, to delay her date, or merely to attract her date.

You know now that I have hurried around the four blocks, made a completely new entrance into the neighborhood, and at the new building next to the house quickly dropped from sight down the driveway into the alley, am over the fence, through the back yard, across the neighbor's front porch, up Stradella's driveway and onto her back lawn without appearing beneath one lamp or being seen, as far as I know, by one person.

Passing a bedroom window down the alley behind the new building next door, I overheard the most delicate female sighs of love and passion at the precipice, but I was in no mood to enjoy or empathize with these sounds, my own feelings being somewhere else at the moment. But I digress!

Thus, to the open window! Crown peak of places to peep, hear and hide! I must admit I made the usual blunders along the way, and the usual errors in judgment that cut down my score in the game of eavesdropping, but there were enough successes to compensate for all the errors, and I was able to begin to formulate an accurate picture of my love.

If you persist in asking why I did all this spying, I can only refer you to the feelings I have expressed in previous chapters. For "letting go" is sometimes harder than "starting up," and not all loves which start casually end so, nor do those which start hard necessarily end easily. And sometimes a love is valuable only to the lover for the lessons it teaches him in changing to non-love, and the moments of harmonious bliss which usually seem so climactic are important only insofar as they lead up to the true climax which sometimes occurs only after the love is thoroughly dead.

And if you persist in knowing why I so readily confess to an act generally regarded as criminal, I can only cite the classical treatises on persons of self-flaying bent. We are, one and all of us, predisposed by our deeds to our punishments, and sometimes are thoroughly bored, perhaps even disgusted, by the crimes we must commit in order to reap the punishment we secretly desire.

I have reached the peaceful part of my story, though perhaps to some the most troubled—which is only a matter of attitude, for isn't an old soldier happiest when most desperately involved in the battle, whereas a merchant would be miserable in the same situation, and can't peace consequently be found in a hell by a nature so inclined? Bear with me, healthy reader. Perversion must have its out.

I recall the night only Stradella's bed lights were on when I arrived. In front of her house a black Mercedes-Benz was parked. It was after 3:00 A.M.

Tossing caution to the wind, I felt the hood. My heart sank in terror and panic. All lights in the house save for the bedroom were off. The hood hot. They were together!

Getting myself quickly into the back-yard viewing position, I saw and heard her under the soft lights. She was holding a man in her arms. Neither was dressed. It was over. I was paralyzed.

However, have no fear—I shall bore you no longer with my feelings. Sick I was. You know it. Whether I experienced joy or sorrow matters little. It is not really necessary to go into the pathetic state of my feelings. By then, they barely existed. I was burning pain itself. Before you judge me, I ask only this: stand in my place; think of the anguish you'd feel. Would you refuse to believe your eyes and your ears, or would you, as I, look and listen even more avidly? My woman lay there as so many times she had lain with me. And I watched. Watched! It's as though I sneeze on the ground as I say it. My muscles contort. My body thrusts forth a spasm. I must admit it ignobly, for all the self-hate and truth in Stradella it implies.

Watched I did: and as the one who watched, I now record it. And you, my accusers, who condemn me for the vile peeping Tom I must be, are no better than I, for if I committed a crime so do you now who read these pages. In reading these lines you also— watch! Watch as I watched! My God! How do you feel? Does it give you pleasure? Scandalous hypocrites, crimemongers who would punish me for the very crimes you yourselves commit—

But enough—not too far. There is yet more to read, more to *watch*.

35

The house Stradella bought was high up in a canyon; it was approached by a road in the bed of the canyon which climbed steadily. "Sort of gives you a lift," she'd said. The house itself was reached by a side road that cut suddenly off to the left and performed some frightening twists as it clung like a snail's line to the edge of the cliff, and spangled itself back and forth, tossing you from one side of the seat to the other, always going up, forgetting both safety and comfort. The road mounted in a thin line straight to the top. "Going home is like having an orgasm," Stradella said.

From the little road in front, her home looked both rural and modern. The concrete was black. She'd painted it. The house was white and the doors were black. The small shrubs had been pulled out and white pebbles resembling snow had been poured on every spot that exposed the naked ground. A lattice-work was installed to disguise the carport and a little cupid with a birdbath at his feet contemplated all persons who approached the door, and smilingly urinated in his bath. The porch lamp beside the door had been pulled out, and a Persian incense burner had taken its place. A red light installed inside it gave Stradella some chuckles.

The furnishings inside were primarily in marble, both black and white, and peacock feathers and velvets adorned the rest. The feathers and velvets were done up in various shades of lavender. Each bathroom had a motif. You could go to the Persian bathroom where the principal feature was a floor entirely covered with sand, and on the doorsill a brush to scrape off your feet so you wouldn't track it, because the motifs of the other rooms called for no sand at all.

The bathroom was draped like a tent in red material, and shiny bronzed fixtures holding toothbrushes, nail files, an electric razor and enough mouthwash for the fussiest of men.

One wall was adorned entirely with mirrors, each of a different size and shape, each in a different-sized frame, so that to see yourself clearly, you first had to decide exactly which frame would suit you best.

The sofas were internally heated, and stereophonic music poured out of the fireplace and the footstool all day long, because the stereo changer was automatic and could not be turned on or off except by a complicated alarm system.

Over the bar hung a canopy which also sheltered a potted plant placed near the bar stools. In the hallway grew some ivy which was threatening to invade the kitchen.

The kitchen was automatic. To enter was to stage a production. Lights went on, dials turned. Stove, refrigerator, broiler, oven, disposal, juicer, opener, roaster, toaster, and a dozen other beautifully concealed devices worked electrically in order to relieve the cook of her burden. All she had to do was find them.

The mistress's bedroom was adorned by the plum of all plums: in the center of the room, of course, was a round bed, the largest, highest, softest and most canopied bed in the world, with a crest like a throne, all of it richly draped in red. It was the bed of all beds. I don't know if you'd want to sleep in it, or if you wanted, I don't know that you'd dare.

The view from the bedroom was superb. From the full-length windows that lined one entire length of the house you had a sweeping view of Los Angeles that was almost sexual in aspect, for the mountains on either side of the canyon had a way of swooping along in the view and finally, at the farthest point, coming together into a gently sloping and curving "V" like the round curves of the thighs, and closing. Stradella was positively aroused by a Los Angeles that "lay out through that crotch in the distance."

It was easy to slide open the windows, which were also doors, and step onto the porch that ran the whole length this side of the house. But here, if you looked down, if you dared to look down, I would say: hang on. There was nothing beneath the house for two hundred feet. It was suspended in mid-air. It was glued to the wall of the cliff by luck as far as I could tell. Some beams protruded like arms and held it. Cantilevered is what they call it, and any house that is built in mid-air and suspended over space with only a couple of stilts to poke up at it from the underside has to wear this big name, but as far as I can tell, it's still more airbound than earthbound for my comfort.

You can of course see at once, the primary advantage in owning such a house is that you don't have to buy any ground to put it on. You've just got to insure the whole neighborhood, and a good stretch of the highway that winds like a ribbon up from the canyon two hundred feet directly below the bedroom. Of course I'm kidding a little bit there. You have to buy the cliff that goes under the house so that no one else will try to glue another dwelling directly beneath. But I think you will share my apprehension, as you look over the balcony edge, and promise yourself to tread a little more lightly around the rooms, especially on rainy days, and not invite too many people in at once.

When you look over the edge, and if you're frightened you might look up quickly, a road will be the first thing you see, for directly across the canyon, on the opposite wall at the same level, a road winds, and on this road is a curve which is just opposite the bedroom and living room. There is a white fence used as a guard rail on that curve where many small bushes have grown up to be large bushes, so little frequented is the road, or the guard rail, or any other part of that lonely area.

But it is used sometimes. For instance, it was used by me.

I sat there on the afternoon of the second Saturday in the month of August. You will recall the famous fire of Laurel Canyon, Coldwater Canyon, Benedict Canyon and Beverly Glen Canyon. It destroyed thousands of acres and made many people miserable. But it didn't touch a blade of grass in this canyon. Stradella had moved here.

I sat in the bushes because it was Stradella's birthday and I didn't go to her house. She'd not invited me. But I sent flowers. I sent her the largest bouquet of orchids I was able to purchase. It took almost all I had, but they were beautiful, the most beautiful flowers I'd ever seen.

When the sun set in the "V" of the canyon, I noted the people in the various houses below putting on the lights in their swimming pools, the distant lights of Los Angeles winking, and a cool breeze sweeping up through the grass. I shivered, but I remained.

About 9:00 P.M. a trail of headlights winding up the canyon began to turn up the far road, and I saw two police cars among them. They parked up above on the knoll, but the officers walked back down to her house. Other cars also came and climbed and parked. People arrived in mysterious waves in mink and white gowns and tuxedos, and wended their way silently into her house.

I saw them arriving by the droves, removing their wraps, glancing in the mirrors, taking their drinks and mingling. The furs, the blue and silver minks, the ermine, the white fox and even the rabbit were heaped like a luscious sea on the satin covers of her luxurious round bed. Jewels were glittering all over the dressing table. Every crevice was sparkling.

The women were coiffured in majestic hairdos. Some had their tresses swept up into hives, combed and honeyed. Others had tumbling hair like water-falls that splashed as wild and loose as Bridalveil Falls itself. Some wore their hair bound into one tress that glided down their necks. Others wore marvelously meshed braids that looked like Medusa's serpents. And some were even shaved short like Joan of Arc while others had half-curtained their eyes with hair.

The gowns were open down to the bosom, or wound and bound and sealed up to the throat, or open down to the navel and in one case down to the base of the spine, and in other cases closed like a mummy all the way up to the ears and forehead like a scubie diver's suit, showing nothing but chin and eyes and ankles and feet and hands.

The faces were bright and painted or dark and marked, were tinkling and pale or bronzed and mock-ing; were silent; were serious; were frightened; were innocent; were young; were old; were faded; were wide-eyed; were slit-eyed; were painted-eyed; were shut-eyed. The faces of the women were enigmas and open books, volumes of despair and chapters of ignor-ance. The faces of the women were responsive and reflective. Some were mirrors. Some were frames. Some were frames without pictures. Some were not even frames.

The men were dark and light, brows bushy, brows thin, hairlines retreating, wigged, well-shaved, and powdered, or mustached and broad-grinned, cigar-chomping, cigarette-holder-wagging or pipe-puffing. Some wore tight-fitting watches and others wore rings with big stones. Some wore wedding bands and some wore name bracelets dangling around their wrists. Some held their drinks in two fingers. Some clutched their glasses like clubs in their fists.

Some hands played on other arms. Some hands

slipped unseen into pockets. Some hands slipped unseen into clothes. Some hands pulled off bow ties, both the clip-on and knotted types. Bare feet with gold toes rubbed tuxedo-trapped ankles and slender freshly shaven legs wrapped themselves around trouser legs.

Little colored waiters hurried through the crowds with trays of *pâté* over their heads. Black maids in white caps handed frosted glasses to groping fingers. Men leaned over the balcony and argued and waved their hands and tapped their fingers and girls played with necklaces and men admired their rings. Cigarettes paused before lipstick-smeared mouths and cigarette lighters flicked. Boys smiled through their make-up and kissed men on the cheeks. Middle-aged women with beautiful faces and some creases burst out in heavy-chested laughter from where they perched on stools.

The movie stars were there. Joan Creamfluff moved about in her white evening gown as though in a spotlight. James Barnstorm wore a tuxedo, white shirt and a tie like a gag, but Richard Crockett had no shirt with his tuxedo and tie and women sparkled their tinsel smiles and ran their thin fingers and long nails through his matted fur chest. One kissed it and left a red heart of lipstick on his hairy skin.

A dark girl with almond eyes, dressed like an Arabian concubine, began to move her midriff and spangle her arms in the air over her head like two snakes doing a love dance, and someone stuck an olive in her navel.

A group of ladies commenced to sing hymns and a homely brunette ripped her skirt on a chair and some man laughed and pulled at it. Another joined in and another, and they pulled it off piece by piece until she stood naked before them. One of the men fell back and roared and pointed for several others. No one had stopped to think even she might not be wearing underwear. Someone crowned her head with a turned-over bowl of cream cheese and she fell down on the floor and cried.

A worried man with his hand caught in the cushions of a sofa tried to pull it out and a woman immersed in conversing with another woman without even noticing, sat down on it. He smiled and went to sleep.

Then I saw in the bedroom protruding from the furs the eight bare feet of four people and I could not tell whether they were men or women or both, though at times an arm rose out of the sea of mink, and a shoulder, but because they were bare they had lost their identity and all the feet had five toes and all the hands had five fingers and all the shoulders were round.

But on the floor around the fur bed were shoes of boys and men and girls, golden slippers and sandals and patent ambassadors and boots. And on the chairs and tables were draped their forgotten costumes—bow ties and bras and suspenders and dresses. And among them, I saw her red dress—the red dress Stradella had worn—tossed away from the pool of ermine and fox to a discarded and forgotten heap by the wheels of the TV set which was aimed at the bed like a gun, playing, broadcasting, I believe, the extremely erect, sober news of a distinguished, unflinching commentator seated scholastically behind his desk.

The rest of the party was still well mixed. People were leaning on the balcony talking. I didn't notice her at first, moving through the crowd. She must have just arrived. I recognized her bearing, for she walked very straight with a righteous grand-lady manner. Then I noticed she'd brought Rodney too. They were invited, of course. Then the poodle got in and Rodney leaped for it, and the poodle got excited and ran away.

But what was she looking for as she moved through the crowd? Hadn't she been told I'd not be there? She seemed to be asking for something. Some people stopped to answer her. Judith Pendant laughed and tossed her head back. That fellow, the young building contractor who had long ago shown his amazement that Stradella and I were together, shook his head gravely when they spoke, then Judith Pendant took his arm and led him two steps and folded herself into his embrace.

The dog barked several times, I heard that. Then I looked once more and she was gone. Why had she come? Where was she going? Several minutes went by as I pondered.

Mother was a famous woman. The blush of youth had long made her a glamour woman. Now the blush was more or less in permanence, but mighty was she, as a woman.

Ariadne Berlin, born in Sandwich City, Great Sandwich Territory, in the state of Montana, made her mark at twenty-one in Hollywood, to which she came with promise and a gift for music.

Mother had been legendary—the greatest star of 1932, and unsurpassed by anybody till the war, to which she danced with sparkling eyes and gaiety that made the soldiers valiant.

Little Ariadne, said they—who leaped full of innocence, with natural tomboy grace, in situations onto horseback, riding with her long hair flowing to bring news of Victory, and fell into nextdoor Freddy's arms exhausted, having saved the village—sang and danced and country-girled her way to glory, virginally.

Now she had rhubarb-colored hair, was full-mink coated and defended by the sparkling diamonds of her necklace and two twinkling rings. She drove a Cadillac. She smiled and she nodded to the people that talked with her and she kept her posture straight, for she had been twice injured—once on horseback in the pictures back in 1939, when she was injured by a serious fall along the forest trail in that great chase scene where the Maid of Lochinvar is riding from the

clutches of the Evil Merlin of the Court to Robin
Hood's protection in the Wood—and then her back
was broken in an auto accident with A. A. Montreau,
crossing Golden Gate Bridge up in San Francisco.

Mr. A. A. Montreau was (and is) the brother of the
former Chairman of the Board of Gargantumite Pictures, Mr. A. E. Montreau, father of Odile, and Mr.
A. A. was an active film producer till that accident
when he was paralyzed, and totally, so that (and still
today) he never left his house and lay upon a special
bed and was, most truly, a forgotten man.

Ariadne Berlin finished with the pictures when
the soldiers took over on the screen, but kept her
independence, and her courage, and she still refused
to have a chauffeur or a servant living in her house.

She was the kind of woman who went places, met
the people, played a little tennis, took the flowers
offered her by sturdy younger men, and went along
with comedy dressed up and brash in rhubarb pink
and listening to compliments, only to say at the end,
with never fading smile, she was sorry but she didn't
have her checkbook with her and it was a great time,
none the less, she had with them, and smiling, the
brown and glitter-gleaming eyes right through the
naked orgy sparkling, not participating, she would
flash her teeth at them until they vanished from
existence.

"That's right Archie! Fun's fun but you can't die
laughing! Life is real and life is earnest but the grave
is not the goal. Dust thou art and to dust thou returnest
never was spoken of the soul. I'm a country girl.
That's all I am, a country girl. I haven't got a friend
alive. I haven't got a relative worth punk."

But she passed many days alone each year, along
the beach at Carmel walking, wearing old clothes,
gathering up driftwood, taking home the better pieces
for her work, wood carving, and perhaps remember-

ing when she was only nineteen and had played a concert for the king and now she touched the piano nevermore, it having cost and brought too much.

She whistled like a bird, and sang. "Golden Days, in the springtime of our happy youth. How we laughed, with a gaiety that knew no song. Golden days, full of innocence, and full of truth. . . ."

No one ever knew, I think, her hair was really "mouse brown" as she laughed and called it, that the famous rhubarb of her later years was only purchased, that she left the diamonds in the safe-deposit vault, the mink coats in the closet, and wore camel's hair and imitation glass. But everyone has someone they've called mother, once.

A deep hush gradually fell over the party. The guests in the living room stopped mixing and turned toward the hall near the Persian bathroom which led to Stradella's bedroom.

They were looking at something. The little old man who was Stradella's voice teacher entered. The little old man was blind and hung his white cane from his hand and felt his way among the women with his hands, his white hair flowing. Mr. X, I called him, for Stradella said he was a wise man who had taught her how to speak and use her chest, and I had waited many hours outside his small house in Baldwin Hills while she had taken lessons on the best way for her to use self-projection.

He had taught her exercises. He had made her sit down on the floor cross-legged. He had told her to undress, that he was blind, it was all right, and told her to stand on her head and spread her legs out one to either side and talk with two or three bananas in her mouth, reciting favorite poetry.

At one point he had said that she must soak her breasts in lukewarm milk, enunciate as follows, on her hands and knees, her head tossed back so she could see the chandelier:

"The woman standing, saggy-baggy, by
"The crooked, wilted candle, with her breasts
"Like water wings, deflated and hung down
"Beyond the age of buoyancy, the tempest
"Of erection, in her eyes the gaunt,
"Harsh stare, the vacant feeling of despair,
"Until she utters some pained phrase born out
"Of her emaciation which has lost
"Emancipation, vaguely groping for
"Release with blunted hands and hardened arms,
"Produces nothing going nowhere in
"A tortured haste of hurry like she knew.
   "Knew what? The art of loving is concealing.
   "Those who love not are, to hide, revealing."

The master, Mr. X, had also given her instruction in the art of eating. First the diet was important to the proper intonation of an artist's speech.

Before she'd give off cooful and alluring sounds, he'd have her swallow eggs with ground up walnuts powdered in them, and drink down a shot of sherry to ignite her eyes.

Before she'd enter into anger he would have her gargle with green vinegar and salve her gums with vaseline, and then say at the top of her voice, after putting mustard on her nipples:

"Foe! Fie! Fee! Fum! Fickle bubbles burst the drum! Anger lurches at the door and I am threatened, pure no more!"

She had a special way of talking, nasally, you know, which they found that she lost by acting lessons—imitating birds by flapping round the room, and dogs by squatting, barking, panting, thanks to Stanislavsky's method, naked—and simply sitting, nude of course, on ice blocks with her feet up to her ankles in large pans of horse intestines which she purchased specially, her arms outstretched and stuffed in sleeve-length muffs of fur.

I'd had her tell me once, "It's auto-analysis Archie!

It's really very good. The state of mind improves."

Finally, when Stradella had perfected her inflection and achieved deep breath control, the master, who was blind, had asked her to hang from the balcony— and there were special stirrups for her feet to hook in for the exercise.

She hung like this, two hundred feet or so above the canyon floor, her long blond hair draped down. Then he turned on the fan which was directly over her and blew a cool breeze at her thighs, while an assistant, an adept young woman from Lahore, and her twin Pakistani sister in the sweet and veiled silk sari, from the Valley of Swat, poured champagne down her legs, which rippled on her stomach and ran up and through her hair and off.

The master put a Spanish goatskin wine bag in her hand, which held Sangrilla, and instructed her to shoot it in her mouth while there reciting:

"Where is the prize for virtue and does it
"Exist? The faces I see on the street
"Proclaim in loud disdain and proud neglect
"Of me the innocent, that my race has
"Ascended or descended to some different
"Place. Please, if there is no prize on earth
"Then call me back to home where I can join
"The love of strange companions without pain.
"For my force is a fortress to the life
"Of good, and virtue is my goal without
"A single mortal stain. I shall not break
"And degradate myself in slops of hate.
    "For what I am I shall be always, strong.
    "But set me free of loneliness, 'fore long?"

Stradella told me, "I don't care what you think of his methods to teach me to speak, Archie. He has given me a sense of personal and spiritual identity and made me realize that the True God of the World is in Myself. He has unveiled my Hidden Holy nature and revealed the living light of the Eternal Spirit in me, Archie. He has taught me that I am a Personal Daughter of God."

Stradella's little sister, as you know, became a sensual guru, and she led us one and all to contemplate divine laws and the Everlasting in our proper natures through the muscular control of body movements as we meditated, when she came out here to Hollywood once Stradella had attained Enlightenment and Truth-hood and gone in the monastery.

The party was in full boom at Stradella's now. I could not hear a thing, but see it all with clarity I did, my telescope assisting me most perfectly.

The people in the hush that had come on the room were looking at the master. Stradella's curtain was drawn and her lights were out. The blue haze of the TV glow was all that penetrated outward and I could imagine that prompt, sober, gray and proper announcer giving out the weather in that sealed and empty, silenced room.

I am sure that in the party not an ice cube tinkled as Stradella did her exercise to demonstrate her voice, the blind man groping in his white suit through the costumed throng. Then I heard the dog bark—woof woof!—repeatedly. Some seated people stood up and one man took off his party hat.

Elmira, the poodle, came running through the crowd, Stradella's dress locked in its jaws. It dodged quick left and right with energetic playfulness. When the dress caught on the heel of a lady and wound round the legs of a man, the poodle tugged, turning and sinking its paws in the thick carpets, shaking its head until finally it pulled the dress free.

A man with a sheepskin for a graduation exercise rolled it up and coughed.

Someone had arrived in costume as a bear and he was grabbing hold of the young lady with the olive in her navel, who had lost her dress through comic taunts to those men earlier who had been playful.

He, the bear, black fur agleam, swept her, the girl, up in his paws and grinned and glistened of white teeth. A pansy dressed in ostrich feathers was attempting to make up a tune that he could whistle while he hopped around on one foot and out to the edge of the long balcony where he leaned forward and sent forth a rising, arching, peepee stream, beside Stradella, who was hanging upside down.

An old dame with a triple chin removed the jeweled cigar holder from her teeth and socked the fellow behind her in the stomach with a fist. He doubled over on a potted plant beside the ivy.

Rodney came bolting from somewhere to catch the dress the poodle had. The little silver dog ran to the balcony, the skirt still in its teeth, between the legs of a young woman on her hands and knees whose eyes were shut and face was squinted. She was pretending to play peekaboo with a real midget lying on the floor, laughing and then giggling as two plush babes in overalls massaged him with electric paintbrush guns, and one babe finally fell down on the floor beside the other and submitted to the paintbrush guns electrically herself, her face a scream of gargle grins and gladness like a speckled sunburst washing through her. A lady in a costume like a nun blew bubbles from a holder made for bubble-blowing games. She didn't even move or budge as mister midget scrambled underneath her robes, and reached out with one hand and took the fire poker from the hearth beneath her robes with him as well. Someone else whose outfit was designed so it resembled a green tree laughed and shed like the autumn when her suitor with a rubber ax began to chop her down.

Rodney leaped around the people after the gay poodle. The poor dog ran down the porch. Fast Rodney dove for it and only barely caught the dress. The poodle slid on over the porch edge, and hung on by its teeth to the cloth of the dress.

But the zipper was undoing and the next thing that the friendly, playful poodle mother named Elmira knew, still barking, it was plummeting straight down, and turning long slow circles in the air till there was only the road black and flat beneath it, and it landed in the path and headlights of a screeching car.

Some people had rushed to the edge to watch. Rodney came down the porch with the torn dress in his hands. He stepped before Joan Creamfluff. He ran up to Richard Crockett. He spun around to James Barnstorm and raised his face. James Barnstorm was Rodney's hero.

Then he faced our mother.

Slowly, with that ominousness you all know, he stepped back two paces. His voice rose up high and loud. It carried clear across the canyon. He was leading the eyes of the people to him.

"Grrr—raw!—Yahoo! Yahoo! The glorious night of the year!—Mother Flum to the rescue! Hooray! Hooray! Mother Flum again, and yahoo! Hooray!— Mettle for medals! Pluck, over the top! Run the gantlet! Charge the lair! Take the bull by the horns! Hooray! Peerless are they, and saintly! Hooray! Smut out the mut! The seraglio survives! Fun's fun but you can't die laughing! Dust thou art and to dust thou returnest never was spoken of the soul!"

He ran to the other end of the porch. He leaped up on the rail. He ran along it as if it were a tightrope, two hundred feet above the canyon floor. Nobody moved. Only frozen eyes followed him, as ice cubes collapsed in their glasses.

"Bring on a small strumpet, let me be a satyr! Toss me a trollop, we'll trull till the dawn! Mix me a minx, I'll jab a jade joyously!"

He leaped for the roof and caught it and swung up. He ran along the flat top of the house, accidentally surprising a man dressed in a donkey suit and Judith Pendant, who was draped over his lap like a frail, broken swan, and pale white was her delicate neck exposed, where they had been still for some time beside the chimney pot.

The people below were crowding the balcony, squeezing and leaning out to look up and get a glimpse of the roof, and the officers of the police car on the door patrol outside turned their spotlight up toward the spectacle, grumbling awake and snarling with aroused malice, mystified.

Rodney was scooping up handfuls of the small white pebbles that covered the roof. He tossed them in the air. They fell like hailstones and rattled on the roof and porch with the sound of a snare drum.

Then Rodney stood quite still on the roof, out of range of their vision, and two movie reporters ran to their flashbulbs and note pads as radio beams glurped out of the police patrol car: Rodney Flum, younger brother of the famous record-making singers, The Three Sisters Flum, and son of retired star Ariadne Berlin, Tonight Made Hollywood History to emerge as the most promising Boy Star Of The Decade!

Rodney was motionless in the night air. There was only the blackness and the stars behind him and everything else below, the one spotlight from the police patrol car pinning him against the night, his feet delicate and hobbling on the sharp white roof's bright pebbles.

Rodney seemed to be looking for something. He turned his head gravely in every direction, and he looked, and looked, and looked.

It was suddenly music time: A hand somewhere in the house below put the needle to the disk. The Three Sisters Flum In Paradise! Yay-yay-rocka-boomy-dee! they sang, an organ quite religiously supporting them, Bop Bach.

"Your little boy is going to be a star tonight. You'd almost think Stradella threw this party to launch his career in movies, Mrs. Berlin," someone who looked like he counted looked like he was saying to the stanch and straight and stiff austerity that was our mother there, imperious, unbending.

Then mother left the party and drove off alone in her uncovered Cadillac. Someone had put the body of her poodle on the seat behind her. Down the canyon in her car she wound.

Then, taming his stentorian voice, he whispered, Rodney did, perhaps directing his words to an ear unknown straight across the canyon, as his name went up already into news lights around the tote board of Times Square, and got set up in headlines Coast to Coast, and his last shred of private self there vanished.

I am sorry, I could hear him say. I am so sorry. O my brother, I heard him. I heard him choke his breath back to prevent the crocodiles. He was only a little boy, the genius, following my footsteps, the fool!

I got up and crawled out of my bush.

How my heart had changed. Now I, cold calculator, knew it, realizing the only pathway to pleasure was misery and the only truth comes from lies, and most of all, the best-planned seduction of woman is deception and the best conception's rejection. Because here I rose like a pyramid to downfall, in all my sallies celebrating the victory of deeds over dreams. Banishment of ideals was the beginning of new ideals, for which I no longer cared. I was hungry.

The voice of Stradella was in me and addressed me. "You know what, Archie? I was in the station with Valencia to get my tires pumped up and the person servicing me asked to go out for a date or something, you know? I turned him down. You know what? And I didn't even recognize him till Valencia pointed, then I realized. That was Johnny Jenkins, my first husband. You imagine? Funny, isn't it? Real funny, like. I wonder if you'll ever be around me, and not know, someday? I wonder if someday you'll—Archie? . . ."

So woe be to youth and virginity, I thought, that

they must age and be whored in order to satisfy their purity. But why, I thought, as I walked away, does this head always revert to exaggerating what I was doing and feeling?

This little world was good to me by not always being so kind. The more it left me out, the more was left to find. We were the silent members of the forgotten generation. We were the sealed-out citizens. Who was it that amused us? All the winners, champions, butterflies. We were the quiet, forgotten and unneeded ones—who watched and picked the tab up when we were amused. We were the plagiarists of pleasure, going lightly after all. The heroes went there first. We were the safe and smug, the last of the cream eaters. Royalty.

I had nothing to complain of. I was lucky that Stradella lost me. I was just taking a moment to hang onto my little coat and keep my small shred of dignity straight and my smile tucked in, when all of a sudden there was a horrible cry nearby, and another bush started shuddering terribly and reeling about like a stunned thing and finally rising up and flying toward me, roaring. It was Dinky.

"Get out! Get out of here, you peeping Tom! You spy! Get out of here! Leave my sister alone! You're no good for her! You're a bum! You're a typical Hollywood phony! Get out!"

But as he came toward me—if you remember, I have described that guard rail in the overgrown bushes —his raised hands brandishing a stick, I think, or perhaps a rock, he stumbled on something, what, I don't know for sure. He cried out as though in pain. Possibly he had twisted his ankle. He lurched and vanished.

I looked up. I looked down. I ran to the edge and looked around. It is a long fall down that cliff, perhaps two hundred feet. There was a swimming pool directly below us, and around the swimming pool, concrete.

The water was lighted inside and resembled a turquoise jellybean. There must have been fifty such pools spotted below me in the canyon, lighted kidneys against the night. I didn't know where he was. I couldn't, in the darkness illuminated only by this, hope to find poor Dinky. So I started down the hill for help. It would be a long hike to Sunset Boulevard to telephone an ambulance—at my regular coffeehouse where they served cheap tea—and I hurried.

I wondered what Dinky's last thought might have been. Was he still thinking his sister was a virgin—at least as far as grown men were concerned? Was he still convinced of that?

But you know, as I think back on it, myself, and I do, I begin to believe a little bit—yes, I really do, without hardship at all—believe perhaps he was right: Perhaps Stradella was, in the pure sense of the word, a virgin.

. . . And the rest you have not read in the papers. . . .